Heart of the Highlands:
The Beast

Protectors of the Crown Series:
Book One

April Holthaus

Heart of the Highlands: The Beast

Edited by: One More Time Editing, LLC
Published by: Grey Eagle Publishing, LLC
Cover Design by: Zak Kelleher
Printed in the United States
First Printing: July 2015
ISBN-10: 1500615153
ISBN-13: 978-1500615154
All rights reserved.
10 9 8 7 6 5 4 3 2 1

Copyright © 2015 April Holthaus

This book is a work of fiction. Names, characters, places and events are used fictitiously. Any resemblances to actual events or persons are purely coincidental. No part of this publication is allowed to be reproduced without the author's written permission.

Dedication

To all of those who have helped me improve my writing. Your insight and advice has helped me become a better writer! And thank you to those who support me by helping me spread the word about my books!

To my husband for your love and support.

To my son…I do all of this for you so you can have a bright future!

Acknowledgments

Janet Greaves, my critique partner! Thank you very much for all of your help and insight and for being such an awesome person and friend!

Denise Marie Stout Holcomb, thanks for being a part of the story and giving Keira her name!

One More Time Editing, thank you for all that you do! I am very glad to have you as part of my team!

Heart of the Highlands: The Beast

Contents

Chapter 1..9
Chapter 2..22
Chapter 3..33
Chapter 4..47
Chapter 5..58
Chapter 6..67
Chapter 7..79
Chapter 8..91
Chapter 9..104
Chapter 10..116
Chapter 11..126
Chapter 12..131
Chapter 13..145
Chapter 14..155
Chapter 15..162
Chapter 16..174
Chapter 17..184
Chapter 18..193
Chapter 19..205
Chapter 20..215
Chapter 21..229
Chapter 22..236
Chapter 23..243
Chapter 24..255
Chapter 25..265
Chapter 26..275
Chapter 27..284
Chapter 28..296
Chapter 29..307
Other books by the Author..........................323
About the Author.......................................325

Heart of the Highlands: The Beast

Heart of the Highlands: *The Beast*

Protectors of the Crown

Heart of the Highlands: The Beast

Chapter 1

Scotland, 1537

This was not her mother's gown. Keira looked at her reflection in the mirror one last time. Standing still as if she posed for a portrait, the image she saw was as distorted as if created out of broken fragments of glass. She imagined this wedding would be more of a public affair than the simple wedding she'd always dreamt about.

Instead of her mother's white lace gown, she was draped in dark, red velvet with rich-colored gold trim and felt as if she were to be put on display like a trophy instead of a virgin bride. The waistline fit her snugly and the bodice had been laced so tight she could barely breathe. The skirt flared out like the wings of an eagle; so wide she wondered if she was even going to fit through the door. It was a dress fit for a queen, though she was nothing of the sort. On most days, she barely passed for a lady.

Keira was everything a daughter of a powerful chieftain should be. She was well educated, trained in the domestic arts, and quite popular among the eligible bachelors at court, but at heart, Keira cared little for the glamour and attention that went with her title. Keira's father had spoken at great length about maintaining a certain appearance at court, but she knew that this dress was nothing more than a ruse to mask the truth about their clan. Keira desperately did not wish to play a part in his theatrical absurdity. She did not feel they belonged among the nobles as her father believed, but he refused to see reason.

After a series of poor investments and a midsummer drought, her clan was on the verge of poverty and at risk of losing everything. Due to her father's questionable business decisions with several other Scottish Lairds, it was Keira who had to pay the price. Doubly cursed as the laird's firstborn and the eldest of the laird's five daughters she was the first to be wed.

If only her mother were still alive, Keira would never be forced into marriage. Especially to a man she had never met. Her parent's marriage had a similar beginning. Arranged marriages were not uncommon. The only exception was that her father had known and loved her mother very much, even before their marriage was arranged, while her mother had despised her father as long as she'd known him. Was that Keira's fate as well, to walk in her mother's footsteps to end up miserable and unhappy with an unfaithful husband? Even the advice from her father's countless mistresses about the joys a marriage could bring did not calm her nerves.

Keira only learned of her father's desire for her to marry less than a week ago. The news came when the tax collector last visited the castle. Her father had not collected enough coin to pay the monthly tax and after much deliberation, they settled on a marriage contract to make up for the loss by finding a wealthy benefactor. Keira's father, Magnus Sinclair, told her that if it were not for the King's good grace they would have had to surrender more land, and they only had a meager few hundred acres as it was. She felt it was unfair to be a pawn in her father's political game, but what other choice did she have? It was her lot in life to be ultimately ruled by her father.

Keira was well aware of her father's wishes, and the import of an alliance between her clan and another. Her father did, however, had allowed her to choose between three respectable suitors who'd decided to pursue her hand in marriage: Abraham, Ennis, and Thomas.

Abraham, Chief of Clan Gunn, was older than her father. He was a widower with two wives already in the ground. His clan was directly to the south and only a short ride from Castle Sinclair, but his promiscuous lifestyle was far beyond what Keira felt would make a suitable husband.

The second man was Ennis, the son of the Earl of Strathaven. He was a younger man of only fifteen summers. Keira did not find much comfort in the idea of marrying a man who was more than three years her junior, not to mention no one could understand him. The heir to Strathaven spoke with a horrible stutter.

The third, and in her opinion, the best choice of her three options, was Laird Thomas Chisholm. Thomas was well-respected by her father. He was a man of means and wealth, and according to her younger sister Alys, who had seen him once at court, he was a handsome man. Keira had never laid eyes on him herself. She knew nothing of him, except for the stories her father told her of their times together on the battlefield.

Keira chose Laird Chisholm, frankly based on the simple fact that he was the only one not in need of an heir. He had several children from his previous marriage, as well as a good handful of illegitimate ones scattered throughout the Highlands. Surely, a man with eight bairns already was not in need of another.

It was not that Keira did not wish to bear a child of her own; she had a secret fear that she would suffer her mother's fate and die a terrible death during childbirth. Had she her own way, she would have given her life to God and to the church. The life of a nun seemed far more appealing than that of a wife.

Keira stood, gazing at herself in the mirror. From this moment on, the life she had always known would forever change and she would no longer be Keira Sinclair. Amazing how a name could be so important. It was as if she were losing a part of herself.

A familiar sadness bloomed in her heart as a single tear fell to the floor. Wiping her tears away with the back of her hand, she thought that even though she would have preferred not to wed, she would not have wished this fate on any of her sisters, either. As the oldest, this duty fell on her. She prayed her father would allow her sisters to have the opportunity to find their own husbands, though the chances of that were as slim as a strand of hair.

Raising her head high, she fought back her tears. At nineteen, she was nearly a spinster, and according to her father, it was time for her to wed.

If she were to survive her misfortune, she had to be her mother's daughter. Before her untimely death in delivering her youngest daughter Abby, Catriona was a brave and noble woman. She was the strongest woman Keira had ever known. Catriona never backed down from a fight or an argument and she never allowed people to question her morals. The daughter of a powerful chief, she helped lead Clan Sinclair to great victory, though Keira's father would deny every word of it. After Catriona's death, Keira's father had led their clan into a whirlwind of debt and turmoil.

Since Keira was the oldest, she had helped her father raise her four younger sisters. To keep their mother's memory alive, Keira often regaled her sisters with stories of their mother so that they would never forget her. Keira, however, was already starting to forget. She had forgotten the exact brown of her hair and couldn't remember if the blue in her eyes matched the sky after an afternoon rain or the mist that lingered over the ocean before dawn. She had even forgotten her smell, a mixture of sweet primrose and rosemary.

Keira turned from the mirror when she heard commotion outside the chamber door. She shuffled toward it, picking up the long train that dragged on the floor behind her, thinking it felt as if bricks had been sewn into the hem. Turning the handle slowly, and thankful for the well-oiled hinges, she poked her head out and peeked down the long hall. The light was dim as only two of four sconces were lit.

As she turned her head to look in the other direction, she saw her father silently follow a man into the room right next to hers and close the door.

With the hall empty, she scurried out of the room, but rather than rushing down the hall as she'd intended, she stopped at the door through which her father had just passed. She put her ear against it, curious about with whom he spoke.

The thick hardwood made it next to impossible to hear the muffled voices rumbling behind it. Keira pressed her ear against the door to block out the noises that echoed within the corridor. Straining to listen, all she heard from within the room was the rise and fall of her father's booming voice. Silently making the sign of the cross, she prayed her fortune had changed.

"Keira, what are ye doing?" her sister, Alys whispered as she crouched down by the door next to Keira.

Startled by Alys's unexpected presence, Keira bumped the door with the side of her head and froze with fear that her father would open the door and see both her and her sister pressed up against it. When several moments passed and the door remained closed, Keira hushed her sister with a wave of her hand. After several more minutes, Keira righted herself and stepped back from the door, keeping her eyes on the dark wood planks and the iron handle, even when Alys spoke.

"What has gotten into ye? Sneakin' about and eavesdropping like a wee ferret. Tis no' like ye to behave in such a manner."

Not that Keira needed reminding. A well-bred lady simply did not snoop about. But she could not help her curiosity. Not when it was her fate being decided just beyond that door.

"I saw our father walk into this room wit' another mon. I wondered if it was my betrothed. But I cannae hear through this wretched door."

"Of course ye can no' hear through it! Trust me, I have already tried! Besides, that is no' yer betrothed in there wit' Father. Tis one of Inverness's guards."

Keira looked over her shoulder at her *all-knowing* sister. They had only taken residence at Inverness Castle for the past two days and somehow Alys knew more about this place than the keep's maids, as if she had been there for years. No doubt she acquired her knowledge from some guard she has already swooned over. Next in line to wed, it should have been Alys in this costume of a dress and not Keira. Alys was the outgoing one who was eager to find a husband and start a family; too eager, in Keira's opinion.

"And how do ye know that?"

"Patrick! I met him this morning in the stables. I think I am in love."

"Ye always think ye are in love!" Keira replied, rolling her eyes toward the ceiling.

Alys's smile was painted on her face. It was nice to see the lass happy in love; or in lust rather. Love for Keira was something of a myth. The matter of love was best suited for tall tales and children's stories; for it was out of duty and honor that she'd agreed to the bloody union with Chisholm in the first place. Love had nothing to do with it. She only prayed that their father would hear out her sisters' wishes when it came time for them to wed.

At the sound of the metal door handle turning, both Keira and Alys bolted upright and ran down the hall. As they neared the end of the corridor, they waited as their father and the man that he spoke with exited the room.

Keira could see her father but the man stood in the shadows with his back to her. She could hear they were still speaking in hushed tones, but could not make out the words. Her father nodded his head. His thin lips, pressed tightly together, looked as if they held back his words. Clearly, he was angry. The unknown man continued heading toward the stairs; Keira never got a good look at him. *Damn!*

Signs of distress, anger and frustration could be seen on her father's face as if the emotions themselves were written by some unseen hand on his forehead. Keira let out a deep sigh. Pulling the tight collar of her dress away from her neck, she loosened its choke hold on her neck. The collar was trimmed with lace and was as itchy as the hemp of a hangman's noose against her innocent skin. It was just one more reason why she hated having to wear the ridiculous thing.

Together, the two girls stepped out of the shadows of the hallway and toward their father. Cursed with no sons, he had little choice but to marry off his five daughters in order for their clan to thrive. Keira had not taken into account the burden he must feel at having to agree to this union, especially to a man with suspicious motives and a questionable family lineage.

Their father let out a short, deep breath through his nose making his nostrils flare. Keira imagined that if he had been a dragon, he would have burned the entire castle down in just one breath.

"What are ye two up to?" her father asked, his deep voice echoing in the hallway.

"Nothing Father," Keira submissively replied.

"Well then, finish getting ready. Ye are to leave within the hour," he advised her.

"Leave? Am I no' to marry?" she asked, feeling a bit of relief.

"Laird Chisholm has requested yer presence at Erchless Castle. He has been unexpectedly detained so he has sent two of his men to escort ye."

"Just me? Will ye no' be attending?"

"Ye are yer betrothed's responsibility now. I have other matters that need my immediate attention. I do no' have the time to travel all the way there and back."

Though Keira did not share as close a relationship with her father as she had with her mother, her heart twisted. Forcing her to wed was one thing, but forcing her to marry without her family was entirely different. A woman's wedding day was supposed to be a celebrated union and now it was as if it were just a union of convenience. She would even be denied the pleasure of her wedding feast and the brief revelry before her life sentence with a man she neither knew nor loved began. Hot tears filled her eyes.

"What of my sisters? Will they be allowed to come?"

"Ye will see them in time. Now say yer goodbyes. Alys come," her father ordered as he coldly walked away.

Keira hugged Alys tightly, not wanting to let go. She felt the trembling of her hands travel to her other limbs.

"Dinna be afraid, sister. I've heard good things of Laird Chisholm. He will be a good mon and a good husband to ye," Alys said, trying to reassure her.

"I will miss ye dearly. Tell our sisters I will see them soon and that I love them verra much," Keira replied, holding her sister close.

"I will. I promise."

Keira had to force herself to let go. She watched as her sister hurried down the hall to catch up with their father as they turned the corner and disappeared from sight. Looking down at her golden-colored slippers, she turned to head back to her chamber. Keira wondered if the Chisholm family would be as standoffish as her father was or if they would take her in with loving arms. She hoped for their approval.

Keira's mind then drifted to her soon-to-be husband, Thomas. She wondered what kind of a man he was; what he looked like, how he acted, and if he would be a cruel or gentle husband. If he was anything like her father, who ruled with an iron fist, she was doomed.

Keira placed the last of her belongings inside the blue satchel that she had brought with her. As Castle Sinclair was so far to the north, Laird Chisholm had originally made arrangements to meet her halfway, in Inverness, to wed. This unexplained change of plans disturbed her beyond belief. What was so important that he could not even attend his own marriage ceremony? And why was it necessary for her to travel to his castle with such short notice? She certainly would not have complained about waiting a few extra days. It was clear to her that he was not as anxious to meet his bride as she was to meet him. Her first impression of him was discouraging at best.

Circling the room to make sure she had not forgotten anything, Keira picked up her bag and set it near the door. The moment she opened the portal, Keira tensed upon seeing two men standing quietly in the hallway just over the threshold. They were not large men and looked awfully young to be guardsmen. Surely, these two scrawny lads were not her escorts. Perhaps they were merely squires escorting her to the carriage, where her escorts awaited her.

"My lady, we are here to assist ye wit' yer baggage and to see to it ye stay safe on the journey. Laird Chisholm offers his apology fer no' attending but he could no' be pulled away from important matters of business," the taller of the two said.

Lord help me! They were her escorts.

Keira nodded and waited as the two men grabbed her bags and followed her down the stairs. Once outside, Keira spotted the carriage waiting for her. It was a small carriage which, by its outward appearance, would barely seat two passengers comfortably. It had a golden metal frame and hand painted Celtic designs on the wooden door panels. With its small window slits, it looked more like a small gilded birdcage than a means of transportation; an appropriate metaphor for how she felt.

The shorter, red-headed escort tied her luggage to the back of the conveyance and opened the door for her, while the other climbed onto the wooden driver's bench and took up the reins of the two horses pulling the carriage. Keira stepped inside and sat down on the brown leather seat. Soon they were off, heading on their way to meet her intended groom.

Chapter 2

Pressing their horses to a full gallop, Ian and his men raced through the open field as fast as their horses could travel. Being exposed was as dangerous as engaging in battle without any armor or a weapon. Their enemies were gaining speed, and Ian heard the thundering hooves fast approaching behind them.

Damn Rylan for leading them straight through Sutherland territory! If only he had listened to sense and reason, they would not be racing toward Fraser land, going completely in the wrong direction. Their mission called for them to head south, not west. This unexpected turn of events would cost them at least a days' worth of travel and if the bloody Sutherlands didn't run Rylan through, Ian would!

They had ridden too far to be delayed any longer and Ian hoped his dispute with the Sutherlands would be addressed another day. Though he was just as bloodthirsty as ever to rid every the land of every last filthy one of them, his duty to this mission was of the utmost importance.

Ian could feel the horses' hooves sink into the sodden ground. His pulse matched their speed causing him to grip the reins tighter. Assessing the situation, their odds of escape without engaging their enemies were slim. At some point, sooner than later, their horses would lose their stamina and begin to slow. And whether it was from the horses or the unfavorable terrain as they near the vast mountain ranges, they would be forced to fight.

Leaving the clearing of the open prairie, they weaved around the narrow turns of trees causing Ian and his men to slow to a steady crawl. Knowing they were outnumbered, and their path was coming to an end as they neared the basin of the steep mountain range, they had little choice but to dismount and face off in battle. Ian raised his fist in the air, signaling for his men to slow their pace.

Dismounting, Ian stood, flanked with a dozen of his men. Amassing over the countryside, an onslaught of Sutherland men ran toward them like a scattering of army ants after a sweet prize. Ian drew his sword from its scabbard and waited as their enemies approached.

One after another, men filtered through the trees, charging toward him and his men. There were at least thirty men against him and his twelve companions. Though the odds were not favorable, they weren't impossible either. Ian had seen worse and his men were well-trained warriors; adroitly skilled.

After all the battles Ian had encountered, each one had a sort of familiarity. Ian was attentive to every detail. From the way his enemy held his sword to the other potential threats around him. The Sutherlands, in Ian's experience, were an unpredictable and disgraceful group of men. Filled with greed, they were fueled by desire for power. And like all thieves and bandits, their claim to his land was illegitimate.

The blade of Ian's sword made contact repeatedly as he battled several men. Like flies to food, more Sutherlands joined the fight. Ian had no idea from where they came. Stepping in a pool of blood, bodies lay slain on the forest floor, including a few of his own men. Ian wiped the sweat from his brow with his arm, and continued fighting.

The sound of battle was deafening and the thunderous clashing of metal drowned out the grunts of exertion and the screams of the fallen. Exhaustion threatened to overtake him, but he continued to swing his sword. Battle not only caused a man to grow physically weary but dulled his mind, as well. Ian fought his body's responses as diligently as he fought the attackers.

The Sutherland clansmen successfully herded Ian and his men out of the forest and back out into the open clearing. Ian heard a volley of arrows whistling in the sky just before they rained down upon them. Without the protection of the forest canopy, Ian thought perhaps death had finally come for him. Making peace with himself, Ian rejoiced at the thought of reuniting with his sweet Sarah. With her death, she'd taken his heart; he'd been left with an aching void that nothing seemed to fill.

It had been almost eight years since he'd lost her. Seven years, nine months and twenty-six days, Ian corrected himself. *Damn it Sarah, why did ye leave me?*

Contemplating death brought Ian back to the matter at hand. He refused to die by the hand of a Sutherland. As the arrows flew toward the apex of their arc, Ian warned his men and they scattered back into the woods for cover. As the Sutherland men chased after them, several of them were hit with their own men's arrows, allowing Ian and his men enough time to return to the horses and escape.

"Did ye see that?" Daven laughed out as they quickly mounted. "Foolish bastards killed their own men!"

"They killed plenty of our own as well," Ian replied as he noticed only five of them returned to the horses. Two of the five were from his own clan, his younger brother Leland and longtime friend Rylan. The other two men, Alec and Daven, were warriors from the McKenna and MacLachlan Clans. "Let's get this bloody mission o'er wit' so we can go home!"

"What about the dead?" Leland asked.

Ian knew that with Sutherlands crawling all over the surrounding area there was little they could do. The only available option they had was to wait for the Sutherlands to leave in order to offer the dead a proper burial, but they had little time to wait and they'd already wasted enough time as it was.

"Tis nothin' we can do, but pray fer their souls," Ian bitterly replied.

Had the men been alive, they would have agreed. Staying would put the survivors in danger. Those who'd died knew the risks they faced with every mission.

Walking past Leland; he continued toward his horse and mounted. Leland turned his head back toward the trees where their dead lie upon the forest floor. Ian watched his younger brother as he slowly sauntered back to his horse. The men they had lost today were brave men. Their laird would have been proud.

Though Ian knew little about them, he felt the burden of their loss as if he had lost his own brothers; because in a sense, they were. They were sons of Scotland; Highlanders who fought together against tyranny and injustice.

The five remaining men rode in silence as they continued searching for the campsite they were sent to find. They had ridden more than three hours with no further sign of the Sutherlands, or the campsite.

Following the riverbed, Ian smelled smoke from an extinguished fire lingering in the air. Slowly and carefully, he scanned his surroundings; checking the trees, the hills, and even looking for strange movement in the tall grass. It was deathly quiet. Not even a bird's sweet melody filled the air.

Ian was not about to chance his men traveling through yet another clearing. With a nod of his head, Ian and his men dismounted and stepped forward, following the scent of smoke. Keeping a watchful eye, they moved through the long grass to the grove of pine trees ahead. This has to be it, Ian thought. Releasing a deep breath, he felt relieved when they found a series of tents up ahead.

For weeks, they had searched for this campsite and now they had finally found it. As plaids were hung out to dry, Ian knew for certain that this was the campsite of Laird Chisholm and his men. Hell, their clan tartans were left out on display like flags waving in the air. The only problem was, the camp was vacant

The tents, which were still erect, and the embers in the fire pit still smoldering, indicated the occupants left in a hurry and were clearly expecting to return. It was odd, however, to find an abandoned camp. Surely, one or two men would have been left behind to secure what meager valuables they had. Even within the enclosure of the trees, the situation did not sit well with Ian. The scene had "trap" written all over it.

Ian and his men searched the tents for good measure but they were empty. Glancing over to Rylan, his most trusted, longtime friend, Ian could sense he had the same concerns about the potential for an ambush. With a sharp nod, Ian and the four other men snuck back to the horses they'd left grazing near the river. Now that they knew where to find the encampment, they would return at dusk. Stealthily, they crept through the bramble of broken tree limbs and fallen leaves until they returned to the river.

Though finding the camp was a success, finding it unoccupied made that success hollow to Ian. He was beginning to tire of this game of "hunt and chase" with

Chisholm. Ian was sure of the facts his informant had given him, as he was a man of proven integrity and devotion to their cause. He swore to Ian that Chisholm was on his way to Inverness but had that been true, Ian would have crossed paths with him long before now. Something must have tipped him off that Ian's men were close on his trail.

"Where do ye think they went?" Rylan asked.

Ian's brow creased as he slowly shook his head in response.

"I dinna know, but they have no' gone far. We are only a few miles south of Sutherland land. It is conceivable that they have gone there for supplies as Chisholm is in bed wit' Sutherland. Based on the tracks we followed, it looks as though they have been camping there for quite some time, or at least 'tis a favorable spot. Now that we know where to find 'em, let's head back to the road. We will return before nightfall. It's only a matter of time before Thomas returns and," Ian stopped in mid-sentence when he heard the sound of horses' hooves kicking up gravel from the road in the distance. "Do ye hear that?" Ian asked as Rylan tilted his head toward the noise.

"Get down! Get down!" Ian called out as his men bolted to the ditch alongside the road.

As the noise came closer, Ian spotted two horses pulling a small carriage. Two young men dressed in Chisholm plaid sat on the bench holding the reins. Just when Ian thought his luck had completely run out and that he would never have the chance to confront Thomas Chisholm, fate had brought Thomas to him instead. For months, they'd played this cat and mouse game, but finally the tables had turned.

As the carriage came in full view, he could see that it was nobly decorated. It was apparent that Chisholm was not trying to conceal his whereabouts riding in such an ornately designed carriage. Had the man wanted to travel incognito, he would have ridden in a whiskey cart with a disguised monk at the helm; unless this was yet another decoy to throw off Ian and his men. After all, the carriage wasn't riding particularly fast, but at a slow and steady pace. A smart man would have known it was dangerous traveling through this part of the Highlands. God damn, Thomas was a tricky man!

Ian had actually never met the man he was hunting. He did not even know all of the charges against him, nor did he care. Thomas Chisholm was only a target. Ian, along with his men were to detain Thomas and return him to Inverness; dead or alive, and that was exactly what he intended to do.

Crouched down in the tall thick grass, Ian and his men quietly waited for the carriage to come closer. Ian looked at Rylan and Leland, and at the nod of his head, they knew to be ready to mount their ambush. For years, these men had fought together. Like a band of brothers, they'd developed the ability to read each other with a mere glance. Within moments, all five men jumped out onto the road, blocking the path of the carriage. The horses veered to the side of the road, startled by the sudden appearance of the men.

Ian drew his weapon before either of the Chisholm men had a chance to remove theirs. Their eyes met Ian's with cold terror. From the other side of the carriage, Rylan stepped up onto the drivers' platform and disarmed the scrawny one. The driver on the right did not hesitate to throw his weapon down. He knew he had no chance with five armed men circling around them.

"Chisholm!" Ian growled out, waiting for him to come bursting out the door of the carriage demanding an explanation for why they had stopped.

But the door remained closed.

"Tis no' Laird Chisholm we are escorting," the younger man replied, his voice shaken.

"Get down," ordered Rylan, keeping the tip of his sword pointed in their direction.

The two men did as they were told; dropping the reins and shuffling past one another. Ian let Rylan do as he wished with the men, for he knew Rylan would not kill them. Their mission was to capture Chisholm and take as few lives as possible.

Ian's eyes diverted back to the carriage. If it was not Chisholm they were escorting, who was inside? These two men were certainly not guards by any means. They were as timid as field mice. Chisholm would have demanded his best guards protect him. It was clear that whoever sat inside the carriage was not someone Chisholm felt was valuable enough to send more than two young lads.

"Get o'er there!" Rylan shouted to the frightened young men as both Leland and Daven sifted through the luggage strapped to the back of the cart. Alec stood back as look out.

"Remove yer garments and take off that bloody Chisholm tartan. Yer braes too," Rylan demanded.

"We will do no such thing!" one of the lads replied.

"Laddie, if ye dinna remove them, I will cut them off ye myself," Rylan warned.

The lads looked at each other, then looked down with shame and did as they were ordered.

"Ian," Daven said as he held up a ladies' nightshift in his hands, draping it across the front of his body as if he was trying to model it.

The shift was white and trimmed with delicate blue lace, with tiny blue flowers stitched along the neckline. For the briefest of moments, Ian's eyes shied away as a memory of his late wife, Sarah crept to the forefront of his mind. Thinking of her was just too painful and he'd tried so hard to forget that God awful day. The moment he saw the nightshift, Ian's chest began to ache as if a sword had just run him through.

"Everything in these bags belongs to a woman!" Daven continued.

Ian glanced back at the carriage door. Why would a woman be traveling unprotected to Chisholm's Castle? Whatever the reason, Ian would make certain she did not reach her destination.

Chapter 3

Keira felt as if she was venturing to a new world; a new life. It was both exciting and frightening. Since they'd left Inverness her stomach felt cramped and twisted like a wet rag being wrung out to dry. Was this how all brides felt before they pledged their life to another?

As the horses began to move, the potholes and bumps in the road jostled Keira from inside the small carriage. For most of the trip, Keira found herself glancing out the small window, the landscape flying past in a blur as she was swept away with daydreams.

She did not know what to expect when they reached Erchless Castle. Rumored to be a majestic fortress, it was inhabited by the entire clan. With no nearby villages, the Chisholm Clan was a mysterious bunch who did not take well to outsiders. She figured that was the reason she was not allowed to bring her own personal attendant.

Keira's thoughts were suddenly interrupted as the carriage began to slow. They could not have arrived already. The distance between Inverness and Laird Chisholm's Castle was at least a good three hour ride and they could have only ridden half of that journey.

Just as Keira was about to scoot over to the window, her bottom slightly lifted from the seat. Jostled around, she hit her shoulder and the side of her head against the carriage wall.

Her hand flew to her forehead to where a slight headache was beginning to form. *What the bloody hell was that*, she wondered as she felt the carriage slowing to a halt. The only logical explanation she could think of was that they had either broken a wheel or a wheel was stuck in a pothole.

Keira heard men speaking but the voices were not those of her two escorts. The voices she heard were deep and angry. They were thick with a Highland brogue and resonated with authority. Though she could not make out their words from inside the carriage, their tone did not sound friendly. Something did not feel right. Too much time had passed and neither escort had come to check on her or summon her. Were they being attacked?

No matter how hard she tried, Keira could not calm her labored breaths. From the small window slit, she could see two men standing to the side of the carriage. But they did not look like ordinary men. They were broadly built, like oxen, and as tall as trees. Hearing the different voices speaking back and forth, her imagination ran rampant. There could easily be ten of them out there, but what if there were more? Why would anyone want to attack her carriage? She was of no consequence, nor did she travel with any coin. Her scattered thoughts overlapped one another as scenarios came to mind.

Were they thieves, highwaymen, *the English*? Keira's stomach churned. She took a chance and peeked out a small covered window at the back of the carriage. The two men she saw looked ragged. Their clothes were dirty, torn, and plain in color. Further, they bore no clan colors or insignia. Her mind settled on outlaws. Though she believed they would be quite disappointed when they found out that they'd attacked a mere woman of no consequence or coin.

Their features were hidden behind a thick layer of dirt, thick grown-out beards, and long tangled hair. They were taller than normal men, with muscles that looked as if they could break the trunk of a small tree with their bare hands. Men like these, she imagined, pillaged villages, raped women, and killed unarmed men for pure pleasure; and now, she feared she would be their next victim!

Pressing her body tight against the inside wall of the carriage, she inched as far away from the door as possible. If the outlaws had not surrounded the carriage, she could have made an attempt to escape, but even if she slipped from the confines of the carriage the thick, heavy skirt of her dress would not allow her the freedom to run.

"Hail Mary, full of grace," she whispered, clutching the small silver cross hanging from her neck; though praying now seemed as useless as a blind dog.

As she heard heavy footsteps near the door, Keira grasped the bench tightly. She would not leave this carriage without a fight. Her eyes locked on the handle as it jiggled. The clatter of metal on wood only added to her consternation. Her hands and knees began to shake violently as her breaths became increasingly unsteady. What ever could they possible want?

Holy Mary, Mother of God, pray for us sinners now and at the hour of our-er, my death. She finished the prayer in a rasping whimper as the rattling of the handle suddenly stopped and the door flew open.

In a flash, Keira stared into the dark blue eyes of an emotionless face. His sandy blonde, unkempt hair and thick beard gave him the appearance of a large bear, a *beast* if she had ever seen one. He wore a brown leather vest that lay over a saffron shirt with a braided leather belt tied around his waist. A rabbit fur lined sporran dangled to one side and the brown of his trews matched the color of hewn red oak.

He was a beast in every regard! His body alone was a weapon in its own right. Large, rounded muscles filled the sleeves of his tunic and the vein along the side of his thick neck was pulsating. The girth of his broad shoulders and chest seemed twice as wide as one could wrap their arms around and his height seemed at least a foot over her head. Even his features seemed sharp and dominating, right down to the slight crook in his nose, which appeared to have been broken at least once.

The look in his eyes and twitch of his lips made him hard to read. She could not determine if he meant to harm her or not, but either way, he scared the hell out of her.

Biting her bottom lip, she met his gaze and quietly waited for his next move.

~*~

The moment Ian swung open the door; the lass who occupied the close quarters looked as if she had seen a ghost. Her face drained of color and she was heaving loudly with each breath as if she was lost in a state of panic.

Ian had certainly not expected to find a lass in the carriage; let alone one so young and without the company of at least a handmaiden. The lassie couldn't have been more than eighteen summers. What kind of a man would allow a woman such as her to travel without real protection? A bloody senseless man, that's who!

Her thin arms and narrow waistline were so small it gave her an unhealthy appearance, as if she had never had a full meal a day in her life. Assessing her looks further, her copper-colored hair was up in curls and braids and her royally inspired gold and red dress was far fancier than was appropriate for a trip such as this.

Ian spat on the ground. She was far too lovely for a Chisholm lass but coming upon her was good fortune. She would be his means to lure Laird Chisholm out from hiding.

"My lady," he said as he reached his hand inside the small carriage to grab her.

As if she had the instincts of a woodland animal, the lass raised her leg to block him and kicked him with the heel of her slipper square on the jaw. Ian stumbled back a step as pain radiated along his check down to his neck. *Jesus and all the saints!*

Ian twitched. He had not expected her to get the best of him. The lass had the kick of a horse, he thought, as he rubbed his hand over his jaw. He would have to keep a watchful eye on her going forward.

The wide, frightened eyes of a startled doe stared back at him. Ian understood the fear she felt. He understood a lot more than he ever let on. He had seen that terror before in the eyes of condemned men. Her eyes glistened as if she fought back tears and Ian took notice of her trembling bottom lip. Instinctively, he wanted to offer her comfort, but decided to stand his ground. After all, he should care naught for a Chisholm lass.

"Tis only a lass," Ian said to his men.

After much effort and a tremendous struggle, he managed to yank the young thing out of the safety of her carriage. He then tossed her into Alec's arms, with a command to hold the lass still. Once the young lass stood in the golden rays of the afternoon sun, her copper-colored hair gleamed like dewdrops on a peach-colored rose and her sun-kissed complexion seemed flawless. She did not possess awe-inspiring beauty, but her simple, even features still made her quite bonny.

"What do ye want of me? I demand ye release me!" she cried.

Brave little warrior! Ian ignored her request but was not ignorant of her fear, made plain by the pitch vibrato of her voice. Ian turned his attention back to Rylan and the two young escorts.

"Be gone wit' ye and tell yer Laird he can no' hide from us much longer!" Rylan instructed.

The two men looked at each other, quickly stood, and scurried off toward the trees.

"Please, dinna leave me!" the lass pleaded, before the two men were swallowed up by the darkness of the forest.

Ian held no fear of the two men telling Chisholm what had taken place. In fact, he was counting on it. Knowing he now held a Chisholm lass captive, there was no doubt Chisholm would retaliate. It was as if fate had brought the lass to him.

~*~

Anger and betrayal replaced Keira's fear the moment she saw her two escorts vanish behind the cluster of trees. *Foolish cowards!* How could they leave me here alone with these men? Keira looked back at the group of Highlanders salvaging what goods and supplies they could find in the carriage. *Thieves!* She couldn't help but wonder why they had chosen not to kill the two young men. The outlaws were well-armed and the two young lads were no match, against even one of them. A tinge of hope that perhaps these men took pity on the weak and vulnerable calmed her rampant thoughts.

There were five of them in all. The first man she referred to as the *Beast* and assumed was their leader, a man with long, dark brown-colored hair who stood across the road, a blonde haired man who looked very much like the *Beast* but not as tall and muscular, a redhead, and the younger brown-haired one, who, reeking of whiskey and sweat, held her tightly, preventing her from running away.

Three of the men wore similar clan colors, and the others wore different plaids. None of them looked familiar, but then again, Keira had never traveled away from home as her father had forbidden it. *Home*, how she wished she was there now. She had not even had the chance to give a proper goodbye to her clansmen, or her sisters, as her father rushed her off to Inverness to meet her betrothed. Thanks be to God that Alys was not here with her now.

"Take only what is valuable and leave the rest. We must return to the camp," the beastly man who'd pulled her out of the carriage, ordered.

Keira's eyes followed him as he went to speak to the dark-haired man across the road. Straining to listen, she heard nothing as they spoke in hushed tones, but she knew with certainty *she* was their topic of discussion as they kept glancing her way.

"What shall we do wit' the lass?" the man holding her called over to the other two.

"We'll take her wit' us," the Beast replied.

"Nay! Please! Please have mercy!" Keira cried out, tears flowing freely down her cheeks.

Keira's body shook as violent as if the earth quaked. Where did they wish to take her, and what did they plan to do with her once they got there?

Keira tried to fight the man's hold but he held a firm grip on her arms. She pulled and pulled until the muscles in her arms hurt, but no matter how hard she tried to get away from him, he didn't budge. It was like being tethered to one of the giant standing stones that littered the landscape. It was impossible. Her hands turned clammy and her muscles stiffened. She felt her stomach burning as fear flared inside her, its flames licking their way to her heart.

"Easy lass! Ye keep on struggling like tha', an' my grip on ye will only get tighter. I do no' wish to hurt ye," the man holding her said.

"Then let me go ye bastard!" Keira shouted as she stepped hard on the man's foot, digging her heel into his toes.

For a moment, the man released her as he winced in pain. Keira should have done *that* in the first place! Taking advantage of her freedom, she sprinted off toward the woods.

~*~

"Oh, bloody hell!" Ian said, shaking his head at the foolish lass. "Where do ye think ye are going?" he called out to her as Leland ran after her.

"Perhaps we should just let her go. We dinna need the trouble nor the distraction. Women cause nothing but problems," Rylan suggested.

"We verra well cannae leave her out here in the woods. Besides, if she has any importance to Chisholm, she might be just what we need to find him," Ian reminded him.

"Well, she will no' be my problem! Dinna say I dinna warn ye," Rylan replied as he turned to walk away, spitting on the ground.

Ian knew that taking the lass was a risk. But she would be safer with them than out here in the woods alone, and far safer than within the walls of Erchless Castle.

Leland returned shortly with the lass struggling and scratching at him like a feral cat.

"If ye would just stop yer thrashin' like a wild boar Lassie, ye would know we mean ye no' harm. We only wish to question ye," Leland said, trying to reason with her.

"Aye," Ian agreed. "But no' here!" Ian stood in front of the unpredictable lass and asked, "Ye will no' cause any more trouble fer me and my men if ye knows what's good fer ye. Aye lassie?"

Ian gazed into the lass's light blue eyes. Her nose was crinkled and she had a look of defiance. Ian pursed his lips at her expression. Perhaps Rylan was right. This lass was going to be a problem.

"I will no' say a word!" she cried out. "No' unless ye tell me who ye are and what ye want of me!"

"And if I do, ye will agree to listen to what I tell ye?"

The lass hesitated but eventually nodded her head.

"I think 'tis safe to let her go. She will no' be running off again," Ian said to Leland though he meant it more as a warning to the lass. Leland hesitantly released her and went to join the others as they finished packing up the stolen supplies. "My name is Ian and what I want from ye will have to wait. We have little time and night is coming upon us fast. We must head back to the camp. T'will be dark soon and I am taking ye wit' us."

"I would no' have been alone if ye had no' denied me my escorts, and allowed us to carry on wit' our journey."

"Twas no other way," he replied.

"What do ye mean, no other way?"

"Lassie, I will tell ye all ye need to know once we reach camp. Ye will be ridin' wit' me."

"And if I refuse?"

Ian lowered his gaze. This lass was testing him! She was daring, he had to give her that.

Lowering his voice so only she could hear, he whispered, "Then I shall tie ye up, string ye to the back of my horse and drag ye back to camp."

"Ye would no' dare! I am a Lady!" she growled.

Ian raised a brow.

"Dinna try my patience lass. I am a mon of my word!"

In truth, Ian would never have followed through with his threat, but little did she need to know that. Keeping her in fear of him was one sure way to guarantee she would not run off again.

~*~

Though she had no intentions of agreeing with anything he said or asked of her, she would, for now, obey his command until she found the opportunity to escape his clutches. She refused to be subdued by outlaws and thieves. It would only be a matter of time before her father or Laird Chisholm came looking for her and she would be safe and far away from these barbarians soon enough.

There were two types of Highlanders in Keira's mind; those who were honorable and those who lacked honor. It was clear which category these men fell into.

Standing near a beautiful russet-colored mare, the *Beast* stood holding out his hand to help her mount. The smug smile made Keira want to slap that expression right off his face. Clutching her fist at her side, she thought it best not to retaliate and bit her tongue.

"I will do it myself, thank ye!" she spat.

Lifting the skirt of her dress with one hand and holding the reins with the other, she raised her leg and slipped her foot inside the stirrup. The horse was tall. Taller than any beast she had ever seen. The height of the stirrup made it hard for her to lift herself onto its back.

Had she not had to hold back the layers of the skirt, it might have been an easier task.

"Damn this dress," Keira quietly cursed as she tempted to mount again.

"Hurry up lass, we have no' got all day," one of the ruffians called out.

She could hear the humor in his tone and could feel the eyes of the others around her, watching her. She could have done without their mockery and boorish behavior.

Before Keira had time to protest, the *Beast* reached for her waist, lifted her into the air, and plopped her down on top of the horse with a hard thud. Keira turned to look at him, narrowing her eyes at his proud grin.

She had no idea where these men were taking her, but she would escape soon enough, even if she had to walk all the way back from whence they came.

Her captor leapt onto the horse behind her with ease and took the reins to lead the horse onwards. Sitting on the horse's back, she held onto its sides with a light squeeze of her thighs. Thankful for the fluff of the horses' mane she grasped in her hand, it allowed her to pull her hips forward, keeping a comfortable distance from him without sliding back against his firm chest.

At full speed, Keira's tightly knitted braids began to loosen. It was only moments before the ribbon that tied the braids flew off with the force of the wind. The horse veered from side to side forcing Keira to grip the horse's withers with her hands which caused her bottom to slip back into the *Beast*. She felt her behind lift slightly and jostle as the mare galloped the uneven terrain. Before she knew it, she was nearly sitting on the man's lap. Securing her atop the horse, he firmly held her waist. Sending a silent prayer to the heavens, she prayed this was not a long journey.

Chapter 4

Ian kept a steady, watchful eye on the lass riding in front of him. Torn between pity and mistrust, he started to second guess his intentions. He would never mistreat a woman the way he had treated her, but his prejudice against Chisholm made the lass an easy target and an easy bargaining chip. There was a chance the lass was completely ignorant of her laird's treachery, but then again perhaps not. Ian could not afford to take unnecessary chances.

He watched as her body was jostled up and down atop the horse. She was barely able to hold on at their rapid pace. Her copper locks blew wildly in the wind and the skirt of her dress fluttered at her sides, revealing the top of her knee and her shapely, smooth calves and trim ankles.

Not easily swayed by a pretty face and a firm backside, Ian was drawn to the wee vixen. Normally, he wouldn't have given much attention to the lass but her grunts and moans were next to impossible for any man to ignore, not to mention her body tightly pressed up against his. No matter how steadfast he was, he was still a man.

Ian found himself finding excuses to glance down at her. Mayhap it was the unanswered questions about her identity that sparked his curiosity; or perhaps the way wisps of her hair tickled his face like a feather, either way he could not draw his gaze from her. Feeling her backside pressed hard against his groin, Ian knew that once their reached camp he would be in need of a dip in the loch to cool his loins.

They had ridden almost an hour and the lass had remained quiet. She had not complained once. He admired her tenacity.

"Is it too much to ask fer us to stop? I need some privacy," the lass called out.

"Ye cannae hold it?" Ian asked.

"I have no' control o'er when nature calls, any more than I have control o'er the weather. Surely ye must know that!"

Grunting, Ian pulled on the reins bringing his horse to a halt as the others followed suit.

"Is something amiss?" Rylan asked. "Why did we stop?"

"The lass needs to piss."

"Dinna she know the dangers of stopping here? We have just entered into Sutherland land."

Ian knew very well where they were. He was reluctant to stop, but knew by the tone in the lass's voice that she was not going to be able to wait any longer.

"Why dinna ye and the rest of the men continue on to the camp? We will be shortly behind ye."

"I dinna think that is a good idea, Ian," Rylan warned.

"T'will be fine. It should no' take more than a few moments."

Rylan nodded to him and snapped the reins. Ian watched as his men took off toward their camp, still another hour's ride south. Sliding down the side of the horse, he dismounted to help the lass down. When he gazed up to her, he was taken aback by the disgruntled lass staring down at him.

The lass's reddened, wind-chapped cheeks and wild curly hair made her look spent, as if she had worked a hard day out in the fields under the heat of a beating sun. No longer looking so prim and proper, the fragile rose he had first seen, she now appeared as a force to be reckoned with. He could only imagine what went on in that delicate mind of hers. She did not look affright one bit, but ill-tempered and feisty. Ian had to admit, she almost looked better mussed than as the noblewoman she had first appeared to be in the royal-looking dress saw was wearing. Somehow, the opulent gown just didn't *suit* her.

"Do ye need assistance, my lady?" he asked, as the lass still sat perched on top of the horse.

He doubted with the thick skirt of the gown she could dismount without falling.

"I do no' need yer help," she ignorantly replied.

Ian took a small step back allowing the lass to dismount of her free will. He watched in amusement as she appeared helpless and befuddled. Ian decided a little humiliation would be good to help the lass learn her place and knock her off that high pedestal she appeared to keep herself on.

As Keira swung her leg over to the other side of the horse, she swayed a moment before losing her balance atop the saddle and started to tumble off. With reflexes as fast as a falcon, Ian stretched out his arms and caught the lass in midair.

She felt as light as a wee bairn. Holding her in his arms, he inhaled, and her lavender scent filled his nostrils. It had been a long time since he'd had any physical contact with a woman. He had forgotten how delicate they were. His skin began to heat up from the feel of her body pressed against his. Her small frame and the curve of her hip fit perfectly against him. Ian's eyes instinctively swept over her, assessing her, before his gaze locked on her eyes. He had never seen such a majestic color of blue before. Along the outer rim, a dark shade of blue outlined the iris as it faded inward to a light blue, the color of ice. They were entrancing, like two blue gems in a crystal cave.

"Are ye alright?" he asked as he reluctantly set her onto her feet.

"Nay, I am no' alright!" she angrily replied.

Ian noticed tears filling her eyes.

"Are ye hurt?"

"Nay!"

"Then why are ye crying?"

"Does it really matter?" she replied making sure he saw her slant her eyes at him as she started walking away.

"Where do ye think ye are going?" Ian asked, stepping out in front of her, blocking her path.

"To piss! Remember?"

The lass stared at him wickedly. She had a sort of demanding nature that Ian admired in a woman. Ian studied her for a moment. It appeared this wee flower had some fire to her that he found rather intriguing.

"There's a spot o'er there that will offer ye some privacy," he said pointing to a cluster of short bushes. "Ye may go but be quick about it. We are no' on friendly territory. I will be right here so dinna think of trying to run off," Ian said, hoping she would heed his warning; this was neither the place nor the time to run after a wayward lass.

~*~

Keira went behind the bushes for some privacy. Lifting her skirts, she had trouble relieving herself as she could hear his footsteps just on the other side of the bushes. She felt violated. Once she was done, she lowered her skirt back down, stood and listened. Peeking through the branches, she hoped to have found her assailant occupied, giving her the opportunity to run, but she had no such luck. His attention was pinned on the bushes and surrounding area, watching with eyes like a hawk. Escaping him was going to be a challenge. Her only hope was to appeal to his male ego. Every man wanted something; she just had to figure out what this man wanted.

Keira came from behind the bushes with many questions flooding her mind. She knew she had to continue being strong, though at times she faltered. She managed to erect a shield of bravado on the outside, but on the inside, she felt like a scared child. There was so much evil in this world she had never known existed. From inside her protective sanctuary at Castle Sinclair, she had never been given the opportunity to explore what the world had to offer, and now she dreaded finding out.

Looking at the warrior who stood before her, a part of her wished she knew more about him and his intentions. At least then she could measure how dangerous he was and if he meant to harm her. Earlier, he introduced himself as Ian. How she wished he would have said his full name. Then, at least, she would know his clan affiliation.

Standing in the ray of sun that shined down from the canopy of the trees, he looked like a Greek God. He stood tall and upright, shoulders back, and his hands were firmly placed on his hips. He was a prime example of confidence, intimidation, and control.

His gaze was daunting. Standing with him alone in the woods, Keira felt unnerved as the tiny hairs on the back of her neck stood on end. Her face felt flushed, her hands, cold and clammy, and her breathing quickened as if he had conjured a spell over her senses. Around him, she felt a sort of dizzy sensation as if the air had thickened, making it hard to breath. What was this tension that filled the air? Why was his gaze like a spear, penetrating her very being, right to the core?

She called him the *Beast* but not for his size or his stature. It was because he was as lethal and dangerous as a fire-breathing dragon. Stand too close and one could easily get burned by his flames. Even the look in his eyes had a way of putting one into submission. She imagined that he was used to getting what he wanted, she only wished to know what it was he wanted from her.

As Keira was about to look away, a blinding shimmer of light caught her attention. Around his neck he wore a golden medallion. The image pressed on the face of the circular medallion was of the Scottish crown with two swords crisscrossed behind it. It was a Scottish crest but none like she had ever seen. It must be of great importance if it represented the Scottish crown, but what? Perhaps it meant nothing. He could have just as easily stolen it, like everything he had stowed away in his satchels. The greed of men! Preying on the weak! Pillaging villages and kidnapping helpless women. Keira turned away from him.

"Lass, we've stalled long enough. We need to go."

"Please let me go. I mean nothing to ye. I am nobody."

"Lady Chisholm…"

He started, and Keira burst out, "I am no' Lady Chisholm!"

At least not yet! Laird Chisholm had only accepted her hand in marriage, but in truth, she wanted nothing to do with the marriage or the man and she would hold onto that information for as long as possible.

She was no more than a peasant with a good name. The union between her and Laird Chisholm was all her father needed to ensure their clan's survival. Without Chisholm's offering, they would have been left with nothing. But what would *this man* know? He was just an outlaw! He was probably hoping for some large ransom, but he would be sorely disappointed to find out that he'd kidnapped the dowerless daughter of an impoverished laird.

"If ye are no' a Chisholm lass, then who are ye and why were ye traveling on his ally's land in Chisholm's own carriage?"

Keira hesitated for a moment, debating whether she should tell him the truth. But what was the harm in telling him that he'd kidnapped the wrong prize?

"I am Lady Keira Sinclair, the eldest daughter of Laird Magnus Sinclair. And if ye do no' release me I promise ye that all hell and fury will rain down upon ye. The wrath of my father is fierce and he does no' show mercy to…to rotten bastards like ye."

"Sinclair?" his brow rose as he questioned. "Why would a Sinclair lass be traveling through to Chisholm lands?"

"I was no' traveling through Chisholm lands. I was traveling to Chisholm land."

"Why?"

"I dinna see how that is any of yer business!"

"Tis, because I just made it my business. Do no' make me ask ye again!" he warned.

"I was to meet Laird Chisholm this afternoon."

"Why?"

Keira bit her lower lip, almost ashamed of the reason.

"Because…today is my wedding day. *Was* my wedding day," she corrected herself. "I am to marry Laird Chisholm; that is why ye must release me! If word gets to him that ye have stolen his bride I'm sure he will send his forces after ye and yer men!"

Ian's expression went from curiosity to anger. His eyes darkened and brow furrowed. He said nothing in response, and his eyes squinted as he looked into the distance. Tension filled the air like a storm was brewing. The silence was deafening and her nerves began to crawl. What was it that she said to cause his change in demeanor? Did it matter that she was getting married? People got married all the time.

"If ye were heading to marry Laird Thomas Chisholm, then ye should be thanking me."

"Thanking ye? For what? Ye attacked my carriage, relieved me of my escort, and now are holding me against my will. Where in this situation do ye think I owe ye any sort of thanks?"

"For saving ye!"

"Saving me? From whom?"

"Laird Chisholm!"

"The only saving I need is from ye!"

Ian snickered.

"Ye have no idea the type of mon he is, do ye?"

Keira ignored his question, yet couldn't help but wonder what he meant. From what her father had told her, he was a good man. And somehow believing that Ian was some kind of knight in shining armor was about as believable as she being the Queen of Scotland!

"Ye told me earlier that if I told ye who I was and why I was crossing into Chisholm land ye would release me. Will ye keep yer word?"

Ian walked back and forth for a moment before stopping in his tracks.

"I can no' allow ye to continue on yer course. But ye have my word that no' harm will come to ye."

The lying whoreson!

"Ye tricked me! Ye never had any intention of letting me go, did ye?"

"Aye, I did and I still do, but first I need to speak to my men," he said as he grabbed her upper arm.

"Where will ye be taking me? Is Laird Chisholm in some kind of trouble? I demand to know! I have a right!"

He stopped and turned to look at her.

"Aye ye do, but I dinna believe I need to tell ye of such things, at least no' yet!"

"Ye bloody barbarian!"

Anger flared in his eyes.

"Forgive my lack of patience lass, but ye are becoming a pain in my arse! Now let me help ye back on the horse."

"Fine! But keep yer hands off me and keep yer distance. Tis nothing like riding wit' a mon who smells of wet dog."

"Damn it woman, ye try my patience."

"Yer use of blasphemies and profane language has no' fallen on deaf ears. Therefore, tis no' just yer manner that offends me but yer speech, as well…ye know, for a Scot and a warrior ye have absolutely no redeeming qualities. That either makes ye daft or no' any different than the bloody English!" she responded, proud of her clever reply.

The warrior muttered a curse, picked her up and plopped her down on the horse. He grumbled but ignored her insult. Keira smugly smiled, realizing that she'd gotten a rise out of him. It would let him know that she was not going to follow his orders without at least putting up some resistance.

The warrior mounted behind her, wrapping his arm around her waist and pulling her close against him. Before she could protest, he snapped the reins, making the horse bolt before taking off at a hard run.

Chapter 5

The lass's revelation baffled Ian beyond belief. How had Clan Sinclair allied with the Chisholm without his hearing about it? Magnus Sinclair certainly wasn't a person of interest, at least not one he was made aware of. Ian had always suspected Chisholm of treason, but was the Sinclair Chief a co-conspirator? The idea did not sit well with Ian. What was more disturbing was that he did not know what role the lass played in all of this. Was she, too, a traitor? Did she know of Chisholm's plot against king and country?

Ian urged the horse faster. He needed to speak to his men and tell him what he had learned. He would then have to decide whether to continue on his course to hunt Chisholm down or to return to Linlithgow Castle to speak to his Sire about the new developments. His other matter of business, of course, was what he was going to do now about the lass. Caught in the middle of a civil war, he certainly could not allow the lass to continue on to Erchless nor could he allow her to return home. He needed to question her further. To find out what she knew and if she could be trusted.

In less than an hour, they arrived at the well-hidden campsite near the entrance of a rocky cave. Ian dismounted, and then helped Keira down from the saddle. She remained quiet and docile.

"What the bloody hell took ye so long?" Rylan asked.

Ian shook his head.

"Leland, tend to the lass. I need to speak wit' Rylan," Ian called out.

Leland walked toward them, but the lass ignored his offer of help, and went to sit down atop a large boulder. Satisfied she wasn't going anywhere; Ian walked toward a stand of trees nearby, and nodded his head to Rylan, signifying for him to follow.

Once they were among the nearby trees, far from earshot of the others, Rylan asked, "What is it?"

"I was wrong about the lass. She is no' a Chisholm woman. She be a Sinclair."

"Sinclair?"

"Aye. She was on her way to Erchless when we intercepted the carriage. She was to marry Thomas on this very day."

Rylan raked his fingers through his hair.

"Why the bloody hell would her father agree to such a marriage? All the chiefs in the Highlands have been warned against making alliances with known traitors."

"I suspect 'tis because he too is a traitor."

"What about the lass? Did she say anything?"

"Nay, and I dinna ask her. No' yet anyway."

"We must get word to James."

"Aye! I think we just found one of the key players in the rebellion."

"What are ye thinking?" Rylan asked.

"I shall leave for Linlithgow immediately. Now that we know where Chisholm's hideout is, we should leave a few men behind to scout and track their movements."

"What of the lass?"

"I'll take her wit' me."

"And what are ye going to do if ye find out that she is a part of this?" Rylan asked.

"Let us just hope she isna!"

~*~

Sitting on the rock, Keira watched as the men erected their tents and tended to the fire. Her stomach growled as she thought of the feast she would have been enjoying at this hour had she made her way to Erchless. Now she was forced not only to starve, but apparently to sleep exposed to the night's cool air.

Surveying her surroundings, reminded her that she had no idea where she was. Nothing seemed familiar. Even surrounded with the group of men, she felt alone. A sliver of anger entered her heart as she thought about her predicament. Had it not been for her betrothed, she would never have been in this situation in the first place. He was supposed to have arrived at Inverness. It was he who was supposed to have escorted her to Erchless, and it was him these men apparently wanted, not her. Had Laird Thomas Chisholm been there now she'd...*spit on him*!

Keira no longer cared about the ridiculous contract her father had signed. There had to be another way to raise the money to pay the taxes. She would gladly work out in the fields herself if it helped. She would even sell her tapestries or her fine linens if she thought she could get a good price for them.

Looking out in the distance, she watched a herd of deer prance through the tall grass. Their freedom saddened her. Not because of her captivity, but because even if she were to escape and return home, her father would just find her another suitor. And she was sure that next time, she would not be given a choice. It felt as if her world was crumbling down around her like a stack of bricks and there was nothing she could do to stop it. She had never felt more alone than she felt at that very moment.

Keira released a deep breath and turned her attention back to her captors. So far, she knew three of their names: Ian, Leland and Rylan, but the other two still remained a mystery. Those two were quiet and kept to themselves. As for Ian, she knew that he was a man of authority, although he had not introduced himself with such a title as Laird or Chieftain. It was however, apparent that he was at least the leader of these men; the governor of outlaws.

As Ian and Rylan returned to the camp, Keira ignored them by fiddling with the hem of her gown, but kept an ear toward the men. Listening to their conversation, she overheard talk of their Laird and the details about their travel, including where they would go from here.

"Ian, what are we going to do?" Leland asked.

Ian glanced at Keira before answering.

"We must speak to Laird Gudeman. If what I think is true, we've got bigger problems. Tomorrow, ye, Rylan and I will take the lass and travel to Linlithgow. Daven, I need ye and Alec to stay and keep watch. Report any activity ye see."

"Aye," the two men nodded in agreement. Keira's brow creased at the mention of their Laird's name. She had never heard of any clan by the name of Gudeman nor was it a typical Scottish name. Perhaps these men were not Highlanders after all, perhaps they were Lowlanders. Of course their size suggested Norsemen as their height and girth were comparable to giants.

Keira hated not being included in their conversation. She had every right to know what was happening, but it was clear that these men were not going to tell her anything. They ignored her as if she did not even exist.

Keira plucked up the head of a dandelion sticking out of the ground near her feet and began taking it apart, one small petal at a time before tossing the stem onto the ground. She welcomed the distraction. Ian stared at her intensely as he and the men continued to talk about their journey thus far. From what Keira gathered, these were men for hire. Hired to hunt down those their Laird ordered them to, and Thomas Chisholm was on the top of their list.

Once their conversation was over, the red-headed man that Ian had called Daven stood and headed over to the horses while the others stayed seated around the fire. Keira's stomach growled loud enough to break their silence.

"Are ye hungry lass? Daven is fetching ye something to eat," Ian informed her.

"I will no' take yer food," she stubbornly replied.

No matter how hungry she felt, she would rather find her own food than share theirs. She thought she could probably go a few days without eating before she would starve to death.

"Suit yerself," he said under his breath.

"Lassie has quite a wicked tongue on her, dinna she?" Leland spouted as the others snickered by his remark.

Keira lowered her eyelids and furrowed her brow at them, then returned her attention back to the *Beast*. His amused smile fueled her anger further. She didn't know why she cared what they thought of her.

~*~

"Ian, we've been robbed!" Daven said, walking toward them, holding onto a small brown cloth bag.

"What are ye talking about?"

"Most of the meat is gone. I only found enough food here in this bag to last us the night."

"How the bloody hell did that happen?" Rylan asked.

"I dinna know, but I saw footprints near the horses. It must have been taken when we were setting up the camp."

"Then whoever took it must no' have gone far. I am going after the thieving bastard!" Rylan said as he stood and made his way to his horse to grab his sword and dagger.

"Well, let's get to cookin' what we still do have. We will have to scare up some bird or rabbits in the morn'." Ian suggested.

As Daven put the food on the spit, Ian glanced behind him at the lass. The forlorn look on her face made her appear vulnerable and defeated. Digging in the bag, he pulled out an apple, and stood. Walking away from his men, he went to stand near the lass. She refused the piece of fruit he held out.

Ian kneeled down in front of her.

"Lass, I know ye are hungry. Ye have no' eaten fer hours now. Go on, take it."

"I'm no' hungry," she whispered, facing away from him.

Ian huffed out a sharp breath, trying to be patient with the lass.

"Tis all the food we have. Ye should eat what we have to share.

Ian took a spot on the ground in front of her, hoping to gain her trust. He had to find out what she knew, and hoped that she would confide in him eventually.

"Lassie, I give ye my word that nothing will happen to ye. I am sorry that I can no' let ye go, but tis fer yer own safety."

"Safety! From what? Why do ye insist on keeping me captive wit' out even giving me an explanation?"

"What do ye know about Laird Chisholm?"

"Nothing! I have never e'en met the mon."

"So yer betrothal to him was arranged?"

"Aye."

"Did yer father arrange it?"

"Aye. But what does my father have to do wit' any of this?"

"Possibly more than ye think."

"My father is a great mon!" she defended.

"I am no' questioning yer father, only his motives. Did ye know he was marryin' ye off to a traitor? Chisholm has allied wit' the English to overrule the king. He is a verra dangerous man. 'Tis why we are searching fer him."

"My father is no traitor if that is what ye are suggesting!"

"For his sake, my lady, I hope ye are correct."

If Ian was a betting man, he would guess that this wee lass knew more than she was letting on, but he decided that he had told her enough for now. Ian picked himself up. With the tip of his boot, he slightly tapped the apple that lay on the ground and watched it slowly roll next to Keira. He confidently stepped away knowing that if the lass was hungry enough, she would eat it. Only a foolish person would refuse to take it and he did not take the lass for a fool.

Chapter 6

"I caught the wee hellion who pilfered the meat," Rylan said, roughly shaking a young lad by the collar of his dirt-stained shirt.

The young boy stood silent and wide-eyed. Ian studied him for a moment. The wee lad looked no more than seven or eight summers.

"I am thinking this whelp needs to feel the sting of my belt on his backside or perhaps I should cut off his hand fer stealing," Rylan suggested.

Ian watched as the blood drained from the lad's face at the mere mention of punishment. Ian held back his smile for he knew all too well that Rylan would never cut off the lad's hand. However, a few lashes might teach the lad a lesson.

"What is yer name?" Ian asked.

"Robbie," the lad replied in a soft whimper.

"Is what Rylan said true? Ye are the one who stole our bounty?"

"We needed the meat," the lad snarled.

Ian always had a soft spot for those less fortunate, but he respected those who asked for charity rather than taking it for themselves.

"Ye ken stealing is a serious offense. And crimes cannae go unpunished."

Ian scratched his rough chin as he thought of a punishment that would best suit the crime, given the age of the lad.

"What clan are ye from?"

"I am no' part of any clan. Me mum and I are alone. We ran away from Clan Ross."

"The Rosses, ye say? What happened to make ye leave?"

"My mum's new husband beats her, so we ran away where the bastard can ne'er find us."

"Does yer mother ken ye steal?"

"Nay."

"Rylan," Ian nodded to him to mete out the lad's punishment.

Keira bolted straight up, ready to defend the young lad.

"Surely, ye have enough food to spare this child a meager meal!" she spat.

"Ye stay out of this," Rylan growled. "Punishment must be given fer such disrespect."

"Then give him my share!"

"Dinna worry lass. A sound lashing can no' cause permanent damage," Ian said, trying to console her.

"He's just a child who is scared and hungry! Where is yer sense of honor?"

Ian looked at Rylan before turning his attention to the lass. Arguing with Rylan, nicknamed the *Wolf*, for his fierce growling voice, never ended well. Though it was honorable of the lass to offer to sacrifice her meal, the provisions were not hers to give away, nor would it save the lad from a good thrashing or two. Regardless of the situation, the lad would not learn his lesson without honest discipline behind it. He must not only hear and understand the lesson but feel it as well, therefore the next time the lad mustered the courage to go thieving, he would think twice about from whom he stole.

After Ian heard the first two strikes of the leather belt making contact with the lad's rump, he stopped Rylan from going any further. The tears in the lass's eyes were as unnerving as if she held a knife to his heart. Had she never witnessed a thrashing before? For a moment, he found himself wanting to hold her and comfort her. Given what the lass had already been through, he couldn't stand to be the cause of anymore pain.

"That'll be enough lad," he said, looking to Rylan, devoid of emotion. "As fer ye, wee Robbie. Ye may take the meat ye have stolen and nay more. Best ye think twice the next time ye decide to steal a mon's bounty," Ian said, hoping the lad would heed his warning.

Rylan released the lad from his hold and Robbie dropped to the ground, obviously nervous and in some pain. Scurrying away from Rylan and Ian, he picked up his satchel and hobbled off into the woods.

"Ye are getting soft," Rylan accused Ian.

"The lad got what he deserved," Leland muttered.

"Aye, but the lass is right. We have plenty of provisions to last us until tomorrow," Ian said.

"*The lass*? What say does she have? Is that the way of it, then? She's the one givin' the orders?"

Rylan stood nearly toe to toe with Ian and boldly held his gaze.

"Back down Rylan," Leland warned, stepping in between the two angry men.

"I told ye the lass would be nothing but trouble!" Rylan said, kicking up dust as he walked away.

Fury burned in Ian's veins. Never had Rylan questioned him before and disrespect was not going to be tolerated. Had they not been such good friends, Ian would have sliced him through. Rylan was as reckless and defiant as his nickname, *Wolf*, implied.

"Dinna mind him," Leland said to Ian as he and Ian watched Rylan saunter off.

It wasn't just Rylan that angered him but the lass as well. Ian was a man of logic and reason. He did not make decisions based on emotions. Allowing his heart to choose for him was not only dangerous but foolish. But this lass made him feel as if the walls he'd erected to protect his emotions were beginning to soften. He felt pity rather than resolve, and that did not sit well with him.

He hated the way she questioned and argued with him. Not only was she becoming a sore on his arse, but she was beginning to make him question himself. If he made decisions based on the lass's tender heart, he would accomplish nothing. Every time he was around her, he felt as if he walked on glass, stepping carefully to prevent injury. He needed to draw a line separating his duties from his feelings toward the lass.

"Ian, I got her tent ready as ye asked," Daven announced.

Ian glanced back over at her. She was looking between the horses and around the sides of the tent.

"What are ye lookin' fer?" Ian asked.

"My bags! They were in the cart when we left but I cannae find them," Keira answered, her voice loud and shrill.

"We dinna take any bags wit' us."

"But all of my clothes, my belongings, they were in my bags. How do ye suppose I am to change or stay warm wit' out any of my clothing?"

"I have a plaid ye can use. We took what we needed and left the rest."

"Does nothing I own have value to ye?"

"Ye can get new dresses once we reach our destination."

"I dinna want new dresses. Ye could have told me. I would have carried my bags myself."

"That would have only slowed us down. Now I suggest, my lady, ye get some rest. T'will be a long day tomorrow."

"I dinna need yer blanket, yer tent, nor yer food. I will stay right here and sleep near the fire if I get cold."

Ian stomped over to his horse and pulled out a plaid from one of the saddle bags, gathering it into his arms. Walking back to the lass, he threw it at her.

"Now get to sleep," he ordered, before turning his back to her and heading over across the camp to lean against the trunk of a wide ash tree.

"Bastard!" Keira mumbled, just loudly enough that Ian could hear when he walked away.

~*~

As the sun sank beneath the horizon, the air began to cool. Picking up the plaid she had intentionally dropped on the ground, Keira wrapped it around her shoulders. The men were quiet. The only sounds she heard were the occasional hoot of an owl in a nearby tree, and leaves rustling in the light breeze.

Keira's mind was consumed with what Ian had told her. Did her father know Laird Chisholm was a traitor? He couldn't have! Keira refused to believe that her father had a part of any plan or scheme against the king. To do so would be treason; punishable by death, and why would her father risk such a thing?

She decided she would sneak away once the men were asleep. Keira looked down at the red apple Ian had left for her, which now lay next to her foot. Her stomach growled. She glanced up at the others before snatching it off the ground and took a small bite. The juice of the apple ran down her chin as she took another. It tasted sweet, and helped curb her hunger. She should have thanked him, but her stubborn nature would not have allowed her to do so.

Keira looked up at the tent Daven and Alec had erected for her. It looked warm and inviting. She figured she needed to at least get a few hours' sleep before attempting her escape. Hiking through the Highlands on foot with little sleep, she would not get far. Plus, if they thought she was in the tent all night, it would allow her a chance to cover a fair distance before they discovered she was gone.

Keira stood and headed over to the tent. She felt the men's eyes following her. Pulling back the flap, she slid inside. Within the tent, was a pallet layered with several warm plaids. She slipped underneath one of the layers and closed her eyes.

Keira slept fitfully inside the tent, wrapped in the oversized, wool blanket Ian had offered. Tossing and turning, worries of what tomorrow would bring kept her awake and restless for most of the night. At what she assumed was just a few hours before dawn, she poked her head outside the tent. Four of the men lay asleep near the low-burning fire. Looking around, she could not find Ian. He was not leaning against the tree where she had last seen him, nor was he one of the men lying near the fire. Keira slipped through the opening into the cool air.

With Ian nowhere in sight, and the men fast sleep, she picked up her skirt and tiptoed toward the trees, trying to be as quiet as a mouse. She made her way just beyond the tree line. Satisfied she had successfully crept enough distance from the camp without being heard, she started to run.

With only the light of the moon guiding her, Keira had no idea in which direction she ran but any direction was better than back toward their campsite.

"Oh the nerve of them!" she muttered to herself.

She tried to put together the pieces of information she had learned from their conversations, but still nothing made sense. As if she were having a conversation with another, she cursed and ranted out loud about Ian and his band of barbarians. Her frustration building, she realized she had more and more unanswered questions. She believed that only her father would have the answers, as he was apparently in on this mess along with her intended groom, Laird Chisholm.

She ran until her legs burned and the bottom of her feet grew sore. After nearly an hour, Keira stopped and rested against a tree, to catch her breath. To the east, the sky was beginning to lighten. She closed her eyes and listened to the sound of her breath, wondering how much farther she had until she reached a nearby village or passed someone on the road. With no food, weapon or coin, she hoped to find someone with God's blessed grace who would offer her aid.

"Tis foolish fer a lass to be out here alone," a male voice said.

At first Keira thought it was her own conscience replying to her. She was beginning to agree that wandering off alone was a foolish idea. But the familiarity of his rough tone brought her back to the present.

Keira's eyes popped open in surprise. Leaning against a tree stood a smug-looking Ian. How had he found her? How had she not heard his approach?

"How did ye find me?"

"I've been following ye the whole way."

"But how?"

"My Lady, nothing gets past me."

"If ye have been following me this whole time, why did ye only now reveal yerself?"

"I wanted to see how far ye'd get on yer own. I must say, I was quite impressed and amused."

"I am no' here fer yer amusement!" she spat.

"I dinna think ye know it, but yer quite bonny when ye banter wit' yerself."

Known for talking out loud to herself when deep in thought, she felt mortified by the things he could have heard, though most of it curses aimed at him and his men.

"So, ye think I'm a beast, aye?"

"I think ye are more than just a beast!"

Ian smirked at her remark.

"That may be true lass. Where is it ye think ye were going?"

"Home."

"And yer plan was to walk all the way there?"

"Aye, if I had to!"

"Tis no' necessary. Once we make our journey to Linlithgow, I will see ye arrive home safely and promise ye, no harm will come to ye. But ye must promise me that ye will no' try running off again."

"May I have yer word?"

"On my father's life, ye have my word."

Keira bit her bottom lip, leery of just how good his word was. The mention of his father sparked her curiosity like flames to dry parchment.

"Who are ye?" she asked.

"I already told ye who I am."

"Ye did no' such thing. Ye gave me only yer given name. Surely ye are more than just one name. Ye dinna tell me where ye are from, or what clan ye belong to. If I am to trust ye wit' my protection, I wish to know who is protecting me."

"I was born into Clan MacKay, and MacKay is my name."

"MacKay? Yer clan hails from just west of mine. Are we allies?"

"My father is at peace with most of the neighboring clans."

"Yer father is Jacob, chieftain of Clan MacKay?"

"Aye, he is."

"And the others? Are ye all MacKays?"

"Nay! Only Leland and Rylan. Daven and Alec are warriors from other clans. I've told ye enough. We must head back. If ye wish to return home, we must leave soon."

"Wait a minute! That's it? That's all yer going to tell me? Ye haven't told me anything like, why are ye keeping me captive? What crime is Laird Chisholm accused of? And who are ye really?"

Ian walked toward her until he stood nearly a foot away. So close, she could smell his scent of horse and leather.

"Lady Sinclair, I do no' have the authority to divulge my orders to ye nor the details of my mission. Can ye just trust that I am only looking out fer yer safety and that I will disclose to ye what I can when the time comes?"

Keira saw nothing but sincerity in his eyes. Perhaps she had been a tad irrational and quick to judge. After all, he had kept his word thus far.

"Alright! Ye leave me little choice but to trust ye."

"Good."

Keira let out a breath and followed Ian. Over a small hill, she spotted his horse grazing on the tall grass. Amazed at the sight of it, she was still perplexed at how he had followed her, on horseback of all things, without her knowledge. Perhaps her banter had kept her from noticing the obvious.

Keira allowed Ian to help her mount the tall creature without dispute. Mounting behind her, he led the horse back the way they had come.

Chapter 7

Ian and Keira returned to the camp just as the men were beginning to awaken. She was surprised to find that she had not gotten as far as she'd hoped when Ian came upon her, as their return trip took only a matter of a few moments. Even if he hadn't found her, based on the distance she'd managed to travel this morning, it would have taken at least a month for her to reach the border of her land. It only proved that she had little choice but to trust Ian and his word to return her to her family.

"Where have ye been?" Rylan asked.

"Fer a short ride," Ian replied.

Keira shot a glance over at Ian. He lied for her. Why? Perhaps he did not wish to anger his men with her rash decision to leave. Whatever the reason, she felt grateful. It was as clear as spring water, these men did not think highly of her and she did not want to do anything that would further provoke them.

"Are ye and Leland packed?" Ian asked.

"Aye, we are," Rylan responded, looking at them both suspiciously.

Ian turned his attention back to Keira. His look was like the calm before a storm.

"My lady, if ye wish fer some privacy before we leave, I suggest ye do so now. I wish to cover as much land as possible today."

"How long will it take to get there?" she asked.

"Tis a two day journey from here. Can I trust ye no' to run?"

Keira bit her bottom lip. She had every right to run, but the scowl on Ian's face had a way of making her feel guilty about her need for freedom.

"Aye," she whispered, speaking the truth.

Ian allowed Keira her privacy but stayed within hearing distance, making sure that she did not back down from her promise.

He had never known a lass to keep her word. One or two had made an attempt to keep their word to him, but in the end, women always did what they wanted if they could get away with it.

"She ran, dinna she? I told ye, she would be nothing but trouble," Rylan said, more as a statement than a question, grabbing his pack from the ground and swinging it over the saddle.

Ian grimaced at his accusation but did not respond. He'd made one excuse for the lass already; he was not about to make another. Nothing ever seemed to get past Rylan. The damn man was too clever for his own good, but that cleverness made him a good warrior.

A few moments later, Keira reappeared. Her eyes were puffy from lack of sleep and it appeared she had to will her body to move. It served her right for trying to escape in the first place!

Ian looked down at her skirt as she walked. He imagined it was hard for the lass to ride with such a large bundle of fabric underneath her bottom. Then an idea came to him. Ian pulled out a small, short-bladed dirk from his belt and tossed it to Keira. She caught the small knife in her hands and studied the blade.

"Do yerself a favor and cut off the under layers of that skirt of yers. All that fluff is no' necessary and removing it will prevent ye from tripping all o'er it when ye walk. Plus it will make ye much more comfortable on the horse."

~*~

Keira looked down at the sharp blade in her hands. How could he have been so trusting to think that she wouldn't use it against him? The small knife wouldn't amount to much in battle but it was enough to slice a man's throat or cause a man to bleed out if she stuck it in the right spot.

Keira had never harmed another before in her life, but that did not mean she couldn't gather the courage to at least make an attempt, especially if her life was in danger. But was it? So far Ian had kept true to his word and not harmed her. And if he had not been concerned for her protection, he would not have followed her in the woods and returned her to camp. Any other man would not have bothered. Perhaps there was more to him than he let on.

Ian's idea of cutting off the extra, heavy velvet was a sound and logical suggestion. Had she thought of it before, she would have torn off and removed the bothersome train earlier.

Finding some privacy behind a bush, she lifted the top layer of her dress and draped it over her arm. Twisting around, and holding the knife with the other hand, she made a small tear along the back waistline. Setting the knife down on a stump, she ripped the fabric from around her waist, pulling it away from the dress.

With a heap of loose material gathered in her arms, she dropped the heavy train, now detached from the back of her dress. The skirt flopped to her sides, sleek and slender. Keira felt as if she had lost nearly twenty pounds removing the excess velvet. This was much better, she thought. It was easier for her to maneuver and undoubtedly going to be easier for her to ride as well. Of course, she never would have needed to damage the dress had Ian and his men not left her luggage back at the carriage, but that was a well-worn conversation and did not need to be brought up again.

Returning to the group of men, she spotted Ian standing near his horse, waiting for her. She made her way toward him.

"Tis much better!" he said, smiling down at her.

Ian hoisted Keira up onto the horse and jumped on the saddle behind her. Cradling her between his thighs, he lightly placed one hand over her stomach and the other on the reins. The close contact made her shift on the saddle but as she tried to move away from him, it only caused him to hold her closer.

As Ian snapped the reins, the horse jolted, causing Keira to wrap her arm over his to prevent herself from falling. Pressing her back against his front had felt too comfortable. She fit perfectly against him and found that she liked the way his arm wrapped around her waist. Keira relaxed her shoulders and leaned against him. Her skin tingled at the feel of his breath on the back of her neck. It caused her stomach to tense and other strange feelings inside her to awaken. Though it was not meant to be a romantic gesture, it was by far the most intimate sensation she had ever felt.

Never had Keira seen such beautiful, picturesque landscape than God's creation unveiled before her that morning. The early morning sun cast hues of gold on the peaks of the mountains and deep within the valley, fog seeped through the trees like a blanket of white smoke. Lush green trees and shrubs dotted the hills and wild alpine flowers were in full bloom, adding a delightful mixture of color. Thick purple heather swayed harmoniously in the light breeze across the fields and small white sheep could be seen grazing in the distance.

The land surrounding Castle Sinclair could not hold a candle to the beauty before her. Unlike the green rolling hills of the Highlands, Castle Sinclair was settled on rocky flatland on the edge of a cliff overlooking the ocean. It was built on top of bedrock and sandy soil, making it hard for crops to grow in abundance. Although the estate was along the shore of the North Sea, the ocean was the only beauty that part of the Highlands offered.

As the sun rose in the sky, Keira was grateful the sun-kissed clouds showed promise for a warm and dry day. This time of year sporadic downpours were common and she prayed the rain would stay away just long enough for them to reach their destination. Once they arrived and they returned her to her family, she wouldn't care if it rained every day for a year.

For what seemed like hours, they rode across the land heading in a southeastern direction. Keira's toes and legs felt numb from staying atop the horse for as long as she had. She thought to question Ian whether they would break soon, but she dared not anger him. He had kept quiet throughout most of the ride causing her to wonder what he was thinking.

As time passed, boredom set in and her eyes began to feel heavy and started to close. Fighting to stay awake was a losing battle. Her eyes were drifting shut, taking longer and longer to open each time. Within moments, Keira fell fast asleep.

~*~

Ian glanced down at the lass slumped in his arms. With her head turned to one side, resting on his chest, he could see every feature on her face from her small nose to her pink lips. Raising his hand, he gently grazed the side of her cheek; moving his thumb as lightly as a whisper against her soft skin. She felt as soft as a rose petal. Had things been different, he would not have hesitated to make an advance or make his intentions known, but he was not the same man he once was. He could not offer her protection nor could he truly give her his heart. He could never be a husband again, or a father. He had given up that life a long time ago.

Ian's loyalty to Scotland was his life. And with all the blood he'd spilled, he was a damned to hell. His only salvation was to serve the crown in hopes of redeeming himself for his sins.

Keira stirred in her sleep. Pressing her back against him, she turned slightly and gripped the fabric of his shirt. Her other hand rested firmly on the top of his thigh. At the moment of contact, an explosion of unnerving sensations shot to his groin. With her buttock firmly pressed up against him, Ian felt his pulse quicken. He willed away his wandering thoughts and physical sensations but as she clung to him, his animal instincts growled within him.

Ian craned his neck, trying to avoid the lass who lay asleep in his arms, but he was failing miserably and his groin reminded him of that fact each time her bottom lifted and settled back down on his lap from the motion of the horse under them.

As if the heavens were answering his prayers, a drop of rain fell from the sky, landing on his cheek. Looking up at the darkened, cloudy sky, he realized he had missed the approaching storm, too distracted by the bonny lass. Another drop fell and then another, and before he knew it, the rain fell steadily. Thank God; he could use the distraction!

~*~

Keira awoke when she felt the tapping sensation of cold water on her cheeks. She quickly bolted upright, straightening her back. All manner of embarrassment came pouring into her mind when she found herself snuggled up against Ian like a wanton whore. She couldn't imagine what he must think of her, nor did she want to know. In the future, she would have to do whatever it took to prevent herself from falling asleep, no matter how tired she was.

Looking up at the sky, she realized that the clouds had turned grey and covered the sky like a thick blanket.

"I had no' expected it to rain. 'Twas so beautiful earlier," she said, making an attempt to dry her face.

"Aye. That's the one thing about the Highlands lass. Ye can experience all four seasons in just a matter of a day," he replied, wrapping a cloak around them both.

Keira gratefully took the cloak and wrapped it over her shoulders, but kept her distance from Ian. She would have protested, but if her choices were between having to travel the rest of the way in drenched clothing or being protected from the rain, she'd gladly choose the latter.

As the rain fell with intensity, the horses slowed their pace. Their hooves began to sink into the sodden ground. The rain hammered down on them like small ice pellets. Keira could feel Ian grip her tighter against him as she started to shiver from the cold. Thankful for the warmth of his chest, she didn't mind in the least.

"Are ye alright, my lady?"

"Nay, I am no' alright but little does that matter! Will we be finding shelter soon?" she asked as rain dripped off the ends of her hair.

"If we come across shelter we will stop. Until then, the plaid will have to do."

They rode for another half hour until they came to a rocky hill with an overhang from a cliff. Ian slowed his horse and called to the others what they had found.

"Is that a shallow cave?" Keira asked.

"Nay! The earth gave way after a heavy rain and created that cavity. 'Tis no' what I'd choose for shelter under normal circumstances, but it's better than riding any further in this pissing rain!"

Ian dismounted before helping Keira down. With her legs sore from riding, she almost lost her balance, and grabbed onto Ian's forearm for support. It amazed her how strong his arm felt under her fingers, as hard as a rock. His skin was much smoother than she had imagined it would be for a beast like him. He placed a hand on the small curve of her back and gazed down at her. For a brief moment, the atmosphere between them changed, and the air seemed to lighten. She couldn't decide if it was because of him, or the storm.

Looking up at him, his eyes were the perfect shade of blue, like two perfectly carved sapphires. Her eyes dropped to his mouth. His lips were full and thick like small pillows and she felt the strange desire for him to kiss her. Suddenly, as if his arm had become too hot to touch, she released her hand from it. She stepped away, wringing her hands.

She was getting dangerously close to her captor. She should hate him, fear him, but she couldn't bring herself to feel that way. Not anymore. Though still apprehensive, she was beginning to trust him.

Keira followed Ian, out of the rain, to the earthen shelter. The muscles in her thighs ached as she walked. Stretching them out, she seemed to be the only one affected by the long travel. Her eyes followed the other two men who seemed to ignore her. Both Rylan and Leland stayed by their horses, digging in their packs.

Digging in his pack, Leland pulled out a small knife from his bag. Swinging the blade at his side, he looked at her and wickedly grinned. She didn't know what to make of his actions, but Rylan had already voiced his opinion of her, and his dissatisfaction that Ian had decided to keep her with them. Rylan was a man she would keep her distance from as much as possible. Keira swallowed hard when he looked at her, and she took a step closer to Ian.

She had learned to trust him but as for the other two, trust would need to be earned. There was no saying what they would do to her if Ian weren't there to protect her.

"Ian, we need to find food. I'm hungrier than a wolf," Leland announced, not lifting his eyes from Keira.

"Aye. I will join ye," Ian replied. Turning around, he faced Keira. "I need fer ye to stay put. Ye will be safe here."

"Yer leaving?" she nervously asked.

"Aye, but I will no' be gone long. Promise me ye will stay!"

Keira nodded her head. After strapping his sword to his side, Ian pulled out a small dagger from his bag and slipped it inside a sheath that hung off his belt and grabbed the reins of the horse, leading the animal into the woods. Keira watched all three men quietly walk deeper into the woods until the trees seemed to close behind them.

Looking around the surrounding area, Keira took notice of the moss-covered rocks embedded into the hard sandstone. The arch of the overhang, and the way the earth had been naturally carved out beneath it reminded her of a magic doorway. It was like the ones she described in the stories she read to her youngest sister, Abby. Only five summers, Abby loved when Keira told her tales of fairies and mystical creatures. Now she had new stories to tell; ones about giant warriors, thieves, bandits and damsels in distress.

Though this was far from what she would call an adventure, the past two days had been the most extraordinary, yet scary, she had ever experienced.

Chapter 8

Ian watched as the leaves on the bush began to rustle. Stealthily, he drew his dagger out of its sheath, firmly gripping the handle. Like a hawk, he watched his prey. Through the leaves, he could see the fine grey fur on its face as it hid in the branches. Only a twitch of its nose and a twitch of its ears gave away its location as Ian took a step closer. The small animal buried its back paws into the earth, hunched down readying itself to flee. Now was Ian's chance.

Like a bird of prey, he swooped down, capturing the frightened hare, which began wriggling violently in Ian's hands. Ian took his dagger and swiftly ended the poor creature's life.

One rabbit did not offer much meat but would at least make a small meal for the four of them. He only hoped Leland and Rylan had been more successful. He had sent Rylan on a mission to find a nearby creek or stream to fill their sporrans with water, and sent Leland out to gather more food. Between the three of them they should be able to gather enough game for the rest of the evening and the next morning.

As the blood drained from the hare, Ian wrapped a leather strap around its hind legs and strung it to his horse's saddle strap.

Heart of the Highlands: The Beast

Clouds waltzed across the sky, chasing the storm away. The rain lightened to just a few sprinkles before stopping completely. Opening his leather satchel, Ian pulled out a fresh, clean tunic and trews. He disrobed and donned the dry clothing, then using his plaid; he wiped the raindrops from his saddle. Placing his wet garb over the back of the horse to dry, he mounted and made his way back to where he left Keira near the cliff, believing Rylan and Leland were not too far behind.

~*~

Keira sat on a rock and waited, resting her head on her hands. The rain had stopped and there was still no sign of Ian and his men. Her stomach ached with hunger, whenever she thought of the food Ian was gathering. She wished there was something she could do to help. She hated being waited on, and she did not want them to feel that they needed to care for her as if she were a child.

Scanning the forest, she spotted several moss-covered oaks trees. At their base, an abundance of wild mushrooms were sticking out of the ground. Unraveling the plaid she held around her shoulders, she stood and headed over to where she saw the mushrooms. *These would make a lovely meal*, she thought.

One by one, Keira picked a handful of the fungi. As she walked around the trunks of the trees, she spotted several other herbs such as parsley, thyme and wild ramson. Though the smell of the ramson was a bit potent, its onion-garlic taste was quite pleasing when served in a stew.

Celia, the healer at Castle Sinclair, had taught Keira many great things. One of those, of course, was how to identify different herbs and the purpose of each. Her cooking skills, however, she'd learned from Brenna, the castle cook.

Holding the skirt of her dress to form a sort of bowl, she placed her findings into its fold. There was a small part of her that hoped Ian and his men would be pleased. She no longer wanted them to view her as a burden. Leland and Rylan were obviously of that opinion, anyway. Ian was different. He was patient and at least showed her a small measure of kindness.

Once her skirt was full, Keira started to head back to the shelter, when she heard footsteps behind her. Relief that Ian was returning eased her tension and melted away her fear and worry, but as Keira turned it was not Ian who stood in front of her.

Keira swallowed. Dressed in a black tunic, blue and green tartan and a broad sword strapped to his side, the man was definitely not one of Ian's men. It was his colors that gave him away. He was a Munro. She would have recognized that plaid anywhere. It was one of the few clan colors she was remotely familiar with. She hadn't even realized they were on Munro land.

The Munros and Sinclairs were allies. This knowledge brought relief. She could ask him to take her to her father and she could escape Ian and his men.

"Ye startled me," she said, dumping the contents from her skirt into a pile onto the ground. "Thank God ye arrived when ye did. I am Lady Keira Sinclair, daughter of Laird Magnus Sinclair. I have been held against my will and I wish to leave this place at once."

The Munro warrior narrowed his eyes as he scanned the trees looking for her assailants. But he stood and said nothing. Surely, he would want to make haste.

"I dinna think ye understand. My captors will return soon. Tis best we leave at once! My father is a good friend of yer Laird. I am certain ye will be compensated for my rescue."

The man turned toward her, one brow raised at the mention of a reward. Puzzled by his silence, Keira felt uneasy and his reaction made her wary of him. Had she said too much? Was he going to help her? Her gazed locked on his.

Licking his dry, parched lips, his eyes lowered, and he looked at her intensely as if he was trying to take her all in. His gaze made her uncomfortable. It took only moments for alarms to go off in her head like church bells. Cold sweat caused a chill down her spine, and hairs stood straight up from the goosebumps on her arms. Keira took an apprehensive step back causing him to mimic her movement, but he took a step toward her, maintaining the distance between them.

"I dinna think we will be going anywhere, lassie," he said, a taunt in his deep voice.

With sly movements, he unsheathed his sword, laid it upon the ground and began unlatching his belt from around his waist. The moment it dropped to the ground, Keira pivoted and ran in a sprint, but it wasn't fast enough. She felt a tight squeeze on her arm as the man grabbed her, tossing her to the ground. Keira screamed out for help but was rendered helpless as he climbed on top of her and covered her mouth with his hand. With his other hand, he lifted her skirt and began unlacing his trews.

Keira fought underneath him like a cat that'd been thrown into a watering trough, as he pressed his hard shaft against her thigh. Bile rose in her throat. Continuing to wrestle, she fought with every bit of strength she could muster.

"Get off her," Ian roared, his voice resonating around her.

Ian lunged. The two men rolled on the ground, fists swinging. Kicking Ian hard in the gut, the Munro warrior regained his balance, stood and ran for his sword. Ian pulled himself to his knees. Unsheathing his own sword, he raised to his feet. His blade collided with his opponent's as they swung their weapons, each man grunting at the force of the impact. Raising his sword up high, Ian's blade sliced through the air making contact with the man's right arm, disarming him. Hitting what Ian felt must have been bone; he pulled the blade back toward him, opening a deep gash in the man's flesh. Blood seeped through the Munro's linen shirt until his sleeve was soaked in bright red blood. But the wound Ian inflicted was not meant to kill him; only render the other man useless.

From a distance, Keira had seen her clansmen battle while on the training fields, but it was nothing compared to watching a real battle play out before her eyes. The anger, the blood, and the murderous atmosphere stimulated every nerve in her body, making her tremble. Panic began to set in. Ian was going to kill him, she was certain of it. She had never seen death before. Not even when her own mother died.

Her eyes were fixed on Ian. He was a born swordsman, and must have spent countless hours honing his skill. He held his claymore above his head with ease as if it weighed no more than a feather. Keira found herself concerned for his welfare, though she knew he was capable. Ian, she imagined, could take on an army, much less just one Munro warrior. But still, the thought of Ian getting hurt caused her chest to tighten and heart to ache.

~*~

The moment Ian saw the man assaulting Keira, fury raced through him like a bolt of lightning. As they fought,

Ian gripped his sword tighter, ready to end this man's life. The warrior lifted his left hand and instinctively covered the wound Ian had inflicted. His reaction gave Ian an open strike. With full force, Ian rammed his sword into the man's shoulder. He howled in pain. To Ian it was the satisfying shriek of victory.

With his boot, Ian pushed him to the ground, removing his blade from the man's shoulder. As Munro lay helpless, Ian pressed his blade to the man's throat. He wanted to seize this moment, to relish it, and rid the world of the bloody bastard for assaulting Keira.

Everything around Ian went black as his eyes focused on the pulsating vein, visible on the warrior's throat. Even the noises around him faded, except for the beat of his own pounding heart. Today, there would be one less despicable bastard walking the earth.

As Ian leaned forward, the tender touch of a soft hand along his forearm brought him back to the present. Angrily, he looked down at the lass, but his anger dissipated at the sight of her mortified expression. In the downward cast of her eyes, he could see her compassion and understanding but there was fear there he had never witnessed, and the forlorn expression on her face was as depressing as afternoon rain.

Ian had become so hardened over the years after giving his life to king and country, he'd rid himself of compassion. But this man did not deserve leniency after what he had almost done.

"Ian, don't," she said softly.

Ian kept his blade firm.

"Please, Ian. Let him go. Ye have done enough damage. There is no need to kill him."

Keira spoke in hushed tones; her voice as soft and sweet as an angel's harp. Ian loosened the grip on the hilt of his sword. Of all the moments in Ian's life, this one was the most significant. It would be the moment he would rise from the ashes.

"Get up," Ian growled, in a deep, threatening tone.

The man struggled to rise. Holding his shoulder to prevent from bleeding out, he stood.

"Fate must be on yer side, as I will no' shed more of yer blood, *this day*!" Ian growled.

Letting the man go was the last thing he wanted but he imagined the man would not last long. The amount of blood he had lost was more than a man could survive. He would probably pass out in the woods and bleed to death. That at least offered Ian some satisfaction.

~*~

Keira sat quietly near the fire as Rylan and Leland began cooking the rabbit, with the herbs and mushrooms she had found, in a large pot. The thought of food now, however, was nauseating. She used to pride herself on being a good judge of character, but she couldn't have been more wrong. Even worse, Ian was completely ignoring her and she did not know why. Bothered by his misplaced anger, she kept to herself.

"Did the mon say anything to ye?" Leland asked as he stirred the pot of food.

She could see pity in his eyes as he gauged her reaction. Saying "no" was all she could respond. The man had no intentions of engaging in conversation with her. When her father learned of what had almost happened, he would demand retribution from Laird Munro. Had it not been for Ian, he would have…would have… Keira broke down in tears.

Burying her face in her hands, she wept. The two men seated with her around the fire offered no comment, allowing her to cry. She at least deserved that! Leland nudged her shoulder. When she raised her head up, he held a bowl of stew out to her.

"Here ye go, lassie. It may taste terrible but I did no' claim to be a cook," he said.

Wiping her tears, she thanked him and cupped her hand around the bowl. She took a small sip, and the hot liquid burnt the tip of her tongue. The taste was bland and could use salt but wasn't as terrible as Leland suggested.

Leland sat down next to her to eat his own meal. Trying to make small talk, he spoke of the weather. He seemed nervous as he spoke. She could not imagine that a mighty Highland Warrior like him could be shy. Was he attempting to distract her or was there something else that he was not telling her?

"I have no' spoken to Ian for some time. Do ye think he is alright? Did he get hurt in battle?" she asked, genuinely concerned.

Leland laughed.

"Dinna worry about my brother lass. When he thinks, he likes to no' be bothered."

"Is that what I am? A bother?"

"I was no' referring to ye lass. I was referring to…"

"LELAND," Ian barked out as he returned to the group.

Leland jolted upright.

"Dinna ye know no' to startle a mon like that?" Leland exclaimed.

"Tend to the horses. We are leaving. I want to get a good distance away in case we encounter other men lurking through these woods," Ian ordered. "Rylan, we leave fer MacKenzie's."

"MacKenzie's? Why the hell are we stopping there? What of Linlithgow, where Laird Gudeman awaits our report?" Rylan asked.

Keira looked at each man as they spoke. At the mention of Laird Gudeman, Rylan's eyes narrowed suspiciously. Whoever this Laird Gudeman was, Keira hoped their paths would cross. She wished to give him a piece of her mind. Perhaps if their laird knew how his men behaved they would think twice about their transgressions the next time they decided to kidnap a lass.

"I wish to seek safe shelter for Lady Sinclair until she can be reunited wit' her family. I will have MacKenzie send a message about our delay. Tis only a half day's ride from here. If we leave now, we should make it before that bastard opens his next bottle of whiskey."

"MacKenzie? How can I trust that I will be safe there? Will he send word to my father? I refuse to go if yer plans are to dump me there and leave," Keira protested.

"Is whining and complaining all ye do? Tis no wonder why yer father could only marry ye off to that bastard son of a whore, Chisholm," Rylan muttered as he walked off.

Keira scowled but remained silent. Rylan was a mean bastard but she would not cower to him. It was clear he, for whatever God awful reason, was stuck in his selfish ways. How could she expect him to care even a little for her?

"Is he always like that?" she asked, nodding her head toward Rylan.

"Rylan? Aye! Ye caught him on a good day," Leland replied.

"Leland, I thought ye were attending the horses?" Ian stated, staring him down until Leland did as he was told.

"Rylan is a good mon, though he may not always be too friendly. He is wanted by the English," Ian explained.

"Is he no' afraid that someone will turn him over to the English?"

"Nay! No true Scot would ever surrender their own, no matter how wicked a mon may be. They'd rather slice him through instead. I think any Scot would rather die at the hands of their own than the bloody English."

"Is Rylan yer brother?"

"Nay, but we are like brothers."

"What do ye mean?"

"When my father was on a hunt wit' his men, they came across Rylan as a wee lad in the woods. He had no home. No family. One of my father's officers, Aldrich Arnett took him in, raised him as his own. He taught Rylan how to be a warrior and direct his anger through his sword."

"What happened to his family?"

"Nobody knows. I dinna e'en think Rylan knows who his parents are and he dunna talk about his past."

"I dinna think he likes me verra much."

"Dinna mind him, lass. Rylan is a hard mon but he means well."

Keira folded her hands in front of her and looked down. This was the first time he had spoken to her in over an hour and now she did not know what to say.

"By the way, I meant to thank ye, for saving me."

"I was no' saving ye any more than I was ridding the world of another bastard traitor. They are like weeds in these parts. *But*...yer welcome."

"These MacKenzies ye spoke of, do ye know them well?"

"Aye. Laird MacKenzie is a good mon. Ye will be safe there. The road to Linlithgow is a dangerous one. Ye can stay at Castle Leod until I return. When I do, I will keep my promise and return ye to yer family. The MacKenzie's are good people and a good clan. I have no doubt they will take good care of ye."

"If ye think it is fer the best, I will no' argue."

"Dinna worry lass. Everything will be fine," Ian reassured her.

If only things were fine! But Keira knew that things were only going to get worse.

Chapter 9

From across the river, Castle Leod could be seen in the distance; blurred by the thick summer haze. Staring out at the castle, Ian hesitated in his decision to leave Keira behind. The only comfort was its high walls and fortified towers provided enough protection to satisfy Ian's high standards.

He had faith in its inhabitants offering the same care and concern for her as he had. His hesitation came from the worry that Chisholm would find her. It would only be a matter of time until he and her father would start looking for her but Daniel MacKenzie, Laird of Castle Leod, was a good man, and he would keep her safe. Ian had met him on several occasions at court and knew that he was trustworthy. These days, there were not many men Ian could trust.

Peering up at intently, Keira asked, "Is that Castle Leod?"

Ian sensed her nervousness. Wanting to offer her comfort and ease her worry, he smiled.

"Aye, Lassie. Its Laird will take good care of ye while I am gone."

"And will he send a missive to my father?"

"Aye. He will. I am sure of it."

Keira gave him a soft smile; it broke his heart that he had to lie. Though in time her father would be made aware of her whereabouts, until Ian reached Linlithgow and revealed what he had learned, only then would Laird Sinclair be summoned.

The urgency to speak to James was driven by the fact that Ian knew an attack was imminent. It could have very well been Chisholm's plan to steer Ian and his men away from the castle by sending them on a wild goose chase while Sinclair, a man no one had even considered dangerous, made his move. Though Linlithgow was well protected by the King's guards, they would have no way knowing that Sinclair was involved. Gatherings of the nobles and Lairds were quite common at Linlithgow and it would be easy for any one of them to be a traitor, walk right in the front gates and kill the king themselves. That alone was the reason Ian felt it best to return to the castle but leaving Keira behind created a void within him that he could not explain.

He made a vow to protect her and felt that he was breaking that promise. He knew his guilt was partly due to what had happened to Sarah. Just the thought of her and his lack of judgment tore at him like a dagger ripping at his own flesh. He tried to convince himself that it was just his sense of honor and duty to care for the lass's well-being but there was something else, a feeling perhaps, he could not explain.

Ian glanced down at the timid lass. Her tender smile filled him with contentment. It was the first time he had seen her smile since he came upon her on the road; then again he was partially to blame for that. Her eyes glistened the way a child would at the sight of a sweet roll; glossy and full of joy. Ian wanted to smile in return but guilt weighed him down. If her father was tried and convicted of treason, he wondered if he would ever see that soft, beautiful smile again.

"When ye leave, will ye be gone long?"

"Are ye in that much of a hurry to get rid of me?" he teasingly asked.

"Nay! I only want to wish ye a safe journey."

"I should be gone no more than two or three days."

"Will ye be leaving straight away?" she asked.

Ian had not missed the strain in her voice. Had he not known better, he'd think the lass acted as if she did not want him to go. It had been a long time since he felt the sense of being wanted by someone. He grinned, but his smile vanished as quickly as it had come. No woman would ever want him again, and in good conscience he could not have her. He was a damaged, broken man. His heart now belonged only to Scotland.

"I shall be taking my men and leaving in the morning."

~*~

As they entered the village, Keira watched the busy men and women tend to their duties. A few young lads were cleaning the animal pens, women were hauling armfuls of linens to be washed, and a few of the older men were hammering away replacing a damaged fence.

The sight of these fine people reminded her of her own clansmen and made her miss them very much.

Keira let out a sigh. It would be only a matter of time before she would see them again, but patience was not one of her strongest qualities.

As they neared the keep, a young lad of roughly fifteen summers ran toward them. Grasping the bridle, he led the horse to a post near the trough.

"Good day, Sir. My name is Jacob. I would be more than happy to care for yer horse during yer visit."

The lad was cheerful. That was a hopeful sign.

"Verra good lad, I'll need ye to fetch the blacksmith as well. The horse has a hitch in his gait and will need re-shoeing. I leave in the morning. Have him ready by then."

"Aye, Sir. I will make sure it is done in haste."

"Good lad."

Ian slid his leg over the side and slid down to the ground. Reaching up, he grabbed Keira by the waist and helped her down. As soon as her feet touched the ground, though, he immediately released her. Untying the saddle bags, he threw them over his shoulder and walked over to his men.

Ian spoke softly to his men, his expression serious, and Keira wonder what matter was so important it had to be discussed in private.

She thought with regret that it was a pity she was not as gifted as Alys when it came to reading lips. For hours,

Alys would practice. Keira felt it was a result of too much time on her hands, but now she understood how the talent could prove to be useful. Though she was younger than Keira by two years, Alys had shown much wisdom for a lass of seventeen summers. She had so much more courage and bravery than Keira. Only now did Keira realize that her sister's many follies and foolish ways had helped mold her into a strong woman. If only Keira had paid more attention to her as a sister and less than acting as a mother-figure, she might have picked up a few useful skills.

"My lady," Ian said as he nodded his head, signaling he meant for her to follow him.

Keira stood tall, mustering her confidence, and followed the three MacKay men inside the large castle keep. As she stepped through the entrance, she was surprised to find that the castle was much smaller on the inside than it had appeared from outside. She followed along the narrow corridor toward the great hall.

As they reached the end of the hallway, they saw men and women already enjoying their evening meal. The tables were crowded with clan members and were full of trenchers containing food, but at the head table were several empty seats. It was odd for the Laird to not be in attendance during an evening meal.

Directly next to the middle seat at the head table sat a lovely, young, blonde woman. Her hair was up in loose curls that framed her slender face with soft waves. She wore jewels and a blue dress trimmed with gold lace. It was obvious by her position on the dais she was the Lady of the Keep.

Ian stepped forward, and all eyes followed him. Voices hushed, and Keira watched as men reached for the hilts of their swords as if they were preparing for battle. The atmosphere became uncomfortable and she shifted closer to Leland, praying these men would do them no harm.

The room was dark, with only a few tapered candles lit. Keira, however, was still able to make out the dark eyes that bore into Ian as he stepped forward, approaching the head table. They may have been a good clan as Ian suggested, but they surely were not a trusting bunch!

"Lady MacKenzie, it is always a pleasure to see ye," Ian said, bowing his head.

"The pleasure is truly mine, Ian MacKay. I do hope you will be staying with us longer than your last visit," she responded.

The velvety tone of Lady Mackenzie's voice was as smooth as melted chocolate. As she spoke, Keira's jaw fell open just enough for her to take in a sharp breath. She had not expected that the Lady of such an esteemed Highland clan would be French! Keira had never met a Frenchwoman and she was amazed by fluidity of their accents. It sounded beautiful, like a songbird singing for its mate.

"Nay my lady, I am only passing through. I have need to speak to yer Laird."

"My husband is not here. He has taken off to the market in Aberdeen. We have had a good and profitable year. We do not expect him to return until tomorrow evening. But as always, you and your men are more than welcome to stay in the guest house."

"Thank ye, my lady. As yer husband is no' here. May I speak to ye in private?"

"But, of course," she said as she stood from her chair and led Ian behind a closed door, with two of her guards following closely.

Keira looked up at Leland.

"Dinna fash, lass. Lady MacKenzie 'tis a good woman."

~*~

Ian stepped through the doorway into the Laird's private chamber, following Lady MacKenzie. Her guards joined them. Ian took notice of the stack of letters on the desktop with broken seals. It took only seconds for him to recognize the king's seal. There was one, however, with the seal still intact. It held the royal British seal and was set apart from the others sparking his curiosity.

"What is it you wish to speak to me about?"

"My Lady, I have a young lass traveling wit' me. I found her on the road in enemy territory. I fear she is in danger, and I ask that she stay here wit' ye until I return."

"And how long do you plan to leave her here with us?"

"I will be gone only a few days. I have business near Edinburgh. She is far from her home and I have offered to provide her safe passage. But I have other pressing matters to tend to first."

"I see. Well, as long as she is not any trouble, I would be more than happy to allow her to reside here for the time being. Now, where is this girl? I wish to meet her."

As the guards and Lady MacKenzie turned, Ian quietly snatched the letter with the British royal seal and slipped it inside the inner pocket of his shirt. With a smile, he took Lady MacKenzie's arm and escorted her from the chamber, then went in search of Keira and his men. Outside in the bailey, he found Keira standing in between Leland and Rylan who were conversing with one of Leod's guards.

"My Lady, this is Lady Keira Sinclair," Ian said as he introduced the two women.

"My Lady, tis a pleasure to meet ye," Keira said, speaking softly as she gave a formal curtsy.

Lady MacKenzie politely smiled.

"Tis a pleasure, Mademoiselle. Good heavens, what are you wearing? Your dress is torn and you are soaked to the bone!"

Out of the corner of his eye, Ian saw Keira turn the color of wild strawberries in spring. Lowering her head, she hid her flushed appearance, which pulled at Ian's heartstrings. She was such a bonny lass and had no reason to hide her beauty; no matter if she did look bedraggled from the journey. Had she worn a potato sack, she would still catch the eye of those she passed. Ian fought the urge to lift her head, reminding himself that to do so would probably embarrass her further.

"We traveled through a spot of rain," he explained, hoping to save Keira from some embarrassment.

"Well, come, Dear. Let's get you properly dressed and into something warm," Lady MacKenzie suggested, holding her arm out to the lass.

Keira looked to Ian, her eyes full of wariness. Ian let out a breath.

"I will check on ye soon," he assured her.

Keira gave him a soft smile and nodded. It was the second time now in one day she'd smiled at him. How he loved to see her smile. Beneath the worry, the politics, and the fear, Keira was a fine young woman. A woman whose heart any man would be lucky to possess. She was feisty, passionate, and had a way of driving a man crazy with the want of her. Ian felt tempted to forcefully grab her into his arms and press his lips against hers. But it was when she smiled that he felt completely undone. Unlike the many other women who had passed through his life, there was something about her that had him bewitched.

~*~

Keira followed Lady MacKenzie up three flights of stairs that led to a large solar. Inside was a large walk-in wardrobe, full of dresses made of fine fabrics in various colors; dresses far too fancy for everyday wear. These were dresses one would wear to court. Lady MacKenzie told her to pick one that she liked. If necessary, they could have it altered to fit. As Keira rifled through the gowns, she had a hard time finding a simple dress. Not wanting to take up too much of Lady MacKenzie's time, Keira settled on a light gold-colored one.

The mantle of the dress was made of pure satin and its kirtle underneath was a smooth, white linen. It had a square neckline and flowers stitched along the trim. The sleeves fitted tightly almost to the elbow then hanging open, tapered such that they were wide at the wrists.

At the creaking of the door swinging open, an older maid stepped in.

"My Lady, there is a bath prepared for Mistress Sinclair."

"Very well, Marguerite. Thank you."

"Marguerite will help ye bathe," Lady MacKenzie announced.

"Thank ye fer yer kindness, my Lady," Keira said.

Keira followed Marguerite into the next room. The steam from the hot bath looked as welcoming as a warm bed. The water beckoned her. Her bones and legs ached from riding atop the horse for the past two days, and she was certain the moment she relaxed inside the hot tub she was sure to fall asleep.

Disrobing, Keira stepped into the bath water. Tension, stress and nervousness melted away. Marguerite lathered up the soap in her hands and began washing Keira's hair. Between the scent of lavender and the fingers massaging her scalp she was in bliss. Had she been forced to endure one more day out in the woods, sleeping atop the hard ground, she was sure to have gone mad.

Washed and relaxed, she sat near the fire allowing her hair to dry. Wrapped in a towel, she stared into the flames of the fire, burning brightly inside the large hearth. She wondered what Ian and his men were doing at that very moment. Perhaps, *hopefully,* they too were able to bathe and don fresh clothing. She did not know how much longer she could tolerate their stench, though she kept quiet about their unpleasant bodily odor.

Her thoughts went to Ian, who invaded her mind as of late. She didn't know why she cared that he was leaving except that she did not like being left behind; not to mention being left in the dark about what was really going on. She knew there was more to Ian and his story than what he was telling her. As he proved to be the most stubborn man in the Highlands, she knew she wasn't going to get much information out of him, but perhaps she could persuade Leland to tell her. Keira knew that when a man was deep in his cups, there was no telling what he would say. She would set her plan in motion this very night. If she knew why Ian was so desperate to reach Linlithgow, perhaps even more truths would be revealed.

Chapter 10

After a bath, a change of clothes, and a much needed shave, Ian entered the busy hall. Finding his brother and Rylan already sitting and enjoying their meal, he went to sit near them.

"Leland, I need to speak to ye," Ian quietly said, not wanting to draw attention from the others in the overcrowded room.

Leland sat up and followed Ian into the long hall. Passing several servants, they stopped in front of a windowless alcove, so that no one else could hear their conversation.

"Leland, ye are a Protector and I need ye to be that now. I wish fer ye to stay here and watch o'er Keira. Make sure she is safe. With Laird MacKenzie no' here, I dinna trust any of the locals. Rylan and I will continue our journey to Linlithgow. Tell no one of our destination. Once I meet with our Laird, I will hurry back. Can ye do that?"

"Aye, of course. Ye dinna think something will happen to her here, do ye?"

"I dinna know, but I am no' taking any chances. Dinna let her leave yer sight!"

Ian and Leland returned to the hall. As Leland continued filling his face, Ian paced back and forth near the doorway, waiting for Keira to join them. He would have journeyed up the stairs to find her, but was assured by the maid that the lass would be down shortly. He convinced himself that the only reason he cared was that he felt honor-bound to protect her. He'd made a vow; one he was not going to break. It was the only reason; the only logical explanation he had; to explain these feelings toward her. For now, she was *his* mission. And like all of his missions, he would see to it until the end.

From the corner of his eye, he spotted the lovely lass dressed in a soft yellow gown that reminded him of spring daisies. Her red locks were loosely braided across one shoulder and a few loose curls had escaped their confinement. Those tempting tendrils gave a bounce as she walked. She was an image that took a man's breath away.

Ian waited as she descended the stairs. He couldn't help but notice the way her hips swayed side to side as she walked, nor could he ignore the way her chest rose and fell with each breath. She was a vision. As Keira reached the bottom of the stairs, she glanced around the room, but paid no heed to Ian who stood directly across from her. Ian's brows furrowed, and he stepped toward her.

"My lady," he said holding his arm out to her.

For a moment, she looked at him with uncertainty as one would look at a stranger. It was not the look Ian had hoped for. He had hoped to see her smile.

~*~

Keira's eyes widened at the Highlander who stood before her. She had not recognized him at first; his clean shaven appearance, his hair slicked back, his formal dress attire, but his eyes were familiar; the perfect shade of blue.

Ian?

Keira was left speechless. With a clean face, a proper bath, and hair tied back, he looked as if he could actually pass for a gentleman. And she had to admit, he was rather handsome.

He did not look as she imagined. Hidden underneath his thick heavy beard, his jaw was strong and angular. His lips, full and plump; no longer covered by an overgrown mustache. For a man, he was beautiful, and not nearly as intimidating as when she had first seen him. He had completely transformed.

"Lady Keira, yer presence lightens this room as bright as stars on a clear night," he said, holding his arm out to her.

She took it, but felt her cheeks blush at his compliment.

"Ye look quite presentable, yerself, if I may say so. I must say, I am pleasantly surprised," she admitted, hoping he would not take her words as an insult.

Ian smiled at her compliment. Stopping in mid-stride, he turned to face her.

"After ye eat, will ye join me fer a walk? I heard Castle Leod has quite the garden."

Keira chewed her bottom lip at his question. According to the rules of decorum, she should not be alone with him. But perhaps this was her chance to get the information she needed.

"Aye, I will join ye."

Ian led Keira to the table where Leland and Rylan were seated, enjoying their meal. In front of two empty chairs were trenchers full of food. Keira sat next to Ian and eagerly began eating. The moist, juicy lamb practically melted in her mouth. As she had spent the past two days eating nothing but apples, Keira did not think she would ever want to look at another apple again!

~*~

"I hope the food meets with your satisfaction," Lady MacKenzie said.

"Tis more than generous, my Lady. After eating nothing but cold, spoiled meat, apples and stale oatcakes, ye could have fed me the dog and I'd be a satisfied mon," Ian joked.

"I have heard many great things your young King has accomplished. I heard he will soon be taking a French bride. It will prove to be a good match, for Scotland and France."

"Aye! Though I know little of politics, my Lady, living only by my sword, I do hear rumors."

"As a Highlander, surely you must know about the rebellion against James?"

"Aye. I have heard talk," Ian added.

"Between you and me, I think the rise of the rebellion will soon be coming to an end."

"And why is that, my Lady?"

"My husband just received his last arrest warrants for several Highland chiefs who are believed to be involved. It should be a great victory for the King of Scotland!"

"Ye are a wealth of information, my Lady."

Lady Mackenzie smiled proudly. Ian finished his meal quickly, anxious for his walk with Keira in the garden. The news Lady MacKenzie shared was not anything he had not already heard. He knew this rebellion was coming to an end, but it was bound to end up leading to something bigger.

Glancing over to Keira, he was surprised to see her plate completely clean. She rested her small hand on her knee under the table. Her fingers looked as if they would be soft to the touch. He desperately wanted to take her hand into his and entwine his fingers with hers. *Damn*, he was becoming an animal!

"Are ye ready fer our walk, my Lady?"

Keira nodded.

Ian stood, waiting for Keira to follow him. Side by side, they walked down the long hall towards the rear door. They walked in silence until they stepped out into an enchanting labyrinth of flowers. Rows of roses, hedges, and a wide variety of fragrant flowers decorated the scenic landscape around the castle. Cobblestone pavers and wooden benches decorated the pathways from one side of the garden to the other. In the middle, two geese and their goslings swam in a man-made lily pond.

"Tis beautiful," she exclaimed.

"Aye, tis," he replied, though he paid no attention to the garden and kept his gaze on her. "Shall we?" he asked as they stepped forward toward the large pond in the middle.

Arriving at the pond, they sat on a bench overlooking it. The sun was just about to set and Ian spotted the moon already high in the sky.

"Thank ye fer bringing me here. I have ne'er seen so many beautiful flowers."

"Yer welcome."

"Ian, does Laird Chisholm have anything to do with the rebellion of which Lady MacKenzie spoke? Is that why he is so dangerous?"

"Aye, one of many reasons, lass."

"So, when ye came upon my carriage, was it him ye were trying to capture? To arrest him?"

"Something like that, aye!"

"So, when ye came upon me, ye thought to use me as ransom to find him. Dinna ye?"

"Aye," he answered, unable to meet her eyes.

Keira nodded her head. Ian finally turned toward her, wanting to know what she was thinking. By the look in her eyes, she looked as if she were trying to process the information she had been given.

"I understand that ye must hate me fer what I have done," he admitted.

Keira looked up at him.

"I dinna hate ye. I did at first, but not now. I do, however, think there is more to the story than what ye are sayin' and I dinna know why ye wish to keep me in the dark."

Ian noticed the pain and desperation in her eyes, though there was little he could say that would make her feel any better. His mission was to be kept secret and she knew too much as it was.

"In due time, Lassie, I promise to tell ye. But fer now ye are just going to have to trust me. Would ye care to go inside? I am sure ye need yer rest."

"I am fine. Is it alright if we stay fer just a wee bit longer?"

Had she asked to stay for the entire night, he would have been happy to oblige! Inwardly, he smiled.

"Of course, Lassie."

They sat in silence, watching the goslings play in the water like children playing follow the leader. Keira's brief giggles were like music from heaven. Ian was surprised to find himself smiling, too. He kept glancing her way, not able to take his eyes off her. He wanted her, needed her, but damn if he could have her.

~*~

Keira fondly watched the young geese splash in the water. As the sun sank beneath the horizon, the orange sky began to fade, gradually replaced with dark blue. Behind her to the east, a few stars shone brightly as they twinkled in the sky. It would be only moments until the sky turned black, and was covered in stars.

Keira yawned. It was late, and the day had been long. Ian would leave tomorrow to complete his task, and soon he would return to take her home. In the meantime, she would offer her aid to Lady MacKenzie as payment for her hospitality.

"It's late. I should probably head in. And where will ye and yer men be sleeping?" Keira asked.

"There is a guest house near the stables. If ye need anything, that's where ye will find me."

As he lowered his head, his gaze smoldered. Keira could almost feel the heat radiating from him. His proximity caused her heart to beat faster in her chest. She did not like the way he made her feel, but every nerve in her body was screaming at him to hold her the way he had when they were riding together.

Though she tried to resist him, she couldn't stop herself from falling for his devilish charm. Only now did it occur to her that the day he ransacked the carriage he was actually rescuing her from a doomed future. He was a Highlander through and through; with honor as steadfast as stone and the ignorance of a mule.

"I am sure that I will no' need yer help at this late hour," she said as she scooted away.

Ian must have sensed her hesitation as he shifted toward her. She tried to look away, but Ian gently touched her chin, returning her gaze to his. She had not expected him to be gentle. *Could a beast be gentle?* Lifting his hand, he brushed a loose tendril of hair over her ear. Grazing his hand down her cheek, he touched her lips, then her chin, and raised her head up slightly so they were eye to eye. She knew he was going to kiss her. *Damn him*; because if he did, she knew she would not resist. The way he touched her, looked at her, even spoke to her, made her feel soft and vulnerable. Even her thoughts were too addled to focus on anything other than him. She wanted to be kissed; to be touched; to be loved.

"Ye have bewitched me, lassie," he said as he leaned toward her.

Panic, excitement, and anticipation coursed through her veins. Her breaths were labored as he gazed at her lips. Unconsciously, she licked them before biting her bottom lip. The world around her seemed to fade away. Keira opened her lips slightly and drew in a breath. Ian combed his fingers through her hair and pulled her toward him. Forcefully, he pressed his wet lips against hers.

At the moment his lips touched hers a fire grew in her belly and her skin tingled right down to the tips of her toes. His kiss was possessive and demanding but she was a willing partner. It was when Ian broke the kiss that

Keira realized what she had done. She had enjoyed it immensely. Was that wrong?

She thought to blame the drink she had at supper for her foolish actions. But if that were true, why did she so desperately want him to kiss her again? Standing quickly, she bid him goodnight before embarrassment set in, and then took off at a near sprint back toward the keep.

Chapter 11

With stars still shining bright, Ian and Rylan had ridden several miles away from the castle before its inhabitants even knew they were gone. Not wanting to be questioned about their intended destination, they thought it best to leave before dawn.

It was not Ian's desire to leave without bidding Keira a proper goodbye, but it was for the best. After what had happened last night, he highly doubted the lass would wish to see him off. He would not be surprised if she even wanted to see him again. He acted on instinct as his passion flared and though he had no regrets, he couldn't help but wonder whether she did. The moment she ran off back toward the castle told him that she must have. He didn't know whether to feel guilt for his actions or relish in the pleasure he'd felt.

Memories of the heated kiss he'd shared with Keira replayed in his mind. She was becoming more than just a mission, as he'd viewed her in the beginning. Selfishly, he wanted to claim her as his. He was too involved now to just walk away.

Ian and Rylan were experienced riders and used to traveling great distances. They rode their horses hard; hoping to reach their destination by midday. As it was, they were already late. They were expected to have arrived at Linlithgow two days ago but their detour to Castle Leod caused their delay.

Remembering the letter in his pocket, Ian pulled it out, broke the seal and began reading its contents. It was a warrant for Rylan's arrest, just as he'd assumed it would be. Holding the letter out to Rylan, he waited as Rylan steered his horse closer and snatched it from him.

"What is this?" Rylan asked, as held the letter up to read it. "Says here, the reward fer my head has been raised from ten pounds to twenty! Pompous English bastards!"

~*~

Rylan had dark secrets. Many of which resulted in this warrant; others only known to God. Though he wanted his slate clean and to be free from sin, he knew his past would one day come to catch up with him. He had hoped by joining Ian, he could earn God's mercy, but it seemed that anywhere Rylan went, trouble followed. It was hard being a man who lived two separate lives, lying to Ian and his adoptive family about his past. His hope was that after all these years, he could leave his past behind and become the man others believed he was.

~*~

"Had I needed the money, I'd turn ye over to the English myself," Ian teased.

Rylan returned Ian's sarcastic look with an unamused scowl.

"I only jest wit' ye. If ye are bound to hell, ye know I'd go wit' ye!" Ian vowed.

"Aye, I know."

Though Rylan never explained in full the details behind his encounter with the English, Ian knew whatever he was being accused of, Rylan would do it all over again without hesitation. Even the Scottish King could not lift the charges against him. Rylan was a determined man; probably more so than most. Only by staying on Scottish soil and avoiding any run-ins with the English, could he ensure his freedom. If not, Rylan would be facing death.

Once the mission their Laird had ordered was complete, Rylan was to head south to the Lowlands to petition the Duke of Annandale to request a pardon on his behalf. Charles, the Duke of Annandale was a dignitary and a noncombatant. Though he was an Englishmen, his ties to the Scottish Crown made him an ally, and favored by the Scots. He had the authority to pass requests to London to seek pardons as well as hold trials on Scottish soil when it concerned English patrons. He was great and powerful, but still only a man, and could not always be trusted. His acceptances always had a cost. The only assurance Rylan had was that the Duke and James had a common enemy, Archibald Douglas. Ian knew that Rylan would have to use that angle if he were to get the man to listen to his requests, though it would be at a heavy price.

From what Ian knew, the Duke of Annandale had removed himself from English politics when Henry, the King of England parted from the church. Henry's heresy is what helped Scotland keep their bond with France strong. To continue this growing relationship, it was King James's decree that any man or women who committed acts of heresy are either condemned to death, imprisoned, or be exiled.

Ensuring that Scotland stayed loyal to the Catholic Church, Rome had continued to offer their support by funding Scotland. However, if James failed to control those who had become manipulated by King Henry and his faulty ruling, the Church would seize those funds immediately, a result which James and Scotland could not afford.

For years, Ian had served King James, by joining a secret society of men called the *Protectors of the Crown*; men who swore their life and allegiance to King James. They were his eyes and ears throughout the Highlands though no one knew this group even existed. Like shadows of the night, they met in secret and Ian was one of them, along with Leland and Rylan.

During his most recent mission, Ian had joined the expeditions sailing across the North Sea on orders to seek and obtain enemy vessels and secure the ports. Though Ian did not consider himself a privateer their assignments were quite similar. The only one in Ian's clan who'd learned of Ian's recent activity was Rylan, though he only stumbled upon this information through his cleverness, not to mention his disregard for privacy. Once Ian discovered that Rylan knew the truth, both Rylan and Leland were initiated into James's faction.

Their current mission, which was not going as successfully as Ian had hoped, was to capture and detain Laird Chisholm for recent criminal activity against the crown. Associated with James's step-father, Archibald Douglas, Chisholm had been caught taking bribes and relaying messages between Douglas and the Highland Chiefs who were in a feud against the King. Chisholm possessed the one thing that could destroy Douglas, as well as end the rebellion against James; a detailed list of the names of everyone allied with Douglas. *They had to get that list!*

Chisholm, however, had covered his tracks at every turn, until Ian came across Keira. His marriage to her proved that Laird Sinclair was somehow involved. And had Chisholm married Keira, her father would have had the safety and security of the English army behind him as well. It was Ian's intention to expose both men for their treachery and to keep Keira out of harm's way.

Chapter 12

Ripped from a heavy slumber, Keira woke to an urgent, repetitive tapping at her door. Sitting upright, still half asleep, she stretched out her arms.

Yawning, she called out, "The door is open."

The door opened and Marguerite shuffled inside with an armful of gowns.

"Good morning to ye, Mistress Keira. Lady MacKenzie insisted I bring these to ye," she explained as she laid the dresses over the back of the chair and began hanging them in the wardrobe. "It was said that ye came here wit' nothing but the bit of linen yer sleepin' in," she added.

"Aye, my luggage was lost during our travels. Twas verra kind of the lady to provide me somethin' to wear."

"Well then dinna mention it. Lady MacKenzie can be quite persistent. If ye wish, I can help ye get ready. Food has been served down in the kitchens where ye can break yer fast, then it's off to the church wit' ye."

"The church?"

"Aye, lassie, today is Sunday, the Lord's blessed day."

"I guess I did no' realize the week had gone by so fast."

"Aye, well, let's get ye dressed. Lady MacKenzie is already downstairs and we dinna want to keep her waiting."

"Are the MacKays wit' her as well?" Keira asked.

After what had transpired in the garden, she'd hoped to avoid Ian all together. It was not that she didn't trust him, but that she didn't trust herself when she was around him. Admittedly, she'd enjoyed the kiss they'd shared no matter how sinful it was. He made her feel things, things she had never felt, and feelings she secretly wanted to explore.

In the back of her mind, she wondered what made him want to kiss her in the first place. She had heard that the fragrance of certain flowers and the light of the moon could do strange things to a person, stirring wayward emotions from even the most obstinate.

Marguerite turned to her and looked at her with a somber expression.

I'm sorry my lady, but two of the three MacKay men left this morning."

"Left? Which of them left?"

"'Twas their leader, Ian, and that rascal, Rylan, milady."

"He left wit' out saying goodbye?" Keira asked, and the maid shrugged her shoulders in response.

Frustration filled her heart and mind. He'd had the audacity to kiss her but not the decency of bidding her farewell!

"We really should get ye ready fer the day, my lady," Marguerite insisted.

Keira slipped off the bed and allowed Marguerite to help her into one of the gowns. She refused to allow herself to shed any tears on behalf of Ian MacKay and from this moment she would force him out of her mind. Keira finished dressing and followed Marguerite downstairs. Keira was escorted to Lady MacKenzie, who was enjoying her morning meal alone in a small room just off the kitchen.

Dressed in another beautifully designed gown, Lady MacKenzie was everything a Lady should be. Her dark green dress matched the color of her eyes and her long blonde hair hung loosely over her left shoulder in tight curls. Raising her head, she glanced at Keira and smiled.

"Lady Keira, I am glad you have joined me. Did you sleep well?"

"Good morning, Lady MacKenzie. Aye, I did. Thank ye. I wish to offer my services today to show my appreciation fer yer gracious hospitality. I can do anything ye wish, from washing to dusting."

"Nonsense! You are my guest and I am happy to oblige. And please, we are not at court so there is no need for formality. Ye may call me Lorna. You must mean a great deal to Ian to have him so concerned for your safety. I saw how he practically fell all over you. A woman in love herself can recognize it in the eyes of others. And I must say, I have never seen Ian look at any other lass the way he looked at you," she said in her accented, smoky voice.

"I honestly dinna think he cares that much about me, my lady. He made a vow and is simply keeping his word."

Lorna offered her a sympathetic smile.

"Are you hungry this morning? Cook has made her delicious pear filled pastries. Won't you join me?"

Keira took a seat next to her and picked up one of the pastries Lorna offered. One bite of the sweet roll made her mouth water. It truly was delicious.

"Will the others be joining us?" Keira asked.

"No. This is my private dining room. My clansmen eat in the great hall as does my husband. Their loud chatter often gives me a headache. I prefer peace and solitude when I eat. Only during great feasts do I join them. The lifestyle here is much different than that of France. When I first married Daniel MacKenzie, oh how I thought he and the God-forsaken Highlands were barbaric. Now that we have been married for more than five years, I *still* do!" she teased.

Keira chuckled, and finished her pastry.

"If you are finished we shall take our leave. I wish for you to sit next to me in church this morning." Lorna said.

"I would be more than happy to accompany ye, my lady."

Keira followed Lorna down the spiral stairs to a long outdoor corridor that lead to the door of the church. A guard manning the door held it open and both Lorna and Keira slipped inside.

The interior of the chapel was lit by several tapers mounted in elaborate wall sconces, and flowers of every kind and color were placed in vases around the narthex. A rainbow shone through the stained-glass windows, casting an ethereal glow over the Stations of the Cross, beautifully done in bas relief along the two longest walls. The faintly spicy scent of incense hung in the air, blending with the earthy smell of the fresh rushes covering the floor.

Keira noticed several of the clansmen were already in attendance, sitting on the plain wooden pews. Near the door, at the back of the room, Leland leaned against the wall and watched Keira move toward the first row. Somehow having him there made her feel safe and reminded her of Ian. Of course it was hard not to think of Ian when looking at Leland. The man bore a most striking resemblance to his older brother.

Soon after Keira and Lady MacKenzie were seated in one of pews with a back, reserved for the Laird's family, the processional began, the priest wearing white robes, preceded by two young lads acting as acolytes. Keira found a sense of peace as the whispered Latin prayers, psalms, and responses surrounded her. The quiet, reverent atmosphere was a balm to her weary soul after the strange events of the previous few days.

Suddenly, she realized she had forgotten to go to confession, and she couldn't help rolling her eyes as she let out a sigh. Now she would have to approach the priest to see if she could confess that she had partaken of Holy Communion without having been absolved. As she and Lorna walked down the aisle after the priest and his entourage, she surreptitiously crossed herself and muttered a quick prayer that her penance wouldn't be too harsh.

This priest and the entire mass had been much more formal than she was used to. Brother Bryant, the monk who performed mass at Castle Sinclair was much more approachable than this man of God. She smiled as she remembered Brother Bryant's loose brown wool robe and cowl, adorned only by a full rosary that wrapped around his waist. She'd always enjoyed listening to his stories of the places he'd traveled in his younger days.

Lorna whispered that she wanted to offer a prayer for her husband's safety, and ducked over to the side of the room to leave a small offering and light a candle on her husband's behalf. Once she rejoined Keira, she smiled and offered to introduce Keira to the priest.

"Father Ambrose, thank you for the lovely Homily. I'd like to introduce you to our guest, Lady Keira Sinclair."

"Lady Sinclair. It is a pleasure to meet ye. I am Father Ambrose."

"It is a pleasure to meet ye as well, Father."

"Do ye wish to give yer confession?" the priest asked, his voice hoarse as if he spoke one too many homilies this morning and lost his voice.

"I dinna believe God will hear my prayers, Father."

"No mon is closer to God than a mon of the cloth. And only through the power of confession and absolution will ye be seated at the right hand of God in the kingdom of heaven."

Keira dropped her gaze. It wasn't her soul she meant to save.

"The sins I carry are no' of my doing."

"Then they should no' be yers to bear alone. Come wit' me, child," he said, holding his hand out for her.

Keira let the priest lead her down the aisle to a small booth in the corner of the room; the confessional, where she would receive the sacrament of reconciliation. Opening the door, she peeked inside at the small bench in the private quarters.

"If ye wish to seek absolution, this is where ye will find it," he added. "What ye say within these walls is between ye and God. I am no' there to sit in judgment. My purpose is only to listen and help bring ye closer to God."

Keira looked at him before sweeping her gaze back to the inside of the booth. Taking one small step forward, she entered, the door closing behind her. Keira circled around and took a seat on the bench, uncertain what she should say. She certainly could not reveal all of her truths, but she couldn't bring herself to lie to a priest either. Perhaps she could avoid the conversation all together. She knew for certain that she had much to talk about in regards to her sinful behavior in the garden.

On the other side of the wall, she heard a door swing open and swiftly close. Hearing the priest settle in his seat, a small screened window opened between the two compartments, but neither person could actually see the other. The only light came from a square window near the top of the door through which she had entered, no larger than her palm.

Keira nervously squirmed in her seat. What if he asked certain questions; questions she could not answer? And if she did, would he condemn her? She inwardly prayed that he was a benevolent man and not a religious zealot who believed in harsh penance.

Keira crossed herself, then quietly murmured the words that would begin the ritual, "Bless me father, for I have sinned. It has been many months since my last confession."

"What has kept ye from the church?"

"We have a church, Father, which I do visit regularly, but my clan has no priest."

"And why is that?"

"My father said he was a mon of wickedness and sent him away."

"And do ye believe he was wicked?"

"No, Father!" she blurted out. "Father Bryant was a good and honest mon."

The day her father sent the man away angered many of her clansmen. Father Bryant was an old and frail man; too old to be traveling at his age. He had been Clan

Sinclair's priest for as long as she could remember. It was only after her mother's death that her father disagreed with Father Bryant's teachings, though she never truly understood why her father had experienced such a change of heart.

"And, do ye believe in the Roman Catholic Church, the one true Universal and Apostolic Church to save yer soul?"

"I dinna know what to believe. I am afraid, Father."

"What fear is in yer heart to no' allow ye to attest your belief in Christ and His church?"

Hot tears burned Keira's eyes. It was the question she refused to answer. She knew if she spoke the truth, she would be condemning her own father. For years, he had brainwashed her into believing that the Catholic Church was more about power and control and that what was known as the House of God was corrupted. As the Protestant reformation grew throughout the Highlands, more Scots were renouncing the Catholic Church following those who sought freedom from religious persecution. Her father and many of her clansmen were among them.

Torn between the God she'd grown to love, and the one she had recently been taught about, Keira was at a crossroad. She knew divulging her secrets about her father would condemn him for heresy and she would also be condemning herself. She had sat and listened on several occasions to the teaching of Protestant ideas and opinions on the matter, simply out of curiosity. But spiritually, she herself did not know what to believe.

It was an ever-changing world and Keira desperately wanted to be a part of it. It had only been a matter of a few months that she learned of King James' actions to charge those who acted against the church. But would it be so wrong of her to tell Father Ambrose? He seemed to be a reasonable man, a man of curious nature himself. Perhaps, he would offer her leniency and help answer many of her questions.

Keira allowed the words to flow like a strong current in a stream. She started at the beginning, telling him about the death of her mother, the change in her father, and the Protestant men who came to visit them. She did not realize how desperately she needed to tell someone her secrets. It was true that her father knowingly committed a crime but not the one Ian accused him of.

As the words came, the more she felt as if a weight was lifted off her shoulders; a sense of freedom she had not felt in a long time. She had not realized how burdened she'd been and how it had affected her until now.

As she finished her disgraceful story filled with death, sin, and dishonesty, Keira felt whole and revived, like after a long peaceful rest. The priest, however, remained silent as if he was still processing all of the information she had divulged.

"Do ye think God will forgive me?" she asked, hoping to hear a comforting response.

"God is all-loving. E'en if we spend an eternity in hell, we are still children of God. Ye must say the Our Father and pray the Rosary every morning and every night. Only then will ye earn forgiveness," he commanded.

"Our Father, who art in heaven…" she said as she began to recite the Lord's Prayer, but before she could finish, she heard the door open and close from the Priest's booth.

Has he left? She wondered as she continued the prayer. Moments later, the door to her confessional swung open, and two large men stood outside the door; behind them stood the priest with an accusing glare.

"Bring her to the tower until the Laird has returned and dinna allow her to leave!" the Priest commanded, barking out his order.

Keira trembled. *What have I done?*

~*~

Leland watched as the priest left the booth and walked over to the two guards near the door. Keira however, was still inside the confessional. The grim expressions on the priest's face portended something dire. Keira had clearly upset him. He watched as the priest led the two men to the booth. Forcing the door open, they drug Keira out, even as she still knelt in prayer. Leland withdrew his sword and ran up the aisle toward them.

"What is the meaning of this? Remove yer hands from her at once," he demanded.

The two guards and several other Mackenzie warriors drew their swords, pointing them at Leland.

"We are detaining Mistress Sinclair until our Laird returns," one of the guards replied.

"And what gives ye the authority to do so?"

"She is being held on allegations of acts of heresy," the scrawny priest replied. "She just confessed."

"Codswallop! That is the most absurd thing I have ever heard. I demand ye release her!"

"Tis the truth!" the priest said. "Ask her yerself."

Leland glanced over at Keira, giving her a questioning look. Over the past several days, she had not been so docile. The look of shame in her eyes told him what he needed to know, but he was unsure exactly what this all meant.

"I am her protector and I demand ye release her," Leland growled, gripping his sword tighter.

"There is only one of ye and a room full of us, I dinna see how this will end in yer favor," one of the MacKenzie guards replied.

Leland glanced around the room. A dozen eyes gazed back at him. They were right, for the moment there wasn't anything he could do until Laird MacKenzie returned and he demanded her release. He had to get to Ian, and fast.

~*~

Keira sat alone in the modest quarters of the tower room. With nothing but a bed, a hard wooden chair, a table, and a fire pit that could scarcely contain a log was all the room had to offer. At least there was a small window to allow some light to enter. The guards did not have the decency to give her a candle or basin of water with which to wash.

She had been locked in here for several hours now wondering where in the devil Leland was. When the guards came to bring food, they did not speak. Keira had no idea what was going on. She only knew that revealing her secrets to the priest had brought about much more than the freedom from her burden she had sought. It may very well have cost her her life, or at least that of her father.

Keira had always known that one day, it was only a matter of time before someone found out about her father turning away from the church and forcing his clansmen to do the same. Whether by her own confession, or that of another, Keira's father was doomed. But that did not explain why she'd been locked away in the tower.

Keira had admitted to attending the teachings but only to observe; not as a willing participant. Still, no one would hear her out. And what of Ian? It was clear that any hope she had to return home was not going to meet with success. What would he think of her once he learned the truth? She had accused him of lies and deceit, yet she had secrets of her own. She did not know why, but the thought of his disappointment in her bothered her immensely.

Sitting in the chair, she looked out the window at the bailey below. The clansmen kept themselves busy as they anticipated the return of their Laird this evening. She had no idea what awaited her. Her only hope was that Ian would return soon, though she had little hope that he could help her.

On the windowsill, a small, brown sparrow chirped. Keira glanced over at the food the guards had brought in to her earlier. The food had grown cold; most of it uneaten. Leaning over, she reached for the chunk of bread and broke off a small piece, tossing it to the bird. She watched the small creature enjoy the hearty meal,

"Hello, Sweetling," Keira whispered, as tears lightly trickled down her cheeks.

Ruffling its feathers as it sat comfortably, keeping her company. If only she could sprout wings, she would fly away from here as far as possible.

Chapter 13

Ian walked with purpose as he headed down the dim corridor inside the walls of Linlithgow Castle. His instructions were clear; to discuss an urgent matter with the king.

As Ian walked towards the gathering room, the dim light in the wide hallway with its high, arched ceilings cloaked his movement as he made his way down the long expanse. Had it not been for the sound of a commotion at the end of the hall, he would have been lost for sure as Linlithgow was a labyrinth of hallways, galleries, and rooms.

As Ian approached the end of the corridor, he could hear the commotion of men chattering behind the closed door, like a flock of chickens. Their voices were loud and booming as if they were in a lively debate, each one trying to crow louder than the other. Though the corridor offered little light, Ian could make out two guards standing outside the door. The one to the right nodded, allowing Ian to enter. Ian pushed opened the heavy wood door and stepped inside.

Inside the room, Ian recognized the dozen men from neighboring clans. Many of them were the King's councilmen, gathered around a circular table, and arguing back and forth.

"We need to stress the severity of the situation to our people. If these rebels were to breach the gates of our own castles, how are we to respond? They are bloody Scotts, just like the rest of us. After all, they would simply blend in," Alpin, Laird of Clan MacDuff rebutted.

"T'would be a foolish mon who would allow anyone to enter their gates without question. And only a fool would allow himself to be attacked from within his own walls," Laird Gregor replied.

"We should hear 'em out. Hear their demands before we put more of our own men in danger. They should be given a fair trial. What of the church? What is their position?" Callum, Laird MacDonald asked as he turned to the Abbott sitting at the far end of the room.

"The church, of course, stands by the crown," the Abbott replied.

"The rebels are trying to overthrow the king. They should be hanged for treason. What of France? Is the king aware of our position?" Alpin questioned.

"My alliance wit' France is strong but I will no' engage him wit' our civil issues. And I prefer him to no' be involved. I am planning a trip to France soon as I find myself a bride. But until then, we will have to prevent a civil war between the clans on our own. I do no' wish fer more bloodshed," James of Scotland responded.

Ian continued to listen to the argument. James's hope was to increase the number of his army by more than half, and hold a tribunal for each of the Highland Lairds to assess their loyalty. As for the rebels, he was unsure how to stop them, and their numbers were growing. Henry the VIII, King of England, had thrown the country in turmoil when he renounced the Catholic Church. English sympathizers started to gather, following in his footsteps. And the Roman Church was threatening to cut their funds to Scotland. It was James's hope that his relationship with the King of France and his marriage would help overrule the new reformation and convict those charged of heresy.

Glancing over at the far end of the room, King James stood and listened, his brows furrowed. With his arms crossed, he leaned against the stone wall. The disdain on his face told Ian that he was getting more frustrated by the minute. Hours passed and no conclusions had been made. They decided to meet again in a few days during the tribunal at Inverness hoping by that time more light could be shed on who was behind the attacks.

As the meeting adjourned, the men filtered out of the room. Ian stayed and waited to speak to James.

"Sire, I have news."

"Have a seat," James said, in a gravelly voice.

Walking to the table, Ian waited for James to sit, then he followed suit. Though James was a young man, signs of aging could be seen in his deeply wrinkled forehead and sunken eyes. It looked as if he had not slept in a week. With his hands folded and resting on one knee, he waited for Ian to speak.

"I have no' been successful in capturing Thomas Chisholm but we did find his hideout, and I left men behind to follow their movements. We lost several good men, however, when we were attacked on Sutherland land."

"Sutherlands? Bloody rogues!"

"That's not all. On the way to Chisholm's castle, I came across a young woman who claims to be his betrothed. She's the daughter of Laird Magnus Sinclair and I believe that he may be the mon we have been looking fer. I always thought Thomas had someone feeding him information and sending his letters to England, but I ne'er expected a Sinclair."

"Neither did I, but I will see to it that he is questioned at Inverness along wit' the others. I have sent Laird MacKenzie the remaining names that witnesses have brought forth to stand trial. I can only hope that once ye capture Thomas Chisholm, we will have the ledger with all of those involved. It has been two very long years since the start of this revolt. The execution of Patrick Hamilton was a necessity but has done little to ward off those who wish to follow in Henry's footsteps and renounce the church. Without the church's support we stand to lose greatly. The support from France and Rome is paramount to our survival. The Highland Chiefs must rule under my authority and our church. If we allow Henry's ideas to influence the minds of the weak, war wit' England will be inevitable. We are Rome's and

France's ally, but we must maintain control on our own soil first. Anyone allying with England, or my stepfather, Archibald Douglas, will be banished or exiled! I will no' yield! I want that list naming every Chieftain, Laird, Earl or Duke that resides on my land, who has committed crimes against the church and the crown."

Ian knew the list James demanded would be long, and he already knew a handful of men whose names would appear at the top.

"I will continue to do what I can, Sire."

"Ye have served me well, Ian MacKay. Your sacrifice has been admirable. I will be traveling incognito to Inverness. Once ye arrive, meet me at our usual spot at Margie's tavern," James advised.

"I will."

Ian bid James farewell and went in search of Rylan. He had hoped to return to Castle Leod before noon the next day. Wandering down the hall, he found Rylan sitting in the great hall deep in conversation and well into his cups, with members of the MacDonald clan, longtime friends and allies to the MacKays.

"Will ye be joining us? We are celebrating Ainsley's last day of freedom," Rylan announced.

"Freedom?" Ian questioned, raising a brow.

"Aye, I am to be married tomorrow," Ainsley mournfully responded. "To an English woman!" he added as the surrounding men laughed.

Ainsley, on the other hand, looked as if he was about to be sick. He was a young lad with ginger hair and pale skin.

"Oh come now Ainsley, it cannae be that bad!" his clansmen said.

"Then ye marry her!" Ainsley pouted, slamming his head back down on his folded arms.

"Where is yer bonny bride anyway?" Rylan asked.

"O'er there, speaking to her father," Ainsley mumbled under his breath as he pointed in her direction.

Ian and the others looked in the direction Ainsley pointed. The young woman's high pitched squeal was deafening. She was not an ugly lass, though Ian did not find much beauty in her either. Her hair was a mess of curls, and her face was marred with tiny scratches as if she had recently gotten into a fight with a bush. Not to mention, she had more curves than a sack of potatoes. Ian grimaced but duly tried to keep a straight face. *Poor laddie!*

"Rylan, I wish to speak to ye," Ian said drawing his attention.

Rylan slammed back the rest of his ale and stood from his chair. The two men left the hall and stepped into the corridor.

"What did James say?" Rylan asked.

"Only that we are to continue our mission in tracking Chisholm and retrieving that ledger."

"When do we leave?"

"Tomorrow, first light."

Ian wasn't sure exactly what gave him the sense of being watched, but he slowly turned his head and glanced toward the end of the hall. Three men stood next to each other, staring right back at him. He paid no heed to the two men standing to the right and to the left; it was the face of the man in the middle which started to make his blood burn. It was that murdering son of a whore, Isaac Sutherland. What was he doing here?

He hated Isaac Sutherland with every fiber of his being, along with anyone who bore the Sutherland name. His hatred ran deep, so deep that his bones ached at just the mention of the name. It was more than hatred he felt for the man; it was a desperate need for vengeance. It ate away at him like wounds left to fester.

When the King offered him a pardon, Ian set aside his anger, but only until the day he came face to face with the murderous bastard, Sutherland. Now the man was here, at Linlithgow, walking towards him. The smug look on Isaac's face sickened him.

Though they were within the King's Castle walls it meant little to Ian. He would spill the man's foul blood even if they were in a God damn church! To hell with the consequences! Ian thirsted for his blood. Had it not been for Isaac and his men, Sarah would be alive today.

With each step, Ian's blood burned hotter. Gripping the hilt of his sword, he began to unsheathe his weapon.

Rylan must have sensed Ian's intention as Ian increased his pace, starting to leave Rylan behind.

"Back down, Ian!" Rylan growled quietly, low enough so only Ian could hear his warning.

Ian pushed Rylan out of the way when he moved forward to block Ian's view of the bastard at the end of the hall.

With a sharp shove back, Rylan managed to push Ian into an open doorway. Ian stumbled for a moment, then regained his composure, and readied himself to knock Rylan down on his arse for stalling the inevitable confrontation. Rylan slammed the door behind them before Ian could act, swiftly locking it.

"What the bloody hell do ye think ye are doing? We must away! We can no' afford a war against the Sutherlands," Rylan angrily said.

"This has nothing to do wit' ye. It is my right to slay that mon!" Ian roared.

"No' here! And ye bloody damn well know it! Do ye wish to see yerself at the end of a noose? For if the Sutherlands get their hands on ye, even the King can no' save ye! Now, get yer head out of yer arse! There will always be another time; another place."

Since Isaac had received a pardon from the king absolving him of wrongdoing against the MacKays, Ian would be named a murderer if he killed Isaac. He must have irrefutable proof that the man was the one who'd orchestrated the assault on the MacKay clan if he was to be allowed his revenge. Ian clenched his fist. Turning around, he punched the side of a bookshelf, splitting the wood. His knuckles throbbed but the pain was easy to ignore. His mind focused on deeper matters than a few bloody knuckles.

"Do ye feel better? Or do ye wish to have a go at me as well?"

Ian gazed from under his eyelids at Rylan. Perhaps he should take him up on his offer. A good fight was an honest way to replace pent up anger, but he turned it down. Nothing would satisfy this need like Isaac's head on a stake.

"What is he doing here?" Ian growled.

"The MacDonalds said Sutherland was here to face the King on other matters. Come! We must leave this place if ye wish to return to Leod by morning," Rylan suggested.

Ian stomped after Rylan, slamming the door behind him as they left the storeroom. As they reached the front gate his anger was replaced with pure panic when he spotted Leland riding toward them, alone.

"Leland? What the bloody hell are ye doing here? Ye are supposed to be watching Keira and keeping her safe!"

"Ye must make haste, Brother. Keira has been charged with heresy and treason!"

"What the hell are ye talking about?"

"Lady MacKenzie took Keira to confession. Keira told the priest about some acts of heresy by her father and claims her entire clan has denounced the Church. The bloody bastard priest told Laird MacKenzie of what she confessed. MacKenzie has her locked in the tower and sent men after her father."

"Is Keira safe?"

"I dinna know. They would no' allow me to see her. They locked her in the tower. I tried to stop them. Honestly, I did."

Fear that he had left Keira alone in a wolf's lair shook him to his core. Why hadn't she told him about her father? Was she a heretic as well? If she too were tried and convicted, then she would be equally punished.

Ian felt very protective of her and blamed himself for her situation. He tried telling himself her youth and innocence made him feel the need to protect her, but he knew that was a lie. It was true that she was young and naïve, but that was not the reason he wanted to keep her safe. The true reason was how he felt when he was around her. The feeling he had been denying since the day he came across her on the road. He could not pinpoint exactly why she drew his attention, but he knew whatever the reason, he was not going to allow anything to happen to her while there was breath in his lungs.

His showdown with Sutherland would have to wait. "Get the horses ready Rylan! We are leaving now and we will no' stop until we get there!"

Chapter 14

Keira woke from her spot on the chair, drenched in sweat and breathing heavily. For a moment, she looked about the room as the events of yesterday played in her head, reminding her why she was there. Unable to sleep, she tossed and turned until giving up completely and going to sit near the fire. She did not remember falling asleep but was grateful she had woken when she had. In her dream, all she could recall was running. Running from someone; a sense of impending danger. As the minutes passed, her dream faded to a few scant memories.

Keira stood. The stone floor felt cold beneath her feet. The morning sun had not yet warmed the air, and a slight draft wafted through the window. Pulling the plaid up from off the bed, she wrapped it around her shoulders and went to the window. Leaning against the stone wall, she glanced over the windowsill, looking down at the bailey below and the clansmen at work.

She spotted a group of four women sitting on wooden barrels, weaving baskets while they watched the young ones at play whacking around a small object with a stick. The men throughout the bailey were also busy with their tasks; hammering away building crates, tending the horses, and carrying baskets of sheep's wool to the elderly, who used it to spin yarn. These were dutiful people, good people, even though in their blind devotion to the church they were unlawfully keeping her detained. She had done nothing wrong, but had spoken the truth within the sanctity of the confessional. The priest was the one who should be held accountable, not Keira.

Without even a customary knock, the door to her room flew open, startling Keira. Her head quickly turned toward the door as a large Highlander swept in with the priest shuffling in behind him.

"Lady Sinclair, my apologies fer my late arrival, I am Daniel MacKenzie, Laird of this castle. I trust ye have been well cared fer," he said.

"Unless it's yer nature to lock yer guests in the tower room, I would most certainly say I have no' been treated well, yer lairdship!" she angrily replied.

"Aye, well I spoke to the priest about the nature of yer visit here as well as the information ye have divulged about yer father."

"I thought confessions were sacrosanct," she said, staring daggers at the priest who cowered behind his master like a dog.

"What ye did say and what ye didn't does no' matter anyway. Yer father has already been implicated in conspiracy with the English. He sits imprisoned at Inverness until trial."

"What? When?"

"It just so happened when ye arrived at Inverness a few days ago to marry Laird Chisholm, yer father was arrested. What he failed to acknowledge was that Laird Chisholm had set him up, and was never intending to join ye at Inverness."

"If they already hold my father in custody then why am I being held against my will?"

"Fer questioning!"

"About what? If I may be so bold as to ask."

"Yer loyalty! Father Ambrose here told me about yer confession. Since yer father is to stand trial, and ye have no witness to verify yer innocence, ye too will be questioned at trial."

"At trial?"

"Tis the way of it, my Lady. These are the king's orders. Ye are to stay here until the trials. I have accepted custody of ye and will take ye to Inverness in the morning."

"This is the most ridiculous thing I have ever heard!"

"Take it up wit' the king! Ye shall see him two days hence," he said as he turned to walk away.

As Daniel closed the door behind him, out of sheer anger Keira picked up the only thing in sight, a pillow lying on the bed, and flung it at the door with all her might. The soft thud of the pillow hitting the door, did little to assuage her anger.

Keira just then realized that her greatest fear had come to pass. Her father was involved. It explained everything; why he'd refused to travel with her, the important business he had to attend; it even explained why he wished for her to marry Laird Chisholm. If the king were to discover her father's treachery, Chisholm would have offered him protection and she was the price her father had to pay. With Keira safe on Chisholm land, she would have been out of harm's way. Had Ian not intervened, she would have been married to a traitor.

~*~

Ian raced passed the gates of Castle Leod with Rylan and Leland riding by his side. Jumping down from his mount, he left the mare unattended in the middle of the bailey and took off in a sprint toward the castle door. Brushing past the guards, he marched into the great hall where Daniel MacKenzie and several of his clansmen were sitting down drinking ale.

"Where are ye holding the lass?" he demanded.

"Tis good to see ye too, Ian," Daniel replied dryly.

"Lady Sinclair. Where is she?" he asked again, his patience wearing thin.

"She is under my care. I have taken custody of her."

"Why? What has she done? Leland said ye have arrested her; under what charge?"

"Heresy," Daniel replied, matter-of-factly.

"I have sworn to protect her. Therefore, she should be placed under my custody!"

"Are ye even listening to yerself? The girl has committed a crime. Therefore she will be tried. She has admitted to knowledge of her father's treachery as well as attending unorthodox meetings against the church."

"That woman has been corrupted by Satan!" the priest added in an accusing tone.

Ian snarled. He did not take too kindly to others speaking ill of her. Priest or not!

"She has no benefactors who can attest to her innocence, so she is therefore guilty by association. She has the blood of a traitor. She will be taken to Inverness on the 'morrow to stand trial in front of the Sherriff of Ross-Shire."

"What if I testify fer her?"

"Ye have no authority to do such a thing. Ye have no claim on her."

"But, if we were to marry, it would be sanctioned by the Church. The King would have to listen to my plea," Ian said before he even realized what he had just offered.

"Ye would marry the daughter of Sinclair? The daughter of a traitor?" Daniel asked.

"Aye. I would."

And that was the truth. If he could not bring himself to let her go, marrying her was his only choice. She would be his, forever.

"I can no' allow this discussion to go any further. My answer is nay."

"And ye can also no' allow five hundred MacKay warriors barging down yer door either," Ian threatened.

Daniel's eyes narrowed on him. Not accustomed to be threatened, he knew Ian was true to his word and if that's what it took, then Ian would see to it in order to rescue

Keira. Having been gone merely two days, he already missed her soft, warm smile.

"Verra well. Guards, take him to the tower. Ye have one hour. If she agrees to marry ye, so be it."

Ian nodded and left the great hall following the guards. Barreling down the hallway, Rylan and Leland joined Ian.

"Have ye gone mad? What of yer obligations and duties." Rylan paused. "Ye have no' told the lass yet, have ye?"

"And tell her what exactly?"

"Ye know bloody well what I'm referring to!"

"What is it ye expect me to do? If I dinna marry the lass she may verra well find herself locked in the tower to rot, or hanging at the end of a noose like her father."

Rylan grabbed his arm to stop him.

"Ian, ye cannae be serious about marrying the lass. No' wit' out telling her what she is in fer."

The look in Rylan's eyes was serious and unyielding. Like a brother, Rylan always kept an annoyingly watchful eye on him, but Ian knew he was right. He had kept his identity a secret for so long he had forgotten who he really was. Living under the ruse of an outlaw, he'd left his life of luxury and comfort behind to serve James the best way he could. Taking a wife, however, would ultimately change all of that. Though he would still serve the crown, he would have to return to a place he had not called home for many years.

Being the eldest son and the eventual Chieftain to Clan MacKay was not the only secret he had been hiding. As a member of the Protectors of the Crown, every moment he participated in his missions he was not only putting his own life in danger, but the lives of his family members as well. Could he marry her knowing the dangers that he might make her a young widow?

Ian looked between Leland and Rylan.

"I know what I am doing."

"Good. Well, I will no' keep ye. I am sure ye are anxious to speak to yer bride," Rylan replied.

His bride, words Ian was not yet ready to hear.

Chapter 15

Since the moment Keira saw Ian ride through the gates, she had paced the floorboards. Anxiousness and nervousness buzzed through her; she could not keep still. Would he rescue her? Condemn her? She had never felt as sick to her stomach as she did now. She was desperate to see him, to speak to him, but then again felt completely terrified at the same time. She was making herself sick with all this worry.

Her nerves caused her hands to shake and knees to wobble. *Where is he*? She felt the passing of time begin to slow. If this was not torture she did not know what was.

Her biggest fear was whether he would believe her, if, and when, she finally had the opportunity to speak to him. If she could not convince him of her innocence, how could she convince the king?

Loud footsteps could be heard climbing the three flights of stairs toward the tower room. Keira jiggled the door handle, but the door would not budge.

"Hello? Hello?" she called out, but there was no answer.

Keira took a step back from the door. She could hear someone jiggling the handle from the other side of the door, then the sound of a key turning in the keyhole. Keira held her breath, waiting for the door to open.

"Keira?" Ian said as he pushed open the door and stepped in, closing the door behind him.

Rushing toward her, he placed his hand on her cheek. Keira closed her eyes at his touch. For a moment, she felt as if they were back in the garden. She felt safe and knew that as long as Ian was near, she would be protected.

"I'm sorry, lass. I did no' realize bringing ye here would cause ye trouble. Are ye well? Have they hurt ye?"

"Nay. I am fine."

"Ye must tell me, lass, everything that happened."

Keira lowered her head, her eyes filled with tears. Ian gently placed his finger under her chin, and raised her head.

"Tis alright, lass. I'm here now. Ye have nothing to fear. No one will ever harm ye. I swear it!"

As Keira gazed into his eyes, there was a fierce resolve and passion in his expression. She wanted so desperately for him to wrap his arms around her; to kiss her and hold her close. She did not want him to leave her side ever again.

Keira wiped her tears away and sat on the edge of the bed. Ian kneeled down in front of her. His beautiful dark blue eyes looked up at her, filled with worry and concern. With a deep breath, she explained in detail what had happened since the morning he left, trying to remember everything. There was no point now to hold anything back from him. She had to trust him.

"Why the bloody hell did ye no' tell me? How did ye suppose I was to protect ye keeping secrets such as that?"

"I did no' lie to ye and I am no' a heretic!"

"I bloody know that, but tis no' me who needs convincing."

"Ye...ye believe me?"

"Aye! I believe ye, Lass."

Keira bent over and wrapped her arms around his neck, filled with relief. She'd half expected him to hate her. Ian, however, did not return her embrace and kept his hands firmly at his sides. It caused a small emptiness inside her.

Pulling back she asked, "What's going to happen now?"

"Ye have been charged by the Church, but those laws and laws of Scotland are verra different. They have agreed to let ye go under one condition."

"And what condition is that?"

"Ye have to agree to marry."

"Marry? What does that have to do wit' anything?"

"Lassie, ye have no benefactors, no witnesses to back yer claim, and the word of a woman means little in the eyes of the church. If ye were to get married, yer husband can vouch fer ye."

"And who is it I am supposed to marry?"

"Me! I have offered fer yer hand," Ian softly replied as if he expected her to argue in response.

"Ye? Why would ye commit to such a thing?"

"If ye've no' wish to marry me, ye can always take yer chances at trial," he suggested.

Keira felt numb, in body and mind. For the first time, she had no words. Even her face was devoid of emotion. Marrying Ian in name only wasn't entirely a bad idea. After all, by Ian's account, it was the only choice she had. She assumed she could have the marriage annulled once her name was cleared of all charges. It should be a fairly easy task as the marriage would not be consummated. This wasn't exactly the result she had hoped for, but little did that matter now. Oh, how her head started to pound.

Ian placed his hands on top of hers. He looked at her with honesty in his eyes.

"My lady, I am sorry, but ye have little time to decide. They are downstairs awaiting yer answer. I know this may no' be the marriage ye were hoping fer, but I promise to be a good husband to ye and to protect ye until my dying day, if ye will have me."

Keira took in a breath.

"How can I answer when I dinna even know who ye are? Do ye have a home? A family? Or are ye and yer mates outlaws living from place to place?"

~*~

Ian laughed at her question. There was such innocence on her face. It made Ian want her even more.

"Lassie, despite what ye think of me, I am no outlaw."

"I dinna understand. Most honorable men do no' go around attacking carriages, pillaging camps, and kidnapping women!"

"Fer yer information, Lass, I did all of that fer yer protection. As fer who I am, I dinna lie to ye when I told ye my name is Ian MacKay and my father is Laird of our clan. I am the eldest, and next in the line of succession. As my father is alive and well, I have left my home to join the cause for Scotland's freedom. And I do so under the king's authority. I am nay a rogue, my lady. I am a Protector of the Crown. My missions are kept secret as our king's life depends on it."

"Are yer missions always so dangerous?" she asked.

"Aye and deadly at times."

"And Leland and Rylan are they also Protectors?"

"Aye, they are."

Keira chewed her bottom lip while mulling over what he had just explained. From her expression, he could almost see her thoughts grinding away like a wheel in a mill, trying to process all of the information.

"I will no' force ye to make a decision, but ye must see reason. I am offering to marry ye, to protect ye. I can no…"

"I will marry ye," she blurted out, interrupting his last words.

Ian rose and held his hand out.

"Come."

"Where are we going?"

"We have a wedding to attend."

Ian grabbed Keira's hand and led her out the door, passing the two guards that stood watch. As they turned the corner to head down the stone staircase, tiny hairs on his arm stood erect as goose bumps emerged like spring daisies. In his core, excitement and nervousness churned. The woman holding his hand was his wife to be; a woman who would bear his children and forever sleep next to him in his bed. The thought both excited him and made him feel uneasy. He did not want to second guess his haste in offering to marry her. It was the honorable thing to do and he wasn't getting any younger. Already eight and twenty, he should have taken another wife by now, but he could not shed the guilt when his thoughts drifted to Sarah.

As they made it to the bottom of the stairs, he met Rylan and Leland standing in the hall waiting.

"The lass has agreed to marry me," Ian announced.

They nodded in unison, as Rylan wiped his hand down his face. The four of them went to speak with Daniel MacKenzie and the priest.

"I take it the lass has made her decision," Daniel assumed.

"Aye," Ian said in response.

"Verra well. I will fetch the priest," he said as he left the room.

"Let me be the first to welcome ye to the family," Leland said, smiling as he nodded to Keira, but she remained quiet and aloof to what was happening.

Within moments, Daniel returned with the priest and Lady Lorna.

"I was hoping there would be a wedding. I already have everything prepared," she joyfully announced.

"Will ye stop yer jabber woman?" Daniel barked.

"In my country, weddings are to be celebrated not mourned," Lorna replied with a smirk.

The group followed Daniel and the priest toward the chapel. Ian smiled down at Keira. She was as beautiful and vibrant as a newly blossomed rose. With her bright red hair and sparkling icy blue eyes, she could have easily hypnotized him, bewitched him to marry her instead of the other way around. He felt intoxicated just by her presence.

Her tightly-fitted burgundy dress teased him as it covered almost every inch of her from her neck down to the long sleeves. He could not help but wonder what she looked like underneath all that unnecessary material but knew that he would soon find out. Gazing down at her made the beast inside of him urge to break free. It was a natural impulse that stirred his groin. This wee lass was his for the taking. And he couldn't wait to indulge, caress and touch every inch of that creamy light-colored skin. In a few short minutes, she would be his wife and he would show her everything a marriage could offer.

~*~

The chapel was decorated with roses and thistles. Keira thought the thorns were a nice touch as it was a clear reminder of the position she was in. She trembled, but Ian kept a firm hold on her hand steadying her as she walked. She could not believe she had agreed to this. What was she thinking?

Keira felt the neckline of her dress around her throat, reminding her of the noose she hoped to escape. Her chest rapidly rose and fell as she attempted to prevent the embarrassment of fainting.

Leland and Rylan sat in the front pews of the church, snickering and whispering, though Keira found no humor in this situation. No doubt they were making fun of Ian for having to marry her. Keira turned to look away from them and took notice of the two men standing near the front of the chapel. Standing behind the altar were the priest and Laird MacKenzie. Keira wanted to plead to them to listen to her argument, but Ian, sensing her apprehension, pulled her closer to him.

"Ye are a mon of honor, Ian MacKay. I am sure she will make ye a fine wife," Daniel said.

Ian's gaze swept from the top of her head to her toes and he replied in a very pleased tone, "She'll do just fine."

Keira's jaw went slack. *She'll do?* He looked at her as if he were buying cattle. And she looked at him as if she were only moments away from clawing his eyes out. If he hoped for a submissive wife, he should have offered a solution other than marriage to *her*.

Ian grabbed her elbow and snuggled her close to his side. Instinctively, she wanted to run and escape this moment, but she stood, frozen to the spot, unable to move another step. Her hands began to tremble.

Vaguely, she was aware of the priest's voice beginning the wedding mass, the Latin words droning on as a backdrop to her thoughts. The thought of Ian as her husband overwhelmed her. Though he had shown much kindness, there was still much to fear about him, so much she still did not know. In truth, she knew nothing of him other than his birthright. She did not know if he would be a harsh husband and would beat her if she spoke her mind, or if he would be kind, but in a few short minutes, she would be his to do with as he pleased. He would be her lawfully wedded husband. Oh God, *her husband*! Even the words seemed threatening.

"My Lady, did ye hear me?" the priest asked, his eyes narrowing on her.

"Forgive me, Father," she responded weakly, her mind having wandered far from what was happening.

"Place yer hand upon his," he mumbled.

Keira hesitated. With cold, shaky fingers, she raised her hand and placed it on Ian's warm, rough knuckles.

The touch sent chills down her spine like tiny spiders were crawling over her skin. Ian cupped his other hand over hers, rubbing her knuckles with his thumb.

She peered up at him; a soft reassuring smile adorned his face. For the moment, she felt comforted in an odd sort of way. She had confidence that he would keep his word and would protect her, but she never considered what he would want from her in return. It had not dawned on her until this very moment that he, too, was making a sacrifice.

So focused had she been on her own problems, she'd never thought to ask why he'd offered marriage in the first place. Surely, there were other lasses he had thought to wed, ones who would not have caused him so much trouble. Her mind was filled with so many questions but she realized she would have a lifetime to have them all answered.

Rushing to the altar was not exactly how she had imagined her wedding. But had it not been Ian standing beside her, it would have been Laird Chisholm, a traitorous man, who had caused her to be in this situation in the first place.

Keira made a mental note to question Ian further about what he knew of Laird Chisholm and of her father's dealings with him. She had no doubt there was much more to the story than she had been told. Perhaps he felt it was too much for her to handle and wished to spare her feelings, but regardless of the reason, she needed to be told.

When the time came for Keira to repeat her vows, the room felt smaller and her head began to spin. Had she forgotten to breathe?

"Ye may now kiss yer bride," the raggedy priest said to Ian.

Kiss? Kissing him was the last thing she wanted. When she kissed him in the garden, she swore to herself that was the last time she would ever allow herself to be so foolish. But there was a part of her that yearned for his kisses no matter how badly she tried to ignore it.

Ian lowered his gaze, causing Keira to unconsciously lick her lips. Gently, he placed a hand on her cheek. She gulped as his lips descended upon hers. The kiss was demanding yet tender. Lips slightly open, Keira felt a warm energy shoot through her as if he breathed fire like a dragon. His hand rubbed down to the middle of her back, pressing her closer to deepen the kiss.

Slightly parting his lips, the tip of his tongue grazed her bottom lip. The feel of his arms around her and the sweet taste of his lips were intoxicating. The kiss felt sinful and it was definitely not a kiss suitable for the house of God, but she found herself liking it; liking it a lot.

Keira pulled herself away, taking a deep breath. The priest scowled as he announced them as man and wife.

Rylan and Leland cheered as their hosts remained unamused.

~*~

"Will ye be joining us fer supper to celebrate yer nuptials?" Daniel ceremoniously asked.

Ian looked to Keira before turning back to Daniel. The distressed look on her face tore at his heart.

"Nay, thank ye. My wife and I will take our meal and accommodations in the village. Ye understand of course," Ian politely said, though he wanted to cut the man down for how he and his men had treated Keira.

Ian grabbed Keira's hand and led her out the chapel door. Together, they walked down the path toward the village to make arrangements for their supper and a room. There were plenty of accommodations at the village inn, and from what Ian recalled, their food wasn't half bad.

After Daniel insulted Keira by locking her in the tower, Ian was not about to ask her to dine with the scoundrel. She was his wife now, and he would see to her every comfort.

Chapter 16

Ian managed to acquire a decent room within the village for the night, for tomorrow they would be on their way to Inverness for the trials. Though Keira would no longer have to speak in her defense, Ian would have to produce the legal documentation of their marriage to the king for the charges to be dropped. There was the matter of Keira's father, his *new* father-in-law, of course. He certainly did not want to see the man hanged for treason or burned at the stake, but he knew some form of punishment would be served. Until Ian became fully aware of the charges against him, there was nothing he could do to save the man.

Ian and Keira joined Leland and Rylan at a table as their meal was just being served. The patrons who sat near the bar laughed and clapped loudly to the music being played on a small stage near the fireplace. It was quite a lively place and reminded Ian of home. On several occasions, minstrels had been brought in from the village to play a cheerful tune for his clansmen and visitors.

As Ian sat down, one of the barmaids came to the table and dropped off two small mugs of ale. Ian pushed one of the mugs in front of Keira.

"Here, drink this," Ian advised.

Ian hoped the beverage would make Keira feel relaxed and comfortable, not to mention make tonight's bedding easier for her. Not that he wished to bed a drunken corpse, but the liquor would help numb some of the pain she would endure. From what Ian knew, losing one's maidenhood was painful and he did not wish to cause Keira any discomfort on his behalf.

Upon their plates was a hearty helping of roasted lamb, potatoes, and stewed carrots. Rolls were served on the side as well as a creamy dipping sauce.

"No one goes hungry in my kitchen," the server said, as he set down the last plate in front of Leland.

Not having eaten all day, Ian greedily ate his share. He couldn't remember the last time he had a full meal. But as he was half way done with the food on his plate, he noticed Keira had barely touched hers.

"Tis something the matter?" he asked.

"Nay. I am no' verra hungry."

"Eat. Ye need yer strength."

Especially fer tonight. His wicked thought made him smile. Keira began picking at her food like a bird.

"Is there something the matter wit' yer meal, Mistress?" the barmaid asked.

"Nay, its fine, I am just no' feeling verra well. Perhaps I should go lie down."

"Are ye sure ye are alright?" Ian asked.

"Aye, I will be fine."

"I can take ye to yer room Mistress," the maid offered. "Perhaps if ye like, I can send up a bath fer ye as well.

The warm water always feels good on these old bones. Perhaps ye will feel better once ye bathe."

Keira nodded.

"I will come and check on ye soon," Ian assured her as she stood up and followed the maid up the stairs to the bedchambers.

"I can no' believe it! I was there, witnessing it fer myself and I still can no' believe it!" Leland said.

"Aye. Whoever would have thought that ye would take a bride," Rylan agreed, taking a swig of his ale and then setting the mug firmly on the table.

Ian scratched his head and wiped his hand down his face. It had been a long day. His thoughts were drawn to his beloved Sarah. Flooded with guilt, he felt he had betrayed her, though he knew better. Sarah would not want him to spend eternity unhappy and alone, nor would she want him to continue mourning her death. She was a good woman and saw the best in him. Sarah would always and forever be his love, but was it possible to love another? Had Keira been some angel sent to heal his heart?

Ian was confused by his rash decision and nervous about taking her as his bride. He just wondered if Sarah knew what he had done, would she forgive him once they were reunited in the afterlife? But Sarah was gone and there was nothing he could do to prevent being hurt again, short of living alone for the rest of his life.

There was no mistaking his feelings for Keira. He thought the capacity to love had died the day Sarah left this world, and though he still loved Sarah greatly, Keira had somehow inched her way into his heart. He did not know why, but he needed her. Perhaps to rid himself of his longing, but it was a desire he did not want to live without.

"Had ye told me yesterday I would be a married mon today I would have thought ye gone mad but I do no' regret my decision."

"What did she say when ye told her about the Protectors?" Rylan asked, scooting his chair closer to keep others from hearing their conversation.

"I told her what she needed to know and nothing else."

"So, how are ye going to convince that poor lassie to bed ye? No doubt the priest is gonna be coming 'round here in the morning wanting proof of a bloodied bedsheet," Rylan asked.

"There's no' way she is gonna bed ye! The lass is too damn proud and too damn stubborn. She is going to put up quite a fight! I bet my horse it'll be yer blood on those sheets in the morning," Leland said in a fit of laughter.

"Are ye suggesting, I dinna know how to handle my women?"

"Nay, I am only suggesting, dear brother, that ye are no' going to be able to tame that one. I dinna see Keira as a docile wife," Leland answered.

"Then I will just have to seduce my wife," Ian said as he grabbed a mug filled with ale and proudly sauntered off, up the stairs and to their chamber.

~*~

Keira followed the maid up the wooden staircase to one of the bedchambers at the far end of the hall. As she walked along the open balcony, her eyes stayed affixed on her husband. She wondered for how long she would have to stay married to him while her name was being cleared. She could deal with a few days, perhaps a week or so, but any longer than that and she would summon the Pope himself to grant her a divorce.

The maid stopped at the door at the end of the hallway.

"This will be ye and yer husband's room."

"My husband? Nay, I will be sleeping alone tonight," Keira was quick to reply.

Yes, they were married, but in name only. That certainly did not mean she meant to bed him, nor would she be so willing to kiss him again. He had stolen enough of her kisses.

As she stepped through the door a cool draft from the window caused her skin to pebble and made her hope that bathwater was nice and hot. The room was dark except for a sliver of light that shone in from a small window. The air smelled musty and stale as if it had been years since it was last occupied. A cold shudder tickled down her spine.

As the maid crept further into the room, Keira watched her grab a candle, light it, then head to the hearth to start a fire. As the tiny candlelight flickered, shadows danced across the room.

With the room well lit from the candle and the fire burning brightly in the hearth, Keira examined the room, taking note of the bed. *The marital bed.* The oversized bed looked as if four people could sleep comfortably in it. The chestnut-colored headboard and matching four-drawer chest complimented the barren room. Laid on top of the bed was a pile of plaids and furs along with two feather-filled pillows. Keira gently dragged her hand across one of the soft furs as she examined the room further.

"I trust this room will be sufficient fer ye, my lady," the woman said.

Keira offered her a soft smile and replied, "Aye, it will do."

"If I may be so bold in asking my lady, are ye alright? Ye are no' scared of yer husband are ye? I have known yer husband fer many years and I can tell ye wit' certainty that Ian MacKay is a gentle mon. As a married woman of twenty-seven years, I can tell ye that ye have nothing to worry about. The first time only hurts a little."

Keira's eyes widened at the woman's remark and heat rose to her cheeks.

"I see," the woman responded, smiling. "Tis the things we dinna say that truly matter. Ye like yer husband; that is obvious. Love…maybe. Dinna try to seek perfection in an imperfect world, Lassie. You'll only find yerself disappointed."

"I was forced to marry Ian MacKay. In truth, I know nothing of him, so how could ye suggest I have any sort of feelings for him?"

The auld maid smiled and took Keira by the hand.

"My lady, the foundation of any relationship must first be based on friendship. If ye want a mon's respect, ye need no' demand it, but ye must treat him wit' the very respect ye want him to return. But dinna be too hasty to think things will change. It will take time. I am sure that a bonny lass such as yerself will have no issues capturing his heart. But ye must make him work fer it. Ye have more power than ye think when it comes to a mon. Most men act tough like stone on the outside when they are as soft as a bairn's bottom on the inside. If there is a beast inside that mon, ye will have the strength to tame him," the maid assured her.

"Capturing his heart is the last thing I want. And besides I am sure he probably feels the same way about me. I do no' love my husband and I dinna like him verra much either."

"Aye, ye say that now, but I know better. Take yer husband fer instance; stubborn as a boar. He has spent the greater part of almost past ten years in mourning. He acted like 'twas him who died and no' Sarah. But I've seen the way he looks at ye, like a blind man who now can see. Give yerself time, lass. I believe ye will find what ye are looking fer."

"Who is Sarah?" Keira asked.

"His first wife."

"Wife? He's been married before?"

"Aye. Did he no' tell ye?"

"Nay," Keira hastily replied.

"My apologies, my lady. I did no' mean to upset ye. I should no' have gone sticking my nose in other people's affairs. I am sorry, my lady."

"Tis alright. Ye dinna know. Please tell me. What happened?"

"I really shouldnae, my lady."

"Please!"

The maid looked at her with heartfelt sympathy. Keira took a seat on the bed and waited for the maid to share what she knew. She was completely taken by surprise by this new revelation into Ian's dark past. Up to this point, she'd only viewed him as a selfish bastard with a heart made of steel. But now she knew why he was the way he was. He had been broken. To break a man, especially one as resilient as Ian, would not have been an easy feat and not one from which he would easily recover. Her heart lightened, thinking about the pain Ian must have endured. She had been so quick to judge, and at every turn he had surprised her. Perhaps he wasn't the Beast she accused him of being. If anything, it was she who had been acting out of anger and selfishness.

"From what I know, they married young. Ian was away on a mission when their village was attacked. No one saw it coming."

"Who attacked them?"

"They believe 'twas the Sutherlands but they were never charged or convicted, as it was MacKay's word against theirs. No' to mention Isaac Sutherland was traveling in England at the time of the attack and made no' mention that he'd ordered such a thing."

Keira tried hard to keep a straight face at the mention of Isaac Sutherland. On several occasions, her father had entertained Laird Sutherland and his men. They'd even welcomed him into their home; shared their meals with him. Keira never paid much attention to the reason, other than he was a dear friend of her father's. She thought it best for now to keep that knowledge to herself, but for how long? If Ian knew that her clan and Sutherlands were allies, he may feel anger towards her.

"That's all I know. I must be heading downstairs now, my lady. I will have the lads send up the tub fer ye."

"Thank ye," Keira said, her voice trailing off as the woman left the room.

Keira sat quietly mulling over the new insight into Ian's past. Every day since she'd left Castle Sinclair, she had been given bits and pieces of information, like pieces of a puzzle. A puzzle she was desperate to solve.

Keira did not know how she was going to ever forgive her father for what he had done. When her father had announced his decision to leave the Catholic Church, she had not fully understood the new religion her father was pursuing, or his reasons for leaving the Church. But perhaps his sins were so great that he would have shamed the Church as well as his family, and hoped to find redemption elsewhere. As a child, she had always looked up to him, but she did not think she could ever look at him the same again.

Chapter 17

Ian tapped on the chamber door, turned the handle and entered. He found Keira sitting on a chair near the fire, with a leather-bound book in her hands. The soft, orange glow of the flames created an inviting and calming ambiance and the earthy scent of burning pine filled the air.

His attention was drawn to Keira, who looked at him with an earnest expression. Shadows of light seemed to dance around her, creating a halo of light, as if she were an angel. By God, she was beautiful. He had thought her bonny before, but in this lighting she looked heavenly.

There was something about the way she looked at him that made it hard for him to resist her. As her soft smile greeted him, his eyes fell to her lips; soft, delicious morsels. Desire surged through him as he wished to taste those lips. With each breath, his pulse quickened. He wasn't sure if it was the drink that had caused his senses to go wild or if it was the tantalizing vixen who stared back at him with equal yearning. He could almost see it in her eyes as well.

The tips of his fingers started to tingle with the need to touch her, to feel her soft skin under his large rough hands. He would take pleasure in showing her all of the ways a man could please a woman, until her body could no longer bear it. He wanted to make her ache for him as he ached for her, with chest-tightening, heart-pounding passion. He would make her his in every way. Ian knew that if he did not distract himself from having these thoughts now, he would not be able to control his actions. He walked confidently to a chair near the fire, turning it so he faced her when he sat upon it. In order to have the satisfaction of bedding his wife, he knew he first had to woo her.

~*~

Keira watched as Ian walked over to the chair and sat down, facing her. He was a hard man to read, for his facial expressions gave nothing away and his mood could change as fast as the wind. He could be kind one moment and belligerent the next. But the provocative look he was giving her now left her uncomfortable. Perhaps, he'd simply had too much to drink. It certainly would have not been out of the question.

Thinking about what the maid had revealed, the knowledge of his previous marriage somehow made him seem more human than the beast she had imagined. To think that his life before had been so much different then, than it was now. That he'd had the tender love of a woman and had returned her love with equal measure. Keira felt a spark of jealousy for the poor dead woman. She had known a side of Ian Keira would never have the chance to know.

Ian stared at her with such intensity; she worried what he could possibly be thinking. Keira shifted in her chair, hoping to divert his attention. She felt a sudden awkward tension between them just as she had that night in the garden, and was reminded once again about the heated kiss they'd shared. Was he thinking about that as well? Licking her lips, she thought to distract herself from the yearning feeling building up inside her, but words escaped her. Lucky for her, Ian broke the silence.

"Tomorrow we are to leave for Inverness for the trials. As yer husband I will be permitted to speak on yer behalf. Ye will no' have to face yer father or the King," he said in a low husky tone.

"But I wish to see my father! I must! I have to know if everything I believe to be true has been nothing but a puddle of lies."

"I dinna know if ye will be able to see him. But I promise, if there is a way, I will make sure of it," he vowed.

"Thank ye."

Up to this point, Ian had promised her many things. But what promises did he expect from her in return?

Moving his chair closer toward Keira, Ian leaned forward, resting his elbows on his knees.

"Keira, I know this situation may no' be ideal but I promise I will protect ye wit' my life."

"I dinna need any more promises or protection. What I need are answers!"

Ian frowned.

"And we will get them, together."

Keira sat back on her chair and studied him. Why was he here? Why was he helping her? It made no sense unless there was a reason of which she was unaware. She had to know.

"Why did ye marry me? Surely, ye must have sacrificed something."

"Truth be told, ye have grown on me."

Keira smiled and shook her head in response. It was clear this man went looking for trouble as she was known to be quite a headstrong lass. Biting her lower lip, she thought to ask him of his first wife but was afraid to open old wounds. She thought for now it was best to wait.

"I like seeing ye smile. Ye are verra beautiful," he said.

Keira thought her cheeks must be glowing red as they started to tingle from his compliment. With her hand, she covered her face in her embarrassment. Other than her father, no man had ever given her such bold compliments.

Ian stood, walked toward her, and held out his hand.

"Do ye trust me?" he asked.

Keira hesitated but placed her hand in his. Pulling her out of the chair, he stood before her. Standing this close, she felt the warmth radiating off his skin, increasing the temperature around her. As Ian released her hand, her skin ached for his touch. What was he doing to her? She should not want his touch but every nerve in her body was betraying her, as she quivered.

He rubbed his fingers down her cheek, across her lips then stopped just under her chin. Lifting her head so their eyes were aligned, he spoke softly.

"Dinna cover yer smile Lass. 'Tis such a beautiful smile, it would be a shame to hide it. It pleases me to see it."

His expression grew grim.

"Tomorrow morning the priest will come and demand to see proof that we have consummated this marriage. *On that*, he will no' compromise. But I want a willing wife. I will no' force myself on ye and I will no' touch ye unless ye ask."

Keira stared up at him in horror but was taken aback by the tenderness in his eyes. She knew there was truth behind what he said, but if the priest required proof, how was he to provide it? Bedding was certainly not in the contract, at least not as she understood things. This marriage was to be in name only, but she had never taken into account the priest's demands. And if she were to bed Ian she would not be able to get the marriage annulled. Could she lie to a priest? Could Ian? They both would certainly go to hell for it.

There was also the matter, of course, of Ian wanting a willing bride. Willing was a far stretch from the truth, though she couldn't help but enjoy his kisses no matter how much she tried to resist.

"How do ye plan to convince the priest that we are married in truth?"

"Dinna worry lass. I will come up wit' something. Ye have nothing to fear. I give ye my word."

Bothered, Keira turned her head to look away but Ian stopped her by cupping her cheek in his hand and gently brought her face back around to face him. His hand lingered there for a moment until his fingers grazed down her cheek to the base of her neck. The light touch sent shivers down her spine and she shuddered. Stopping just above her shoulder, he moved his hand from her neck to stroke down the length of her arm until their fingers met. Raising her hand to his lips, he lightly kissed each knuckle. Turning her hand over, he circled his thumb along her palm and kissed the inside of her wrist.

Keira swallowed hard and felt an intense heat rising within her. Ian must have felt it too. Forcefully, he pulled her into his embrace until their bodies were pressed together. Lowering his head until his lips hovered over hers; breathing her in. Keira's body relaxed against him. Though she wanted to resist, and fight this burning desire inside of her, her body took on a mind of its own.

"I will no' kiss ye unless ye ask," he said as his lips teasingly grazed against hers.

Why must he torture me so?

"I want ye Keira," he growled.

Kissing the side of her mouth, his lips trailed down her neck. The sensation made her knees go weak as tantalizing shivers pulsated inside her. Forcing herself to breath, she felt a sense of losing herself in his arms. She felt overwhelmed and a part of her was desperate to let go and give into this urge.

God bless it!

"Kiss me," she panted, barely muttering the words.

Ian placed several more kisses along her neck until he righted himself. Cupping her face in his hands, his lips crashed onto hers like a tidal wave crashing along the shore.

His lips felt remarkably warm, and she felt as if she was scorched by the sun. His hands wrapped around her back, gliding down to her waist, then up to the back of her head, caressing her and pulling her into him as if he meant to swallow her whole.

This kiss was the most intense, erotic sensation she had ever felt. It felt devilishly sinful but wonderful at the same time.

Ian pressed his tongue on her lips, encouraging her to open. When she eagerly complied, Ian slipped his tongue inside her mouth. She felt breathless as his tongue massaged hers.

As he gently released her, she was slowly brought back to the present. Taking in a breath of air, she was lightheaded and her limbs felt weightless. Using Ian for support, she cupped his forearm. It felt impressively hard underneath her fingertips, like he was built of stone. She looked to him in bewilderment and though at times he intimidated the hell out of her, he had a tendency to make her feel awestruck by just looking at her. Ian looked at her with the same stricken expression. She smiled knowing that her kiss had affected him as well.

Ian grunted and placed a kiss to her forehead.

"Ye should get some rest. We leave early in the morning," he said pulling away and gliding toward the bed.

Keira stood speechless and confused. Sitting down on the bed, Ian began kicking off his boots and pulling the covers down from the top of the bed. His reaction made her feel shameful. Had she done something wrong? Did he no longer want her? He sure tried to make an attempt to seduce her, so why did he stop?

"Are ye no' going to sleep?" he asked, looking puzzled.

"But I thought…I mean, I assumed," she tried to answer, fumbling her words.

"I told ye lass. I will no' touch ye unless ye ask. Now come to bed," he ordered.

Ian turned away from her and slipped his shirt off over his head. Keira stood wide-eyed at his bronze skin, noticing the multiple scars that ran along his back. Scars only a good thrashing would leave behind. Her chest tightened at the sight of them. They looked to have been deep wounds and no doubt were quite painful at one time.

There was so much about her husband that she didn't know. Other than the few tidbits she'd learned, she did not have enough knowledge of him to really understand him or his motives. Perhaps tomorrow she could change that.

Ian laid down on the bed, his back to her. She was grateful the bed was so large. In normal circumstances, she would have protested sleeping on the same bed as he, but as her husband, she knew he would not allow her to sleep on the floor, and she didn't dare ask him to do so. She trusted he would keep his word, and thus far he had not disappointed her.

Keira unlaced her gown until she was left wearing nothing but the shift underneath. It would have to do. Lying down on the bed, she lifted the covers over her and scooted herself as far to the edge of the bed as possible without falling off. Snuggling with her pillow, she closed her eyes and drifted off to sleep.

Chapter 18

Ian woke from a pleasant sleep. The smell of lavender surrounded him like a spring day. He felt warm and comfortable in his spot upon the bed and it was no wonder why. Opening his eyes, he smiled down at the lass whose head rested on his chest with her hand upon his stomach. He stilled his movements and steadied his breath, careful not to wake the sleeping beauty in his arms.

Her hair lay sprawled out across his shoulder and down the length of his arm. It was tempting to run his fingers through her long, soft locks. Had he not needed to rise, he would have stayed in bed holding her in his arms all day.

A loud pounding sounded at the door. Keira woke, sitting up faster than a spooked horse. Her wide, frightening eyes scanned over him when she realized the compromising position she had been in. Ian grinned in satisfaction.

The pounding at the door grew louder. Ian shuffled his feet from under the covers and stood from the bed. Making his way to the door, he opened it, and Leland stood in the door way, on his face a look of warning.

"Ian, I wanted to warn ye. The priest is on his way down to the village."

"Alright. Thank ye. We will be down in a moment," Ian said as he shut the door, turning his attention back to his horrified looking wife.

"Tis time to wake up. The priest is on his way here."

"What are we going to do without proof to give him?" she nervously asked, slipping off the bed holding the covers tightly around her chilled body.

If the lass's only concern was the priest and not the fact that she found herself lying in his arms, today was going to be a good day!

Ian studied the bedsheet for a moment before walking over to his belt lying on the floor. Removing his sgian dubh from its sheath, he pressed the blade against his thumb until it pierced his skin. Squeezing the tip of his finger allowed the blood to flow freely. Walking to the edge of the bed, he leaned over and smeared his thumb across the middle of the bedsheet. It wasn't as convincing as it would have if the lass had been a bleeder, but it would have to do.

Ian pulled the bedsheet from the bed and rolled it up in his arms.

"Get dressed and meet me down stairs. Dinna take too long," he advised.

Ian left the room just as the priest was heading up the stairs.

"Good morning MacKay. I trust ye slept well," the priest said.

"I am no' interested in yer pleasantries, father. Here is yer proof that Lady Keira is truly my wife in fact. Now take it and leave," Ian demanded.

The priest cast a slight snarl but did as he was told. Ian would not show respect to a man who had treated Keira so poorly. Had he not been a man of the cloth, he would have ripped the mon's tongue straight out of his mouth and forced him to eat it for the blasphemies he spoke of Keira.

Below stairs he found Leland and Rylan finishing up their morning meal.

"I see ye survived the night," Rylan said with one brow raised.

"Was the lass's honey sweet or did she sting ye like a bee?" Leland said as he burst into laughter.

Ian smacked the back of Leland's head as he had when they were young.

"That *lass,* mind ye, is my *wife,* and if either of ye say another word, it'll be the two of ye whose heads I'll be knocking around," he warned.

~*~

Keira rushed getting ready as Ian had requested. Slipping into her gown, making haste braiding her hair, and patting her face down with a cloth dipped in a small basin of cold water left out overnight.

She followed the motions of her regular morning routine, but her head was completely in the clouds. How had she ended up lying in Ian's arms? Just the memory of his grin when she woke was enough to humiliate her. She was grateful that he did not mention it and that Leland had come when he had. How long had she been like that? Being a heavy sleeper, she imagined that she could have snuggled up against him in the middle of the night. He would have been all too pleased and eager for the chance to touch her. Making a mental note, she would remember to place a pillow between them the next time she was forced to sleep next to him.

Leaving the room, Keira went to search for Ian. Once downstairs, she found him outside saddling the horses.

"I hope I did no' make ye wait long on my behalf," she exclaimed.

"Nay. I was just finishing packing our supplies I purchased from the innkeeper. His wife prepared us several hearty meals for our travels."

"That was verra kind of her."

"Ye must've slept well last night, for this morning ye were sleeping like a bairn," he said with a smirk on his face.

Embarrassment caused her to suddenly lose her voice, so she was unable to respond. The way the other two looked at her she could only imagine that this morning Ian had boasted about his evening giving them every detail of their kiss, unless he'd lied to them as well. Had they too believed she had bedded him, as the priest did? Even though she was his wife, she still felt the shame of a disgraced whore.

Approaching her side, Ian held out a fruit pastry. Keira eagerly accepted it. Ian helped Keira onto the saddle as he mounted behind her. Being forced to sit so close wasn't as uncomfortable as it had been before. She rather liked the way he wrapped his arm around her and snuggled her close.

~*~

They rode hard over the next several hours. Ian wanted to cover as much land as possible, as Inverness was a full two days ride away. Allowing Keira short breaks to tend to nature's call and stretch her legs, they continued to press forward into nightfall. Ian would have ridden the entire way had it not been for the horses needing to eat and rest. Ian could go days without sleep. A useful practice he'd learned from his days in battle.

Leaving the road, they rode into the woods to find a secure place to camp, though their choices were limited. As the clans continued to feud in these parts, it was getting harder to tell where a safe spot would be. It wasn't just rogue Highlanders they had to worry about. There were also highwaymen, gypsies, and English troops roaming these parts as well, that would not hesitate to start a fight whether they were provoked or not.

Ian settled on a spot near a group of tall pines. It wasn't an ideal place, but it would have to do. Reining in his horse, he called out to the others to stop.

Ian got down from his horse before helping Keira down as well. He decided to send Leland and Rylan out for wood and to search the area. Leaving Keira alone as he had done last time was not an option. He remembered all too well what happened the last time he left her alone and undefended. A mistake he was not going to make again. Unbuckling his pack, he pulled out a large tent from his sack and grabbed two rolled up plaids. Keira stood by quietly as he began setting the tent up. Once finished, he grabbed onto the bag tied to Rylan's horse and walked over to the burning fire Leland had built.

"Compliments of Lady Aggie, the innkeeper's wife," he said, as he pulled out portions of dried venison, bread and sliced cheeses, placing them on a small platter, and handed it to Keira.

"Thank ye," she said tiredly.

The four of them sat around the fire, eating and talking for what seemed like hours. Leland entertained Keira by way of stories of home including a particularly embarrassing one of Ian when he was a younger lad. He would have insisted Leland keep his foolishness to himself, but the sound of Keira's laugh was the sweetest sound in the world, so he bit his tongue. That, of course, did not stop him from staring daggers at his younger brother who was immensely enjoying poking fun at his older brother while he could get away with it. This was one of the few times, Leland could by all means get away with it, but Ian would have to remember in the future when Leland met his own future bride, to share a few stories of him as well.

Watching Keira's bright smile was like witnessing the stars for the first time; bright and radiant. He was astonished by how she managed to have such an effect on him. He found himself caring deeply for her and her safety. And unlike any other woman, he cared about what she thought and how she felt. He had learned a long time ago the mistakes he'd made with Sarah. Mistakes for which he had spent the last eight years trying to atone. But he promised himself that with Keira it would be different.

"There is a loch nearby," Rylan announced. "I think I am going to take a swim and cool off. The water should be warm enough fer ye lass if ye wish to do the same when I am through."

"I would verra much like that. Thank ye," she replied.

"If ye are leaving, I will take first watch," Leland said as he stood up and strapped his sword to his belt.

Ian was grateful the two of them were leaving. He had been waiting impatiently all day for a chance to be alone again with Keira. He didn't know how much longer he could wait until he could kiss her again.

He knew she wanted him as much as he wanted her last night. Though she tried to resist, the way her body responded to his touch made wooing her all too easy. But he didn't just want to bed her. He wanted her to want him. With those two dimwits gone, he would steal himself another sweet kiss, if she'd let him.

~*~

"I really like yer brother Leland. He has a gift of storytelling."

"What do ye mean ye *like* him?" he asked dryly.

"I only meant that he seems to be a good mon. He would get along rather well wit' my sister Alys. She has the same kind of humor that he does."

"Good. I dinna like hearing ye say that ye liked him."

"And what if I did like yer brother?"

"Then I would have to live wit' the regret of killing my own brother."

"Surely, ye jest!"

"Nay. Ye are my wife and I dinna like ye talking about another mon in such a fashion. Whether he be my own brother or no'."

Keira gave him an annoyed look.

"I am only stating the fact that I know more about yer brother from just in the last hour than I know of ye in the past several days. And besides, he would be best suited for Alys."

Had Alys been there now, she would have died from embarrassment at Keira's prejudgment but she would have heartily agreed. Leland was just the type of man Alys had been seen swooning over and probably the first man of whom Keira would approve. He had good character and a sense of honor to him that would make him a good husband. Much like Ian, she supposed.

That realization surprised her. She had been so bent on wanting an annulment she'd thought nothing about what she would do once she returned to her home and her family. There was no doubt she would be forced to marry another man and one not of her choosing. Keira looked to Ian. Perhaps staying married to Ian was not as bad as she'd thought. After all, he was a kind man.

"So, ye want to get to know me, aye?" he asked.

"Must I repeat myself?" she answered.

Ian shifted on the ground, turning to face her.

"What is it that ye would like to know?" he questioned.

Keira bit her bottom lip. There were so many things she wanted to know, but she couldn't possibly learn everything about him in just one sitting. There were things she would have to learn over time. There was one question; however, burning in the back of her mind and that was of Sarah.

"I do no' mean to pry but I was wondering if ye were willing to tell me about Sarah," she asked cautiously.

Unable to gauge his reaction to her question, she winced; worried she was opening old wounds. She had hoped he could be just as open and honest with her as she had been with him. She was his wife after all and if they were to stay married, she would like to know more about the woman who clearly still held his heart.

"Where did ye hear that name?" he asked; his voice dry and brazen.

"The barmaid that escorted me to my room mentioned her."

Ian ran his fingers through his hair and let out a long, deep sigh. Perhaps, she should not have asked but it was too late to take back her words.

"Ye dinna have to tell me," she began to say until Ian interrupted her.

"She was my wife," he said.

Keira could hear the sorrow in his voice.

"What happened to her?" she asked softly.

"Our village was attacked. Twas nearly eight years ago when my Sarah was taken."

"Was it by the Sutherlands?"

Ian nodded, wiping his hand down his face. His brows tightly knitted together as if he searched his memory of the events of that awful day.

"I'm sorry. I dinna mean to intrude. Tis yer past and if ye no' wish to tell me, I understand."

"Nay, lass. I will tell ye what happened."

"Twas my fault she died," he whispered.

Keira's mouth fell slack but she quickly closed it, clenching her jaw. She wanted further explanation but was unsure how much he was willing to share. It clearly pained him to talk about it. Suddenly, her mouth went dry. Licking her lips to moisten them, she thought carefully about what she should say. But how did one respond to that?

"I dinna understand. How could ye possibly be to blame?"

"We were married less than a month. I went away on a mission to Dun Au Noon wit' my clansmen to sign a peace treaty with a neighboring clan. I went to prove myself as a mon. I was young and foolish. While we were gone, our village was attacked by the Sutherlands; they killed thirty of our men and women. When we returned, they had burned our village. When our Chieftain confronted Laird Sutherland he denied any and all wrongdoing on the part of his people. But I know it was him. He killed our people but was never convicted. Sarah's death is on my hands. Had I been there to protect her, she would still be alive."

Keira's heart sank. She couldn't help but feel sorry for the guilt he bore. She now understood why his heart seemed cold and protected at times. Keira felt an unnerving urge to reach out for him and hold him in her arms. She wanted to comfort him and lift his pain. No man should carry such a burden. Her eyes glossed over with sympathy as he spoke.

"I am sorry, Ian, that ye bore such pain and sorrow."

"I dinna need yer sympathy Keira. It was a long time ago. I made my mistakes and must live wit' them. But ye are my wife now and I will no' make that mistake again. Tis my duty to protect ye, and I will wit' my life."

Ian's declaration sent Keira over the edge. She was pleased to hear he cared for her so much. Overwhelmed with emotion, she leaned toward him and wrapped her arms around his neck. No one had ever made her feel the way Ian had. In just the past two days, he had stirred emotions inside her that she could not explain. It both confused her and excited her.

Leaning back slightly, Ian placed both hands on the side of her face. Looking down into her eyes, he captured her lips in a warm, sensual kiss. Keira melted against him as she opened her mouth willingly to him, allowing his tongue to enter.

"God blessed, woman! Ye are making me mad from the want of ye," Ian said, murmuring against her lips.

Chapter 19

In the back of Ian's mind, he couldn't help but wonder how his luck had changed. God must be smiling down on him to have blessed him with such a woman as Keira. She was everything a man could ever want in a wife. Not only was she beautiful and smart but had honor and a brave heart, similar to any Highland warrior. He took pride in her ability, the way she had handled herself thus far. Most women would have broken into a fit of tears. But she was nothing like any other woman he had ever met, nor what he had expected from a Sinclair lass. She was stubborn to a fault, of course, but even that did not bother him. She was perfect; his wee, fierce bride.

Rylan and Leland returned from their trip to the loch and boasted about how warm the water was. Keira expressed her eagerness to wash the day's sweat and grime off her skin.

"I dinna have any soap fer ye lass," Ian said.

"That is alright. The water will be fine, I am sure."

Ian stood. Grabbing his plaid off the ground, he rolled it up in his arms.

"Are ye ready then?"

"Ready for what?" she asked, expressing utter confusion.

"Fer yer bath."

"I am, but where do ye think ye are going?"

"To join ye."

"Ian MacKay, I will no' share a bath wit' ye!"

"Aye, ye will. Ye are my wife. And I too need to bathe."

"Then I will wait right here fer ye to finish. T'would be indecent!"

Out of earshot of Leland and Rylan who looked as if they were positively enjoying their banter, he leaned towards her and whispered, "Listen to me wife, for I will only say this once. Ye are no' leaving my sight. So if ye wish to bathe, yer gonna have to accept that ye will no' be doing it alone."

Keira huffed in frustration.

"I dinna like ye ordering me around, Ian. I am yer wife, and I have no' denied that. But I will no' be treated like I am yer chattel."

"That is where ye are wrong, lass. Do ye always question authority?"

Ignoring his question, she asked one of her own. "Do ye always order people about and tell them what to do?"

"Aye, I do. And they listen."

"Well, if we are to be married in truth, I would like to have a say in certain matters."

"Are ye trying to compromise wit' me?" he asked, finding humor in her sudden display of confidence.

"Aye. I am."

"Alright! I will listen to what ye have to say, but only in our private quarters and ye are never to question me in front of my men."

"There is a verra big difference in hearing what I have to say and listening to what I have to say," she stated.

"I understand. I promise to listen, but ye may no' always get yer way."

"I can live wit' that, fer now."

"Good, now that's settled, I will escort ye to the loch where ye can bathe," he said, having no intention of allowing her to bathe alone.

Keira stood and stormed away in frustration which made Ian snicker all the more. He loved getting a rise out of her. He imagined she would be a wild cat in bed. Ian was unsure how much longer he could go without taking her into his arms and ravishing her. He had thought to wait until they reached his castle where he would properly bed her, but that was almost a week away and the ache in his groin was almost too unbearable. He was full of need, and a week was far too long to wait.

~*~

After the hours spent atop the horse, walking had proven to be a challenge all its own. Keira's backside ached from the hard ride and her thighs burned as if she had been marked by a branding iron.

"Bloody Christ!" she yelped, falling to the ground and quickly grabbing her calf.

Her leg muscle twitched and tightened. The pain felt as if a horse had just stomped on her leg. Vigorously, she massaged the tight knot but the pain in her leg did not abate. Ian rushed to her side and grabbed her calf in his hand. With his large, warm hands, he worked out the knot from her muscle.

He was very tender with her as he caressed her leg. His touch was warm and pleasant. It appeared he had done this before as he successfully calmed her twitching calf. Though the pain had stopped, she held off telling him just yet.

The intensity of the attraction she felt for him grew. It was as if just being near him wasn't enough. She wanted to feel his hands upon her; for him to touch her, hold her. She wanted to feel the warm sensation she felt when he kissed her lips. God was she becoming a wanton woman!

"It's better now. Thank ye," she said, pulling her leg away.

"Muscle cramps are common when riding fer as long as ye have been. Best ye stretch yer legs before tomorrow as we have another long ride."

"How much further must we travel?"

"Another whole day."

Keira sighed at the thought of riding again for so many hours. With her backside as sore as it was, after tomorrow, she would not be able to sit down for a week!

Keira followed Ian through the woods towards the loch. When they finally reached the shore, she felt a sigh of relief as she felt the cool water on the sore muscles.

The surrounding landscape was calm and serene. The reflection of the moon shone over the still water like a mirror. And lightening bugs danced and sparkled over the water as if she had stepped inside the realm of the fairies.

"I'll just be o'er there making sure no' one comes upon ye," he stated as he sat upon the shore, still in full view.

He was true to his word. He really wasn't going to let her out of his sight. The ignorance of him! Well, I don't have to completely undress, she told herself. Removing her gown only, she kept her chemise on and walked into the water.

"Do ye always bathe wit' yer clothes on?" he asked amusingly.

Just to spite him, she did not want to give him the satisfaction of ever believing he would see her naked.

"Aye, husband I do."

"Yer jesting wit' me, wife"

"Are ye so sure?" she asked, keeping a straight face.

"Aye, I believe ye are."

"Then ye have much to learn about me, Ian MacKay," she said as she sank further into the water.

After dunking her head under the loch's surface, she rose up and turned back to the beach, but Ian was nowhere in sight. Had he finally given her the dignity of some privacy?

"Ian?" she called out, but he did not respond.

Then, startling the hell out of her, Ian popped out of the water in front of her and wrapped his arms tightly around her.

"And ye have much to learn about me as well, wife," he said, pressing his lips hard against hers.

Ian reached down, grabbed the back of her thighs, forcing her to wrap her legs around him. Deepening the kiss, he held his hands firmly on her backside, pressing his groin against her. Keira could feel his hard shaft pressed against her as it bobbed in the water. He was naked! Keira blushed and wanted to pull herself out of his hold, but her attempt was stopped by Ian's hands moving up the outside of her thighs. As if her body had a mind of its own, her hips pressed harder against him. She wanted him in every way. Ian must have sensed her reaction to him, as he carried her out of the water.

Gently, he placed her down onto the plaid.

"Are we no' returning to camp?" she asked with a breathy voice.

"Aye, we will. Soon," he said as he nuzzled her neck, sending shivers down her body.

"Ian," she moaned, feeling as if she was about to lose control of her senses.

"Aye, lass," he said, as he continued to kiss and suck on her flesh.

"Ian," she said in a weak voice.

"Say it!" he said, rubbing his hands down the length of her body, stopping between her thighs. Keira could hear the desperation in his voice. He wanted her as well. "Tell me, ye want me!" he softly growled.

Keira felt an eruption of emotion and sensation stirring and tingling every nerve ending in her body. His hands roamed freely, exploring each curve and the warmth of his mouth on her neck caused her to feel as if she could touch the stars.

Her pulse quickened and she trembled beneath him. She no longer cared what anyone would think of her. She was a married woman after all; a woman who desperately wanted her husband's touch and embrace. She did not want him to stop.

"I want ye," she responded, breathlessly. "But are ye no' afraid someone will come upon us?"

"Nay!" he said, carelessly.

Raising her chemise to expose her legs, Ian slid his hand under the fabric to the juncture of her thighs. Keira let out a breath, as he slipped his fingers inside of her most sacred area. At his touch, her skin tingled and every limb pulsated. With her body twisting and twitching, her hips raised, forcing his hand harder against her.

"Ian," she cried out, as a wave of pleasure exploded within her.

Ian's lips descended on hers as he continued his sweet torture, stretching his fingers deep inside of her.

"Ye are so wet for me," he breathlessly uttered.

"Is that bad?" she asked.

Ian laughed softly.

"Nay lass. It means ye want me."

Ian knew just when and where to touch her to make her succumb to him and she was a willing partner. Removing his hand from her, he began helping her out of the wet chemise. She lay there, fully naked in front of him but he blanketed her with his own warm, naked body. His mouth went to her breast and suckled her nipple. The sensation was almost mind-blowing.

Positioning himself between her thighs, without warning, Ian drove himself into her, breaking through her maidenhood. Keira yelled out digging her fingernails into his back. She felt as if he had just knocked the breath right out of her. The pain, so intense, made her stomach clench.

"Ian," she cried out.

"Tis alright lass, dinna move," he ordered.

Keira had not realized that such pleasure could cause such pain. Listening to Ian, she lay still. A few moments later, the pain subsided and the aching desire she had once felt returned in full force

"Has the pain gone?" he asked.

Keira could see the concern on his face. Nodding her head, he slowly pulled out and without reservation plunged himself deep within her again. Wrapping her legs around him, she raised her hips to meet his. She wanted him, all of him. In all her life, she'd never dreamed what happened between a man and a woman could be a wondrous and magical feeling. She did not wish him to stop. She loved the feel of him on top of her and the feel of him holding her in his arms. Each time he moaned, she smiled knowing that she was the cause of his pleasure.

~*~

Ian wanted to be gentle. He had meant to go easy on the lass, but he could not stop from wanting to pound the hell out of her. She felt so good in his arms, he did not want to stop. He tried to slow down but his climax was building and he felt his seed on the verge of spilling. Her skin under his touch was as soft as if he was wrapped in the finest silk. Pressing his lips to hers, she tasted like a sweet apple. It made him want to devour her all the more. There was nothing he would not do for this woman.

Within moments, he collapsed on the ground next to her and gathered her in his arms. Keira pressed her backside up against him. Desire shot to his groin, as her backside pressed against him. He wanted her all over again, but had to resist. He knew she would be too sore and he hoped she would heal quickly so he could make love to her again tomorrow, God willing.

"Ian, have ye been wit' many women?"

Ian's brow rose at her question. He wondered where that had come from.

"A few," he truthfully responded.

"Did I please ye?"

Ian smiled at her question. Though he found her question silly, it was a valid question. She had no experience in such things and could not have been expected to know what to do. But he wondered how she could think that she had not pleased him? In truth, she did please him very much.

"Aye, lass. Ye please me," he responded.

~*~

Keira felt completely drained of energy. Ian on the other hand, walked around as if he felt refreshed. Handing her the gown he had tossed onto the ground, Keira slipped it over her head and stood.

"We should head back to camp before the lads come looking fer us," he suggested.

"I agree. I certainly dinna want them finding us in such a predicament."

Keira and Ian walked back to the camp where Leland and Rylan were already fast asleep near the fire. Quietly, Ian and Keira slipped inside the tent and covered themselves with the plaid. Unlike how she felt the first time they'd slept in the same bed together, Keira did not protest when Ian grabbed her and held her in his arms. She found she rather liked it there. It did not take long for her to get comfortable snuggled inside Ian's warm embrace and she fell fast asleep.

Chapter 20

It was well before dawn when the four of them started their journey north towards Inverness. Ian was hell-bent on arriving at the King's castle before nightfall. The wind blew fierce against their backs as if nature itself had lent a hand, pushing them towards their destination, as if their arrival would affect fate itself.

It was a hard ride for Keira as Ian pushed the horses fast across the uneven terrain of the Highlands. With only a few short breaks to stop and stretch, she felt her legs and backside turn numb, as her bottom jostled up and down on the hard leather saddle. She was not used to riding this hard but she would not complain. She knew Ian's reasons for expediting their journey. They had to cross not only enemy territory but a southern point of Chisholm's holdings as well.

Ian explained to her how dangerous it would be for her to be caught in the middle of battle. If they could safely reach Fraser territory to the north, they could find a safe haven there for her in the event Chisholm attacked.

Rylan took off ahead to scout out the area, leaving just Leland and Ian to protect Keira. She had faith in the two brothers and knew she was well cared for but it did not ease her worry. Traveling across enemy territory did not bother her. It was their destination she feared, and facing her father. She could not imagine what they were doing to him. Despite that he had lied to her, he was still her father.

Unsettling images of her father chained to others in the bowels of a dungeon had haunted her dreams the past two nights. Though he was convicted of crimes against the crown, the thought was still unnerving. She knew one day her father would have to answer for his sins but she could never have imagined his sins were so great.

She loved her father very much but was equally as angry with him. He had put her in the worst sort of predicament. His selfish actions made her and her sisters have to choose not only between him and God, but between him and the king. He was a heretic and a traitor, either of which would ultimately result in his death. Keira realized she could do nothing to save him. This journey had never been about saving him or his soul. It was for her; to allow her closure and to say goodbye.

For hours they rode, long past the setting sun until the moon hung high in the sky. They stopped along the shore of a small body of water, and Keira could see the castle turrets reaching high above the trees on the other side of the loch. *Inverness*, she whispered to herself.

The structure was massive and much larger than her home at Castle Sinclair. Even from across the bay, Keira could sense its magnitude. She thought of the labyrinth of halls and rooms that made up the keep. Though it had only been a week that she had last occupied the castle, she felt as if it were just yesterday that she was within those walls preparing to give her life to her betrothed before this tornado of events had occurred.

How different things would have been had they played out as her father had intended. She would be married to Laird Chisholm and father would have been safely back at Castle Sinclair with her sisters. But had things not turned out the way they had, she would never have met Ian. And if she had met him under different circumstances, they would have been enemies. That thought did not sit well.

"Leland, we are to meet Laird Gudeman at Margie's tavern to let him know we have arrived," Ian informed him.

Keira looked up at Ian. He had made mention of Laird Gudeman on several occasions, saying that he was the man who from whom Ian had received his orders. Perhaps he was one of King James' personal guards.

The three of them walked into the tavern and took a seat at a small round table near the back. A young barmaid offered them a drink as they sat. Within a few moments, a man Keira assumed was Laird Gudeman, judging by the way Ian and Leland took notice of him, came down the stairs with a young buxom lass on his arm. He gave her a kiss on the cheek and sent her away. Walking over to their table, he took the vacant chair that sat across from Ian.

He was a young man of fair complexion. By his clothing Keira would have thought him a mere peasant, but his well-manicured beard, white teeth and clean fingernails said otherwise. He looked familiar to her but she could not place where she would ever have met him before.

While Ian explained their situation and the roles Keira and her father had played, she sat quietly and listened. Laird Gudeman seemed to be in agreement with the others; believing her father was a traitor. Keira, however, had already made up her mind that until she heard the words from her own father's lips, she would never believe it. Gudeman eyed her suspiciously.

"Ye dinna believe it to be so, do ye lass?" Laird Gudeman asked.

"I have only known my father to be a good mon," she replied.

"I would be verra interested to hear yer side of the story."

"I dinna know what else to say. Ian has already told ye everything."

"Do ye believe in the allegations against yer father?"

"I believe, my laird, that until I hear it from his own lips, I can no' say fer certain."

"But ye agree that he denounced the church?"

"I dinna believe it is a simple thing to say aye or nay. I dinna believe he has issues wit' the church, my laird, but with God Himself. My father blames God for taking my mother. It wasn't until my mother died that he banished Father Bryant and stopped going to sermons. My mother died five years ago in childbirth and I think when he lost her, he lost a part of himself."

Keira looked at Ian with sad eyes. She assumed Ian must have felt the same way when he lost Sarah. Turning her attention back to Laird Gudeman, she did not care whether he believed her or not. He was just another man quick to judge and point fingers. For all she knew, he was just another pompous Laird believing he was as high and godly as God himself. Who was he to place judgment?

"I am sorry fer yer loss on both accounts. As fer yer father, there were witnesses who came forward who testified against him, even some of his own men."

"I dinna believe that. None of my clansmen would ever go against my father."

"Do ye no' believe the word of my men?" Laird Gudeman asked with a curious expression.

"If I may speak so freely, my laird, I have come to learn that yer men think more wit' their balls than their brains."

Ian coughed, spitting out the ale he choked on from Keira's outburst. Laird Gudeman's eyes widened in surprise at her harsh words, but he quickly let out a hearty chuckle.

"Aye, that may verra well be true lass," he agreed.

Ian held his hand up to stop Keira from replying.

"Tomorrow we will discuss matters further," Ian said.

"Agreed," Gudeman said as he stood up from his chair. "Lady Keira, it has been my pleasure to make yer acquaintance. Ian MacKay is a good mon, one of my best warriors, and I am sure he will be a good husband to ye."

Keira just nodded her head in response, as it wasn't her pleasure at all to make his acquaintance.

~*~

Ian and Leland led the horses towards the gates where several armed guards were stationed at their posts. By the light shining from the torches that hung from the walls, Ian could make out more than twenty dark figures walking along the parapet atop the castle wall. He did not recall so many men securing the castle during his last visit here.

"Who goes there?" a guard called down to them from one of the towers.

"I am Ian MacKay of Clan MacKay and I'm accompanied by my brother Leland. I have come to provide testimony to the king," he replied.

"A MacKay ye say! Well, ye would be the first. And who is that wit' ye?" the guard asked, looking down at Keira.

Ian could sense that she was about to respond. He glanced down as he whispered, "Dinna say a word." Looking back to the man atop the tower he replied, "She is my wife."

Keira looked up at Ian but he discouraged her questioning look by shaking his head.

"Verra well then, open the gates!" the guard called down to the gate guards. "Leave yer weapons when ye enter," he added.

Ian removed his weapons and laid them inside a large cart full of swords and daggers that sat just outside the gate. Taking the reins, he led his horse through the gate.

A loud pounding echoed around them as they entered the courtyard. Searching the noise, he saw a group of men constructing the platform of the gallows. The smell of burnt flesh lingered in the air as several other men swept up ashes that were still smoldering. Ian felt Keira trembling in his arms. "Tis alright, lass," he whispered before dismounting.

A young red-headed man came running out of the barn to greet them.

"That be a fine beast ye have there, Sir," he said, running his hand along Ian's mare.

"Aye. Her name is Storm Fighter. She once belonged to the King."

"Storm Warrior must be her sire. I'd recognize the similar coat anywhere. Never seen another one like her."

"Ye know yer horses!" Ian said.

"Aye, I am the stable master here at Inverness. I have been running stables since I was a lad. Dinna worry about yer mount. I'll take good care of her."

"I trust that ye will."

~*~

Ian walked to the side of the horse and helped Keira dismount as Leland grabbed their satchel from the saddle bags and came to Keira's other side. Wrapping his arm around Keira, Ian held her close to his side as they walked swiftly toward the door of the keep.

"Ian what's the matter?" Leland asked.

"Just get inside the castle, Leland, I will explain later."

Instantly, Keira knew something was amiss.

The three of them were greeted at the front door by one of the castle's chambermaids who eagerly found them a room and ordered a meal to be sent up to Ian's and Keira's quarters as the evening meal had been served long since, and the tables put away for the night. Keira pitied Leland as the maid insisted he sleep in the guard house.

The maid led them to a bedchamber on the third floor.

"Is there anything else I can get fer ye?" the maid asked.

"Just bring the meal for the three of us, if you please. After that, we wish to no' be disturbed," Ian firmly replied.

As soon as the maid left, Keira could feel the tension in the air.

"Ian, why have ye been acting so strangely?"

Ian looked to Leland before turning his attention back to Keira.

"Have ye noticed when we reached the gate, they no' made any mention of Rylan?"

Keira pondered his question. Had Rylan made it to Inverness, he would certainly have introduced himself as a MacKay, yet she did remember the guards mentioning that they were the only MacKays present. Even the stable master seemed surprised to see a horse like Ian's, but Rylan's horse looked almost identical. Surely, if he'd seen Rylan's horse it would have come up in conversation. Had something terrible happened to him?

"Ye dinna suppose he was attacked on his way here, do ye?"

"I'm no' sure," Ian said.

"Had Rylan been accosted, there would have been signs on the road. We traveled the same path," Leland added.

"Do ye suppose wit' the bounty on his head, he chose no' to come? After all, ye did say that many men were after him," Keira said directing her comments to Ian.

"That may be true, but tis no' like Rylan to go missing. And I can no' go looking fer him either." Turning his attention to Leland, he continued, "Once the trials are over, I will take Keira home to Invercauld. From there, we will search fer Rylan."

"Invercauld? But I thought ye lived at Varrich? That is where Clan MacKay hails from. My father spoke of it many times."

Leland responded, "Castle Varrich was our home. Many years ago, our home was taken from us. It was seized by the Sutherlands shortly after they burned our village. We make our home now wit' our cousins, Clan Farquharson. But it is Ian's hope to one day restore our clan to its rightful place when our father passes. For now, our clans have allied."

Keira looked back at Ian.

"That's why ye left home in the first place, isn't it? Fighting the Sutherlands was yer mission, and that's why ye felt it was yer fault they attacked yer lands," Keira said, affirming what she already knew.

Remaining silent, Ian nodded. Losing his wife was one thing, but his home as well? Pity did not even begin to describe what she felt for her husband.

The more she learned about him, the more she started to understand him. And with understanding came trust and respect, and with respect came admiration and love. *God blessed*! Could it be true? Had she fallen in love with him? Keira wrung her hands together as she thought more on it. She couldn't possibly be!

Keira sat down on the edge of the bed, her eyes following Ian and Leland as they paced back and forth while they were in deep conversation about Rylan. Too distracted, she couldn't keep up with their conversation. They spoke in half sentences as if they had the ability to read each other's minds. Their actions were not completely out of the ordinary, for she and Alys had the same ability.

"Leland," Ian said, "I want ye to stay here and guard the door. I am going to speak to the officers."

"Yer leaving?" Keira interrupted.

"I will be right back. I am going to see if there has been any sign of Rylan, and see if they will allow ye to speak to yer father before tomorrow. The maid will be here shortly. I want ye to stay here with Leland. Listen to his orders. I am leaving him in charge. Do ye understand?"

"Aye. Please do no' be gone long."

Ian walked up to her and placed his fingers under her chin. Lifting her head, he kissed her. But before Keira could kiss him back he was already gone.

Leland and Keira sat down on the chairs and waited.

~*~

Ian left the chamber in search of answers. He decided it was best to speak to the castle steward first. If Rylan had arrived, he would know about it. Ian also hoped to gain permission from the man for Keira to speak to her father in the dungeons below, at least to get her questions answered and say goodbye.

As Ian reached the steward's quarters, he found the man hanging up a ring of keys on a rusty nail hammered into the back wall behind his desk. Cell keys, he figured, by the looks of them. One too many times had Ian seen keys such as those. The man continued to sit at his desk and began reading a ledger.

The steward looked up at him defensively. With no guards present, and no formal introduction, Ian stepped into the chamber. The man gasped and looked ready to run. It became clear to Ian this man was not a military man, but by the look of him he was a man of politics, and ambition. By the smell of whiskey from his breath; he was also a man well into his cups which meant he might be easily persuaded if Ian used just the right approach.

"Good day, Sir…" the steward began, slurring his speech.

"MacKay. Ian MacKay."

"Aye, well it's quite unfortunate that ye have caught me at a bad hour. I am no' taking any meetings today. I'm verra busy as ye can see. Come back tomorrow," he said as he continued his reading.

"I was sent here on behalf of Clan Sinclair. I have escorted the laird's daughter to pay her last respects to the man before ye see him hanged."

The steward looked up at him, giving him a vicious glower with his reddened eyes.

"Visits will take place tomorrow before the tribunal," he said, hiccupping as he tried to speak.

"Aye, I understand. Ye have yer orders. Surely, ye would allow a mon of God to hear the prisoner's confession."

"Ye are a mon of God?" the steward asked suspiciously.

"Aye. I apologize for my attire, but ye know traveling through these Highlands. One feels the need to conceal his identity until he is called upon in times of need." Ian hastily replied.

"Surely ye must understand my position, Father."

"My humble apologies. I do no' wish to get ye in trouble wit' yer superiors. Is there someone else I should ask?"

"Nay. I am this castle's steward therefore all requests go through me."

"Then surely a good Christian like yerself would allow my mistress a few mere moments of yer precious time."

Ian patiently waited for the steward to mull over his request. He was quite gifted at playing the role of a priest when the occasion called for it. And this man made it all too easy for him. As drunk as the man was, he could be talking to the Pope for all he knew.

"I will allow it. But tell yer mistress that I will allow her only a few minutes," he said as he stood from his chair.

"She will be pleased for any time ye will give her. May God bless ye and keep ye."

"Here," the steward said, picking up a small pouch from his desk. "For the good of the church," he said, digging in his bag he handed Ian a few coins.

"Thank ye."

Ian looked at the coins the man offered and slipped them into his inner pocket. Sin or not, if the man was willing to share his riches, Ian was not about to protest the offering. He would put them to good use.

"Before I forget, I did have one more question. Ye havena happened to see a mon by the name of Rylan Arnett of the clan MacKay, have ye?"

"Rylan Arnett? Ne'er heard of the mon."

"Are ye certain? He was to arrive earlier today."

"I am certain of it. My guards keep me well aware of who enters these walls. Perhaps the mon ye are searching fer has decided to stay in the village."

"Perhaps, thank ye again fer yer time."

Chapter 21

Keira nervously paced the floor as she waited for Ian to return. Knowing that her father was somewhere in the dungeon beneath her feet caused her stomach to cramp and tighten as if she'd swallowed a bag of rocks.

Keira thought about their meeting and what she would say. She had so many questions to ask that she knew she wouldn't remember them all. If she could, she would have written them all down just to make sure she wouldn't forget.

"Lassie, ye need to ease yer worry. Ian will be back soon," Leland advised.

"I cannae help it. I hate having to wait. I always have to wait."

Leland smirked, "Tis the way of life, my lady."

"Well it's a way I am no' use to," she admitted just as Ian walked through the door.

Keira quickly turned to face him.

"Did ye find out where they are holding my father? Will they allow me to speak to him?" she asked in one breath.

"Aye, I did manage to convince the steward to allow ye a few minutes below in the dungeons. However I am afraid my request has cost us. Until we leave this place, ye will have to refer to me as Father MacKay."

"Father? Ye told them ye were a priest? Are ye mad?" Leland asked, surprised by Ian's remark.

"Twas the only way I could convince the mon to allow Keira to see her father."

Keira felt terrible he had to lie for her but was grateful for it; though his sin would now be her burden. Since they met, Keira had been counting the number of times she would ask for a reprieve to save his soul; as she highly doubted he could save his own. It was curious, though, how he managed to convince someone of his *sainthood*. A man would have to be mad to believe such a thing. Every bone in Ian's body was sinful. He obviously had the skills of deception, of that, she knew all too well.

"Thank ye Ian, fer yer sacrifice," Keira solemnly replied.

"Ye are my wife, Keira. 'Twas nay a sacrifice," he reminded her. "Come, we have little time."

Keira followed Ian out the door and down the stairs. The two of them stopped at the bottom step just outside a warped wooden door where two guards stood guarding the entrance to the dungeon below the stairs.

"My name is Father MacKay. My mistress has been given permission to speak to Laird Sinclair," Ian reported.

Keira was awestruck by Ian's performance as he conversed with the guards. He spoke with an English accent, similar to that of the Lowlanders. As the guards spoke to him, Ian went into full character citing bible scripts and blessings. It was hard not to laugh. She wondered what other antics Ian had up his sleeve.

The guards granted entrance and opened the two locks that sealed the door. They guided them to a solitary room down the end of a long hall. The smell was nauseating, Keira held her breath as they passed several closed wooden doors. The hall was dim and gloomy and smelled of moldy straw and piss. Beyond the moans and cries of the inmates, sharp squeaks of rats could be heard as they scurried in and out underneath the doors as they searched for food and shelter. Keira almost dug her nails into Ian's arm as her grip on him intensified.

"Stay here," the guard ordered. "I will fetch the prisoner."

Keira's pulse increased at the mention of her father.

"Ian," she whispered. "May I speak to my father in private?"

Ian's brow furrowed at her question. She could tell he was not happy with her request.

"I will no' leave this room. But if ye wish, I will stand near the door."

A few moments later, the two guards returned with Keira's father. She gasped as she saw his bare feet shuffling: there were iron shackles around his ankles and his clothes were ragged and torn. At first glance, she almost did not recognize him. It was not his appearance that was striking but his demeanor. No longer was he the tall, proud man she knew. No longer did he hold his head up high, exuding dominance and confidence. This man before her had been broken; a giant cut down to pieces. What had they done to him?

Instinctively, Keira rushed into his arms, but they remained at his sides. The two guards left the chamber locking the door behind them.

"Keira? What the hell are ye doing here?" her father scoffed. "Ye should no' be here. Ye must leave!"

"Nay!"

"Where is yer husband? Where is Chisholm? He was supposed to protect ye!"

"That is where ye are wrong. Father, I must know, did ye know that Chisholm was an enemy to the crown? Did ye know that he conspires wit' the English?"

Magnus looked at her with a cold blank stare. Keira gazed into his eyes and could see the truth. Shaking her head she refused to believe it.

"Father, please tell me is it no' true."

"Aye. Keira. I knew."

Keira stepped back from her father in horror. Her stomach clenched with nausea. She looked back at him in disgust.

"Then why the bloody hell did ye ask me to marry him?"

"The world is changing Keira. I found refuge with Laird Chisholm. Ye must understand, had it no' been fer him we would have lost everything."

"But we did lose everything! Chisholm never intended to marry me. He fooled ye, father. He fooled us both. He was the one who told the king of yer involvement. While the guards were busy arresting ye, he remains a free mon. Dinna ye understand? Ye sold yer soul to the Devil fer naught. And now ye are to die fer it."

"I am sorry, Keira. But do no' mourn fer me. Death has no' come fer me yet and I am no' afraid to die. But tell me, if Chisholm did no' bring ye here then who did?"

Keira looked over at her husband who was staring daggers at her father. She could not blame him for being angry with her father.

"This is Ian MacKay, my husband," she said waiting for her father's fuming response, but he said nothing.

The two men glowered at each other.

"How did ye become involved in this?" her father asked.

"I was sent to capture Laird Chisholm when I came upon yer daughter before she married the savage beast," Ian firmly replied.

"Then I offer ye my thanks and trust that ye will keep her safe."

"She is well protected," Ian responded.

"Yer time is up," the guard called out as he entered the room.

"Wait, I am no' finished," Keira pleaded.

"I said, ye are finished!" the guard snapped.

~*~

Ian grabbed ahold of Keira's shoulders and pulled her into him. He did not want trouble.

"Keira. Its time," he said gently, trying to focus her attention on him. "Ye have to say goodbye."

Keira looked at him with tears brimming her eyes but he kept his gaze firm. He could see the pain in her eyes, but denying the inevitable would only prolong her suffering. And they couldn't afford to cause a ruckus. As much as he wanted to wrap her in his arms, he forced himself to keep a safe distance. After all, he was a man of the cloth, at least that's what the guards were meant to believe. But once they were alone, he would hold her and comfort her all night if that was how long it took.

"Keira, go!" her father demanded refusing to look at her.

"But Father!"

"Take her away! Keep her safe," he demanded to Ian.

Ian nodded and pulled Keira out of the room.

As they entered the hall she asked, "What will happen to him?"

"He is to be hanged tomorrow after the trials."

"But, what of the trial? What of witnesses?"

"Keira, he has already been tried."

Keira froze in place as if she were the one in shackles. Her face had turned white and she looked sickly. Ian wrapped an arm around her and hurried her down the hall and out of the dungeon. As he led her up the stairs to their chamber, she remained silent. As soon as they entered the bedchamber, Ian held her close. Keira sobbing, buried her face in his chest, soaking his shirt.

"Tis alright lass. We knew this was going to happen. Ye knew we were no' here to save him."

"I know," she faintly replied. "Ian, would that have been my fate had ye no' married me?"

"Nay! Because I would never have allowed anything to happen to ye."

"Are ye worried about the trials tomorrow?" she asked, sniffling.

"Nay and neither should ye be."

~*~

Not worry, he told her! Asking her not to worry was like asking her to keep the sun from rising. It would take a miracle or an act of God to abide by such a request.

The hour was late and Keira had no idea how she would ever sleep knowing what tomorrow would bring. Ian repeatedly asked her to join him in bed, but her mind was too distracted. Gazing into the fire, her mind played out the past several weeks leading up to tomorrow's trial. She felt angry with herself for having been so blind to what was happening in her own household. Her concern shifted to her sisters. Where were they? Were they safe? She needed to find them. Keira turned to ask Ian if he would send someone out after them, but he was already sound asleep.

Chapter 22

Ian escorted Keira to the back bench inside the courtroom. At the front of the room sitting on the dais, a man who introduced himself as Phillip Stewart, the Sherriff of Ross-Shire, waited quietly as the accused were led into the courtroom and taken to their seats on the front row, her father among them. The twelve men sat humbly as they waited for their trial and judgement.

The courtroom began filling with spectators. Many of whom came from miles around to witness the hangings. It seemed the population of Inverness had doubled overnight. Just the number of people attending caused Keira's nerves to twitch and stomach to tighten.

Witnesses began taking the stand offering their testimony against the accused. It seemed that everyone in the room stood against them. Not one spoke up in their defense.

The room of spectators seemed to only want one outcome. *Death*! Glancing around the room, Keira saw only hatred in the people's eyes. After the witnesses gave their accounts, the Sherriff called Magnus to the stand.

"Laird Magnus Sinclair, son of Athol, ye are accused of crimes against the church as well as the King of Scotland. Do ye agree to these charges?" Phillip asked, narrowing his eyes, and looking down at him.

Magnus stood tall, unashamed of his actions as he held his head high.

"I do."

Phillip lifted his head and addressed the crowd.

"As the accused has admitted guilt, he will be sentenced to death by the gallows. May God have mercy on his soul."

At Magnus's confession Keira broke down in tears. Why had he not pleaded for mercy? She could not believe he had done what he was accused of doing. As the guards grabbed Magnus's arms to escort him out the back door, Keira felt herself close to fainting. She did not have the strength to watch her own father die. The image of him dangling from the rope had already crept in her mind and it was more than she could handle.

"Ian, I wish to return to my room," she said breathing heavily.

Ian wrapped his arm around her and was just about to do that, when the door to the room swung open and a commotion commenced. Keira glanced behind her and saw Rylan forcing a man into the room. The room fell silent as they stared at the prisoner. Shuffling in behind him was Laird Gudeman and several guards.

Immediately the crowd bowed their heads and the procession continued down the aisle towards the dais. Laird Gudeman took a seat next to Phillip Stewart keeping his attention on the prisoner.

Noticing the crowd's reaction to Laird Gudeman, she turned to Ian.

"Ian, why is everyone bowing to Laird Gudeman?"

Ian tightly pressed his lips together before answering.

"Ian, who is he?" she nervously asked.

"That mon is James, the King of Scotland. To keep himself safe, he travels incognito as Laird Gudeman so that he can mingle among his people. Only a few men know his real identity and it must be kept that way. I am sorry I lied to ye, but it was no' my secret to tell."

Keira's eyes flew back to James. She felt mortified. The things she'd said to him, the way she'd embarrassed herself in front of him, oh God, what must he think of her.

"He must have thought I was mad speaking to him in such an ill-mannered way!"

Ian shook his head and smiled.

"Nay lass. James is a good judge of character. In truth, I think he rather enjoyed yer conversation."

Keira sat lower in her seat, wanting to hide herself from James's view.

~*~

"I bring ye Laird Thomas Chisholm. A man accused of treason, conspiring wit' the English, and attempting to kill James of Scotland," Rylan stated.

Ian stared in bewilderment. *This* was Laird Chisholm; the most dangerous man in all the Highlands? This man was nothing more than a weak-looking coward. Chisholm was not a very tall man as rumors would suggest, nor was he built as broad as an ox. It was clear these fabrications were meant to warn off his enemies. In truth, the man looked like nothing more than a mere ruffian. To think that this man would have been Keira's husband. That thought alone angered him. Chisholm would not have been able to protect her any more than he would have been able to protect himself. Ian could not believe the audacity Keira's father must have had to agree to such an arrangement.

Rylan picked up the man cowering on the ground by his shirt collar and tossed him onto the wooden bench. Ian studied the man's movements as Thomas squirmed in his seat. The man did not speak a word, nor did he try to fight off his accusers.

Everything about this situation seemed wrong. His capture seemed far too easy. Had Chisholm planned to be captured by Rylan? Ian was sure the man would not have surrendered so easily unless he was up to something. Although many of the rumors about him proved to be false, he was a cunning and tricky man. It would be easy for him to arrange an attack with his numbers of English supporters and Scottish enemies. Ian surveyed the room, looking at the faces of the men in the crowd, gauging their actions. The sheriff silenced the room.

"Thomas Chisholm, ye stand accused of numerous counts of treason, allying with the English and plotting against the King of Scotland. What do ye say to these charges?"

The room anxiously waited for a response but it was Rylan who spoke up first.

"My Laird, Chisholm can no' give his testimony to his charges. He does no' have the ability to speak."

The crowd in the room began to whisper. Rylan continued.

"Before I came upon him, the bloody bastard cut out his own tongue."

The buzzing whispers of the onlookers grew louder. Ian felt the sleeve of his shirt being tugged as Keira clutched her hand around his arm.

Leaning toward him, she whispered, "Why would he do such a horrid thing?"

Ian turned to her. "Probably because he knew that if he were to be tortured, his secrets would go wit' him to the grave."

"Laird Chisholm," the sheriff said, "I assume yer hearing is fine. Do ye admit to these charges?"

Everyone looked back at Chisholm awaiting an answer. He sat upright on his seat and vigorously shook his head, denying the charges. The sheriff looked at James who gave a nod of his head.

"As ye can no' speak and nay one has come forth and offered to speak fer ye, it is my belief based on the evidence that ye, Laird Thomas Christopher Chisholm are guilty of all charges. Therefore, it is this court's ruling that ye shall be sentenced to death."

~*~

As Chisholm was hauled away, Rylan, Ian and Keira quickly left the courtroom before the mass of witnesses came piling out to view the hangings.

"Rylan what happened?" Ian asked, still not feeling right about the situation.

"I came upon a small group of men camped along the border. They had captured Chisholm fer the award on his head and meant to bring him here. I escorted them and kept Chisholm in custody."

"It just does no' seem right," Ian said.

"What do ye mean?"

"Dinna ye think it was odd that it has taken us months to hunt him down and capture him and yet it only took a few men to succeed?"

"What are ye thinking?" Rylan asked.

"I am thinking that there is something else going on."

"That may be but Chisholm is now in the custody of the king's guards. We fulfilled our mission Ian, and now can return home."

"Aye, maybe yer right."

"Are ye no' providing yer testimony to the court?" Keira nervously asked.

"James has already granted ye pardon. I spoke to him this morning," Rylan said.

"He did?"

"Aye. He said that he had a verra interesting conversation wit' ye last night," Rylan assured her.

Interesting was not the word she would have chosen for her outlandish outburst.

"What will happen to my clan? To my sisters?"

"I dinna know what will happen but as of right now ye are the heir to Clan Sinclair, and I am sure James will manage the estate in yer absence. In regards to yer sisters, they are welcome to stay wit' us until they are of age to find a suitor of their own," Ian responded.

"Ye, ye would do that fer me?" Keira stuttered, surprised by his act of generosity.

"I am yer husband, Keira. I would do anything fer ye."

Gazing up at the man she had regarded as the Highland Beast, who had the Heart of the Highlands.

Without hesitation, Keira rose to the tips of her toes and wrapped her arms around his thick neck. Pulling him down toward her, their lips met. Keira kissed him hard and without restraint. Where there was darkness, he brought forth the light. Where there was sorrow, he created happiness.

"Where are we heading now?" she asked, wanting to leave this whole thing behind her.

"We go home!"

Chapter 23

Invercauld: one castle, two Lairds, and a great and powerful army of more than six hundred skilled warriors, that was how Ian described it.

Invercauld was a beautiful grey stone castle that rested between the river Dee and the majestic, snow-covered mountain Ben-a-Bhuird. The castle, in comparison to her own, was twice as tall, and the keep reached high above its great wall. Atop the great towers, handwoven banners waved proudly in the air, depicting the Farquharson Clan colors and crest.

As they rode across the bridge into the bailey they were greeted by several clansmen, both Farquharson and MacKay, cheering for the return of the three MacKay warriors.

At the front steps, a woman ran out to greet them. She was dressed in a black dress and her light brown hair was up in tight braids. As Leland dismounted the woman wrapped her arms around him.

"My sons have returned!" she cheerfully said, wiping a tear from her eye.

Her enthusiasm and smile was contagious. It was obvious she was Ian's and Leland's mother and had missed her sons very much. It reminded Keira of her own mother. Oh, how she missed her.

Ian helped Keira down from the horse. Hand in hand they walked toward the proud woman. Keira felt a pinch of nervousness. She had not expected to meet his mother so soon.

"Mother, I would like to introduce ye to Lady Keira Sinclair MacKay," Ian said.

Keira smiled up at him. She could hear the pride in his voice as he introduced her as his wife. For the first time, she felt proud to be his wife. Standing tall, she stood with her head held high. She was no longer Keira Sinclair, the daughter of a traitor. She was Keira MacKay. Wife of Ian MacKay, a brave Highland warrior.

"Keira, this is my mother Lady Gwendolyn MacKay.

"Tis a pleasure, my lady," Keira respectfully responded by curtsying.

"Ye have been gone fer two years and ye go out and get yerself married sending nay word home to yer own mother! I have raised ye better!" she said swatting Ian on the arm.

"We have only recently married. There was nay time to send word. But we are here now," he advised her.

"Ye sure picked yerself a bonny lass, Ian. Since losing Sarah, I have always wanted me a daughter," Gwendolyn joyfully said pulling Keira into a tight, warm embrace. "Welcome to the family, dear."

Ian's mother then stepped in front of Ian. Her eyes surveyed him from the top of his head down to his feet.

"Look at ye, wasting away. Do they no' feed ye out on the battlefield? Best get ye inside and get ye something to eat. I'm sure Seonag will be happy to see ye. I trust she will fix ye up something fierce."

"Where is Father?" Ian asked.

His mother's face grew grim at the mention of his father. Looking at both of her sons, she cupped her hands together and took in a deep breath before responding.

"I am sorry to tell ye lads, but yer father died nearly six months ago. I tried to get word to yer battalion but it was too late. He fought hard but died peacefully. I saved his belongings fer when ye returned."

Ian nodded his head.

"Rylan, tis good to see ye lad," Gwendolyn said.

"And ye my Lady."

"I'm afraid yer father has gone to the market wit' Laird Farquharson. But I am sure they will return shortly. I know yer father will be anxious to see ye as well," Gwendolyn proclaimed. "Well, let's get the four of ye inside and unpacked. I want to hear all about yer travels and to get to know my new daughter-in-law."

As Gwendolyn led the way, Ian and Keira held back from the others.

Taking his hand in hers, Keira stopped and looked up into Ian's eyes.

"Ian, what did yer mother mean when she made reference to yer battalion?"

"My mother does no' know about the Protectors. As I said, no one does. They believe that Leland, Ryland and I have joined the king's army. As I made a vow of silence, ye must keep this a secret as well."

"I will. I am truly sorry about yer father, Ian," Keira whispered.

"Dinna worry Lass. My father was ill when I left. I am only surprised he lasted as long as he had. Once we enter the keep, I will take my place as Laird of Clan MacKay. But before I start my duties as Laird, I must tend to my duties as yer husband," he said, pulling her into him and passionately kissing her.

"And what duties would those be, my Laird?" she teased.

"Allow me to take ye into our chamber and show ye."

As they stepped inside the great hall, Keira noticed a grand staircase that spiraled upwards leading to the next two floors. The building, Ian explained, was built of modern material and newly constructed. Laird Farquharson had plans for expanding the tower to add an additional three floors. By the looks of the building materials piled alongside the walls, it appeared that construction had only just begun.

Keira felt excited to start her duties as Lady of the Castle as there were so many things she wanted to learn, but she still felt troubled. With two clans sharing one castle, she was uncertain exactly what her responsibilities would entail. Not to mention the lack of space and privacy. The new tower, Ian told her would take nearly two years to be finished, and until then there wasn't going to be room for all of them. She made a mental note to ask Ian later what his future plans were for his clan. With Castle Sinclair open to an attack with no Laird, she had hoped to persuade Ian to return to her castle and perhaps unite their clans instead. But that would be a conversation for later, when she had his full attention.

It truly was not a terrible idea, she thought, as it would satisfy both of their needs. Castle Sinclair after all had several rooms to accommodate Ian's men. And there were plenty of abandoned cottages in the village as most of the villagers had left looking for work elsewhere when her father could no longer afford to pay them. The only thing they lacked was land.

There was, however, one reason that would cause Ian to forbid her to ever speak of it again, and that was that Clan Sinclair was an ally to Clan Sutherland; Ian's most hated enemy. Keira doubted there would ever be a way to get them past their differences. After all, Isaac Sutherland was accused of murdering Ian's wife, burning his village, and seizing his castle.

With everything Ian had lost, Keira wanted nothing more than to see him happy. But the only way he was ever going to be truly happy was returning to his own home and restoring his rightful place as Laird of Varrich Castle.

Suddenly, as if Keira were bestowed the gift of sight, she knew exactly what she had to do to satisfy both clans. She would forfeit her right to Sinclair Castle to Laird Sutherland in exchange for Ian's castle. Even though the idea of losing her home saddened her, the peace treaty between Clan Sinclair and Clan Sutherland would still hold. If they were to unite, her clan would never dare wage war against the MacKays, since they would be united by marriage. It seemed like the perfect plan, or at least in her head it did. Until she set things in motion, she would never know, but she was willing to risk it. She was willing to do anything to make Ian happy, because she loved him.

~*~

As they entered the hall, Ian's mother linked her arm around Keira's and led her to the kitchens to inform Seonag to fix a hearty meal for her returning sons. Lady Gwendolyn began showing Keira the various castle rooms and the garden as Ian patiently waited down in the great hall with his men. It seemed the two women could talk for hours without ever tiring and no matter his futile attempts to steal his wife from her, his mother continued to shoo him away and keep his bride's attention from him.

For over an hour his mother kept Keira occupied with questions and stories causing his patience to wear thin at his mother's constant babble. Now that he was finally home, all he could think of was taking his wife up to his room, locking the door and making love to her. It had been two days since the night he had made love to her on the beach and every day since that memorable night his body ached to touch her again. He was full with need, and he did not know how much longer he could stand to force himself to wait.

He welcomed the distraction of his men as they informed him of the events he had missed the past two years, but it did not stop him from occasionally stealing a glance at his lovely bride.

As the maids entered the hall with trays full of food, his mother asked everyone to gather in the great hall to eat. As everyone began shuffling through the large double doors, Ian grabbed Keira's hand and led her towards the stairs.

"Ian, where are ye going? Will ye no' be joining us fer a meal?" his mother called out.

"I need to speak to my wife, *alone!*" he firmly stated.

Wanting to run, not walk up the stairs, Ian began taking them two at a time.

"Ian, slow down. I can no' keep up wit' ye. What is so important that ye have to whisk me away so urgently? It is rude to no' attend the feast yer mother has so generously prepared fer us," Keira said trying to keep up with him.

As they reached the top step, Ian scooped Keira up in his arms and kissed her before she could utter another word. Grasping the handle on the first door at the top of the stairs, he pushed the door open and stepped through, then nudged the door closed. Gently, he laid Keira upon the bed.

Blanketing her with his body, he captured her supple lips in a fierce kiss. Stroking and massaging every curve of her form, his hands moved along her body as if they had a mind of their own.

"Lass, ye have no idea what ye do to me. Ye make me go mad every time I am near ye just from the want of ye," he said as he began nuzzling her neck.

Keira moaned in response to him. His need grew wild but tonight he would take his time and savor every inch of her silken body.

~*~

Keira giggled beneath him as he nuzzled the arc of her neck tickling her with his scruff. His touch felt different than the first time she shared his bed. When he had taken her virginity, he had barely touched her but now she welcomed it, craved it in a way she had never thought possible. Her skin tingled and ached for his touch and she yearned to touch him as well.

Keira allowed her hands to explore his body. Slipping her hands under his shirt, she felt the strong sculpted muscles along his back as she ran her fingers around his sides to his chest. His skin felt soft and warm under her touch. Ian slipped his shirt off over his head giving her a full view of his chest. Along the center of his chest was a small patch of hair which she eagerly ran her fingers through. Though she pretended not to stare, he was a magnificent example of man and muscle. She thought her husband was the most handsome creature she had ever seen and her attraction to him grew with each passing day.

"I like it when ye touch me," he said smoothing his hands over her breasts over the fabric of her dress.

Ian pressed his thigh between her legs, causing her hips to instinctively rise to meet him as she tangled a leg around his. Deepening the kiss, she parted her lips, allowing him to slip his tongue inside her mouth, taking her breath away. Every extremity pulsated as her heart thunderously beat in her chest. Ian slowly began unlacing the bodice of her dress, in a slow, teasing fashion until he removed it completely.

The extra fabric hung loosely across her chest, exposing the top of her shoulders. With a free hand, Ian slid each side of the dress downwards, kissing the exposed flesh until the top of the dress hung well past her breasts, just above her navel.

Taking her breast in his mouth, he flicked her nipple with his tongue sending a surge of heated passion through her as he lightly blew the tip causing it to harden. Keira moaned.

Ian ripped the dress from her and removed his trews. Kneeling naked before her, she could see every curve, every muscle as he hovered above her. Grabbing her hand, he placed it on his hard shaft. It was hot to the touch and harder than she had imagined it would be. As she wrapped her hand around it more tightly, Ian moaned. She wanted to continue to investigate it further but Ian pulled her hand away.

"Nay lass. I am already about to burst. If ye do that, it'll be over before I even get started. I want to be inside of ye. To feel ye," he said as he placed his hand between her thighs. Feeling his fingers stretching the inside of her, Keira bellowed out in pleasure.

"Ye are so wet," he remarked.

Removing his fingers, he positioned himself between her thighs and thrust forward, deep inside of her. Keira could feel him holding back and he slowly and steadily rocked back and forth but now was not the time to be gentle. She wanted him; all of him.

Grabbing his hips, she pushed him deeper inside of her. Wanting to satisfy her growing need, Ian drove himself deeper. With every thrust, Keira bellowed out. Sweat beaded on her forehead and her breaths were short and fast. Ian had lifted her to the heavens and her body exploded in release. Holding him tightly, she forced his head down and kissed him hard and fierce. She cried out in ecstasy, feeling every sensation coarse through her as her body convulsed.

When they finished their love making they washed up, and Ian left to fetch them something to eat. Keira's stomach had growled when Ian suggested it. He returned shortly with a plate of food to share.

Keira lay in Ian's arms on the bed as they ate. His free hand rubbed along her naked body, caressing her, massaging her; making her want him again.

Looking around the room, she noticed it was a grand room; one fit for a Laird. The walls were mahogany-colored with two tapestries draped on opposite ends of the wall that faced the bed. The large bed had four tall posts nearly reaching the ceiling, and a large stone hearth was positioned in the adjacent corner of the room.

Looking around the room at the various trinkets on the dresser and clothes hanging in the wardrobe, she realized she had nothing of her own. No clothes, no books, and none of the tapestries she had spent so many hours stitching. All of her belongings were to arrive at Erchless Castle on the day she was supposed to have wed Laird Chisholm, but where were they now? It saddened her to think that she had lost all of her valuable possessions.

"Ye are quiet, wife. Something is on yer mind," Ian guessed.

Keira frowned at him.

"I was just thinking that there is nothing here that belongs to me. All of my possessions were sent to Erchless Castle the day before I was to arrive. I only wondered if it was possible to retrieve them."

"Dinna worry lass. If ye be wantin' yer things, I will make sure they are returned to ye."

Keira rolled in his arms to face him.

"But how are ye going to do that?" she asked, hopeful he meant what he said.

"Dinna have such little faith in me, wife. I will send men to Erchless to get them fer ye. I have confidence in my men. In the meantime, I am certain my mother will make sure ye have something to wear until yer things are returned."

"Thank ye, Ian."

"Ye dinna have to thank me, wife. Tis my duty to see to yer happiness. Now try to get some sleep lass. I expect we are to have a busy day tomorrow."

"What's tomorrow?"

"Fer starters, I need to introduce my wife to my clan. No' to mention, there will be a ceremony which I have no doubt my mother has already arranged. Each man in my clan must pledge their fealty to me and to ye as well."

"Me?"

"Aye! Ye are their Mistress. And each man will vow to protect ye wit' their life. Tis their duty."

Keira considered telling Ian of her plan to reconcile his clan with the Sutherlands, but she felt now was not the time, it would only spoil his good mood. Besides, she thought it may be best to convince Isaac Sutherland of her plan before making mention of it to Ian. Perhaps if he knew Laird Sutherland was in agreement, Ian would be more accepting of her proposal for reclaiming his home.

Chapter 24

"My lady, are ye stark raving mad? Ye do me a great injustice having me lie to my Laird," Leland scolded her.

"If I am to right any of my father's wrongdoings, I must do this. The treaty between my clan and the Sutherlands is as strong as if it were written in stone. My mother was a Sutherland. Harming me would be like harming his own blood. I am no' asking to go on some foolish quest, mind ye. I only wish to speak to him. Leland, I believe it is the only way to reclaim yer lands. Ye want to go home, dinna ye?" Keira argued.

"Of course, but no' under the agreement to sign a treaty with Clan Sutherland. I'd rather poke my eyes out wit' hot pokers before arranging a meeting wit' that bloody bastard. Does Ian know of yer crazed plan?"

"Nay! And ye must no' tell him either."

"My Lady, how am I supposed to do my duty to protect ye and follow my Laird's wishes wit' you making such a foolish request."

"Leland, all I am asking is that ye send word fer him to meet me. Isaac is…was a good friend to my father. Our clans have been allies fer years. I know ye dinna trust the mon, but I do."

"If Ian found out," he began to counter.

"He willnae know that it was ye that sent fer him. When the time comes, I will tell him that I did. And if I must face Ian's wrath then so be it."

"My lady, forgive me but ye must either be the bravest Highland lass I have ever come across or the dumbest I have ever met."

"I will no' be offended by yer comment, Leland. And there is no changing my mind about this. I too want to see yer clan back at Varrich Castle where they belong. Tis no' Ian nor yer clan who is sacrificing, but me. By giving Laird Sutherland full control over Castle Sinclair he may be persuaded to leave yer lands in exchange fer mine. It is no secret that Isaac has been pining over my lands fer years. Perhaps if I dangle the bait in front of him, he will take it. As fer my clansmen, I will leave it up to them where they decide to place their loyalty. They are good people."

"My Lady, there is no' doubt yer plan is sound, but even if it works, Ian would ne'er agree to it. Tis too dangerous."

"It's a risk, but one I am willing to take."

"Why?"

Keira pondered his question. In all honesty, she hoped Ian would have done the same for her. She knew that he cared for her regardless whether he admitted it or not. But she cared for him dearly. Was this what love was? To sacrifice for another? If Leland was right and Isaac could not be trusted, he could use her as leverage against Ian and more than anything, she desperately did not want Ian to lose yet another thing he cared about. The poor man had already suffered enough. But leaving him was not her intention. She would never leave him by choice.

"Because, he is my husband and I love him."

She *loved* him! In every meaning of the word, she loved him. She knew it as soon as she said it.

"Keira, I must warn ye, if this does no' work, Ian will have both of our heads."

"Then I must make it work!"

~*~

Ian entered the great hall, where his clan stood waiting for him. He looked around the room at the faces of his clansmen. Many he knew by name and had known for years. They were a good clan; a loyal clan. The clan stood silent as they stared up at him, waiting for him to speak. Ian glanced over at Keira who was standing on the top balcony overlooking the hall.

His eyes followed her as she made her way to the top of the stairs. He smiled at the sight of her. Dressed in a dark blue gown, she proudly wore his colors. A green and blue plaid hung across one shoulder and was secured in place with a silver brooch. She looked positively regal as she descended the stairs. She moved like a queen. She did not falter and every one of his clansmen noticed her composure as they gratefully bowed their heads to her when she passed by them. Ian had never felt more proud.

Keira came to stand by his side. Raising her hand, he placed a kiss on the inside of her palm.

"Ye look lovely dressed in my plaid," he whispered.

Keira smiled at his compliment and took a seat in the chair next to his. One by one, each member of the clan pledged their allegiance to each of them upon Ian's sword.

The whole ceremony took up nearly half of the day, but he had many clansmen who wished to give their allegiance and meet the new lady of the castle. As the festivities concluded and the clansmen left to continue their duties, Ian and Keira were left alone in the hall.

"Would ye care to join me fer a walk? I would like verra much fer ye to get acquainted wit' the castle grounds."

"I would like that."

Ian gently placed Keira's hand in the crook of his arm and escorted her outside. Keira could smell the scent of roses fill the air as they passed a large garden. The roses were beginning to wilt with the cooler temperatures but were still in full bloom

"I do hope that ye like it here."

"I am sure I will. Do ye imagine we will be here long?"

"Nay. If all goes well, I expect to be back at my own castle before the first snow falls."

"What do ye mean?"

"I intend to wage war against the Sutherlands."

Keira swallowed hard.

"War? But ye could get killed!"

"Dinna fash yerself about such things lass. I promise ye, nothing will happen to me. I am a skilled warrior and know how to care fer my own."

Keira bit her tongue before she inadvertently revealed her plan to him. If Ian planned on waging war soon, she had to set her plan in motion sooner than she'd thought.

~*~

Walking along the cobblestone path, they passed the stables and open fields where the horses were grazing. Ian watched as Keira's eyes lit up marveling over the beasts. Looking back at the horses, Ian thought of a way to help win her affections.

"Ye like horses, do ye?"

"Aye. I used to go riding all the time wit' my father, though after riding nearly three days straight, I may never wish to ride a horse again," she said with a chuckle.

Ian smiled.

"Choose one. Whichever one ye like is yers. Consider it a wedding gift, my lady."

"That is verra kind of ye, but tis no' necessary."

"I insist. Which one do ye like?"

Keira looked back at the horses as they galloped around the fenced-in field. Of the five of them a spotted grey mare caught her eye. The horse had a tender look and its coloring was beautiful.

"If ye insist my Laird, I like the spotted grey one."

"Aye, she is a beauty," he said. Calling out to the stable master to come toward him, Ian said, "The lady has chosen the grey mare as her mount. Make sure her hooves are clean and she is brushed down and fit her with a saddle."

"Aye, my Laird," he said scurrying away to catch the horse.

"Thank ye," Keira said, her voice soft and tender.

"Yer welcome. Have ye decided what ye are going to name her?"

"I was thinking about calling her Seraphina. When I was young, my mother told me a tale of a great warhorse that broke free from her master to live in the wild. Her name was Seraphina."

"How did the story end?"

"It was a long time ago, but from what I remember, while Seraphina was on an adventure riding across the lands, she found a wee lass lost in the woods. She had protected the lass and brought her home to her family, but instead of returning to the wild, she chose to stay wit' the lass forever and ever."

"Sounds like a wonderful story."

"Aye, it was."

Ian continued showing Keira the various sights and buildings throughout the castle grounds. He explained the Farquharson Clan's history as well as their kinship. He also informed her that the reason why she did not see many of the Farquharson's within the keep was because the Farquharson Clan took up residence in the west wing of the castle as the MacKays' resided in the east wing of the castle.

"Now that I have shown ye the grounds, ye must promise me that ye will ne'er go out wandering beyond them. Promise me!"

"I promise, but I really wish ye would stop fussing o'er me. I do know how to take care of myself."

"I am sure ye do lass, but if ye dinna need me, I wouldn't be much of a husband to ye."

~*~

They continued to walk the long stretch from the courtyard to the lush green hills where Ian's men trained. Keira enjoyed his stories and the opportunity to learn more. With each story and each new thing she learned about him, the more she found herself falling deeper in love with him. But in the back of her mind, she couldn't help but wonder if he felt the same. He cared for her, that was obvious, but love, that was an entirely different matter altogether, after all much of his heart still belonged to his late wife, Sarah.

The tall grass they walked through swayed like waves along the shore and the heat of the summer sun beat down on her as if she were a dry piece of wood; easy to catch fire.

As they reached the fields Ian's men came into view. Sunlight shone off their metal swords like spirit wisps wildly flying about blinding her. Sweat trickled down the men's bare backs, as they practiced honing their skills. As Ian approached, they stopped.

"My Laird, I did no' expect ye to join us," one of the warriors stated.

"I had meant to join yer scrimmage yesterday but duties kept me away. I am eager to see how the men fare and how much they have learned under yer direction and training."

"Do ye doubt me, my Laird?"

Ian smiled at his question.

"Nay, my good friend. I only wish to see ye in action. And see if any of yer men can wield a sword well enough to best me. No' to mention, I wished to introduce ye personally to Lady MacKay. Keira, this is Roderick. He is my commanding officer. He has served my father fer many years."

"Tis a pleasure my Lady," Roderick bowed. "Well then, ye heard Laird MacKay. Any mon who can best him wins a prize swine to bring home fer yer supper," Roderick called out to the men.

Ian laughed at the challenge. Picking up one of the training swords from the ground, Ian swung the blade over his head and dug his heels into the ground waiting for his first opponent. Keira laughed at the display but prayed he would not get hurt, though the chances of that happening were slim to none. Ian was a warrior, born and raised with dignity and honor running through his veins.

Like his father before him, he was a proud and fierce Highlander.

Ian successfully bested several of the men he choose to fight but Ian's last opponent was a young lad who did not look like a seasoned warrior but more like he was new to the battlefield.

Looking at the other men he had defeated, they were bruised and badly beaten by Ian's brutal attacks. She worried that if he were to fight this young lad he would kill him.

"He is going to get himself killed," she said looking back and forth between Ian and the young man.

"Dinna be too hasty to judge, Lady MacKay," Roderick exclaimed. "I have full confidence in my squire Brodie, regardless of his size. I have trained him well and he is as tough as nails. Dinna ye ever hear of the story about David and Goliath?"

Keira cocked her head and looked at him in bewilderment. Sure, she had heard the story, but David had the blessing of God on his side!

Ian swung his sword at the young lad, who successfully ducked underneath it. Like a wee mouse, Brodie jumped from side to side avoiding each blow. It was the oddest thing she had ever seen. Crouching beneath Ian, Brodie entwined himself around Ian's thick legs causing him to lose his balance. As Ian teetered back and forth, he crashed down onto the ground like a large tree after it had been cut down with Brodie still tangled in between his legs.

Keira intensely watched as they rolled around on the ground. She could not believe that such a wee sized man could take Ian down so easily. Had she not seen it for herself she would never have believed it.

"How the bloody hell did ye do that?" Ian asked.

Keira waited for him to become angry, believing that he would have felt humiliated by the young lad, but instead of thrashing him, Ian laughed and put his hand on his shoulder.

"Brodie is my secret weapon," Roderick proudly remarked.

"Ye have done well, my friend," Ian replied.

Roderick turned to face Brodie. "Well Brodie, my lad, I believe ye have just won yerself a prized swine!"

It was such a delight for Keira to see Ian interact with his men. He was such a different man with his clansmen than when he was away from them. She had not taken into account the struggle Ian had living two separate lives; one life as Laird MacKay and the other a Protector of the Crown. She wondered if now that he was Laird if his secret identity would one day be revealed or if his secret would stay with him to the grave.

Chapter 25

As Ian kept busy with his duties as Laird, Keira spent the following days learning everything she could to help manage the household. Keira was not used to sharing such responsibilities with others. At Castle Sinclair, Keira's father depended on her to keep the staff organized as well as tend to the books, the inventory and preparing the meals. Though she was adjusting well to her new role, Keira had to take into account that she was not the only Lady of Invercauld Castle.

Lady Madeline Farquharson was a young, English woman and one not accustomed to getting her hands dirty. Daughter to an English Baron, Madeline had enjoyed the finer things in life. Being married to Laird Farquharson was not one of them. She complained endlessly about the cold Highland air and the rude manners of her clansmen. Needless to say, she was not making many friends nor did she have any idea how to run a household.

Lady Madeline was young and ill-prepared to take on the responsibilities as Lady of a Keep and she had little experience how to oversee a castle. Keira thought to take her under her wing to instruct her but the maids advised against it saying the Lady Madeline was too selfish to care.

After hearing the horror stories the maids had related, Keira pitied the servants who had to attend to her. On more than one occasion, she overheard the kitchen staff poking fun at their mistress and though she knew it was wrong, she could not help but agree.

"Did ye hear the war our Mistress Madeline started with my lad Peter this morning?" Sorcha whispered to the others.

"Nay."

"Made the poor lad saddle her horse three times with different saddles; complaining that each one of 'em was warped and uncomfortable."

"Heaven Almighty! Laird Farquharson just bought her a new one. I dinna know how he puts up wit' her. Bless that mon."

The maids silenced their voices as Lady Madeline entered the kitchen. She looked as if she was ready to pounce on someone like a wild feline. Her black hair had fallen out of its curls and her green dress was covered in hay. Her eyes were reddened from crying. Before Lady Madeline could speak, Keira quietly backed into the corner as if she readied herself for Madeline's explosive outburst.

"Oh My Lady, what happened to ye?" one of the maids asked.

Spitting out her words as if the women could not understand English, she replied, "That blasted, no good excuse of a lad of yours gave me a wild horse to ride. As soon as I mounted the horse, it bucked. I went flying off into a pile of hay. He did it on purpose I tell you, just to spite me! I could have broken my neck. But that is what you want, isn't it? None of you Scots like me. You are trying to drive me back to England."

For such a young woman, she had a mouth on her a sharp as a dagger.

"My Lady, we would ne'er wish such a thing!" Sorcha said, defending her clansmen.

"Well, I expect you will give your son a proper punishment!"

"Of course, my Lady," Sorcha mumbled.

"Good! I wish to be informed the moment my idiot husband returns, is that understood?" Lady Madeline demanded.

"Aye, my Lady."

A few moments later, Peter poked his head into the kitchen.

"Is she gone?" he asked.

Sorcha grabbed him by the ear and dragged him into the room.

"Petey, what did ye do?" Socha asked smacking him on the back of his head.

"Nothing! Tis no' my fault the horse bucked. The mare does no' like her."

Keira joined the others and spoke up to defend the lad.

"I heard that some animals can sense evil. Perhaps the horse chooses the rider and no' the other way around," she said smiling at Peter, hoping to comfort the lad.

"Aye, well ye leave me no' choice but to punish ye. Run along home. Ye get no meal tonight," Sorcha said.

"But he did nothing wrong!" Keira argued.

"Tis the way it is, Lady MacKay. As we live under her household, we must abide by her wishes."

"Aye, but ye are a MacKay and no' a Farquharson! If we are to live under the same roof, she can no' expect to make all the rules. There are two clans living here and hers does no' have superiority over ours."

"Thank ye, my Lady," Sorcha softly replied, with an earnest smile.

"For what?"

"For being a kind Mistress."

The woman's comment filled Keira with glee. She was happy they welcomed her with open arms. There was not one MacKay she had met that she did not like. They were all kind and very welcoming to her.

As for Lady Madeline, trying to befriend the sour woman seemed as pointless as a dull knife. Instead of trying to make amends with the woman, Keira spent most of her time focusing on her husband's clan; her clan she often corrected herself. She knew that she might as well get used to saying that, no matter if the reality had struck her yet or not.

Keira began learning the clansmen's names as well as their families and where they lived. As she made her way to the village, two of Ian's retainers followed her.

"May I help ye?" she asked them.

"Nay, my lady. But we wondered if we can help ye."

"Nay. I did no' ask fer any help so ye can carry on wit' yer duties."

"Ye are our duty, my Lady."

"What do ye mean?"

"Laird MacKay said that we were supposed to stick by ye and keep ye safe."

"Keep me safe? From what? Am I in danger?"

"Well, nay my Lady. But the Laird gave us strict orders and we mean to follow them."

"Well than ye can inform yer Laird that I am in no' need of protection. I am only heading to the village to meet wit' the clansmen."

"I am sorry, my Lady, but we are no' leaving yer side."

Keira huffed at her husband's silly protectiveness.

"Well, then ye will just have to follow me everywhere I go! What are yer names?"

"I am Seamus Fraser, my lady and this is my brother, William."

"Under normal circumstances I would say, tis a pleasure, but I think we can all agree that any order by Laird MacKay is no' of normal circumstance."

Keira and her two overbearing guards, sent out to visit each cottage to see if there was anything they needed. Seeing to the clan was one of her responsibilities at home so she took it upon herself to do the same here.

The list was long as several things had been overlooked. Many of the homes had been damaged by the recent storms and were in need of repair. There also seemed to be a lack of necessities throughout the castle such as candles and flatware. They did not even keep a moderate supply of salt which was an essential item to have. Organizing her list, she would see to it that the most important items were procured first. Perhaps she could send one of Ian's men to the market to fetch the much needed items.

Keira waited for hours for Ian to return from the fields with his men. But the moment she saw him, he was too busy to even notice her. He sat down with a group of his warriors and began discussing matters of the King and the threats of rebellion. Keira sat down at the far end of the table and patiently waited.

At the end of each conversation a new one began. This was going nowhere and if she did not speak up now, she would never get her chance.

"My Laird, must I have an appointment wit' ye to have a moment of yer time?" she sarcastically asked interrupting one of the clansmen who was speaking to his Laird.

Ian smirked at her, finding her comment amusing. Keira frowned at him.

"Nay lass, ye dinna need an appointment. What is it that ye want?"

Keira stood from her spot and walked over to Ian.

"I wish to speak to ye in private."

"Is it so important that it can no' wait?"

"I wish to discuss wit' ye my concerns."

"And what concerns are those?"

Keira looked at the men whose eyes fell on hers before turning back to Ian.

"Well fer starters, I dinna need yer guardsmen following me around all day," she said looking at her two *shadows*.

"Ye are Lady of Clan MacKay! Ye will no' be allowed on yer own wit' out a guard to protect ye. Tis too dangerous! There is nothing ye can say that is going to change my mind. And what is the second thing?"

Keira grunted.

"While ye have been away I have compiled a list of things that many of the villagers are in need of. Did ye even know that two of yer clansmen are deathly ill? They are in need of a healer but I have no' been able to find one. I would have tended to them myself had it no' been for the lack of supplies I need to care fer them. I insist that ye send someone to the market straight away."

Ian stared at her, speechless, his face blank.

"And how did ye come to learn all of this?"

"I visited each of the clansmen and asked fer their concerns."

"Concerns?"

"Aye. One must always make sure that their clansmen are well cared fer. As ye have no' seen to the task, I have taken it upon myself."

Ian looked irritated by her response. Standing up from his chair, he excused himself from the others and took Keira by the arm. Once they were in private, he continued.

"Lass, I dinna need ye to tell me how to run my clan. And ye must promise me that ye will never speak to me like that again in front of my men."

"Am I no' to speak my mind?"

"Aye ye can speak all ye want but in our private chamber."

"Well, excuse me, husband, but I did ask for a moment to speak to ye in private, and ye refused! I am sorry, my Laird if I made ye feel inferior, but I will no' apologize. As Lady of a castle, tis my duty to help oversee the castle and clan."

"Why did ye feel it was yer duty to follow through wit' my tasks?"

"Because, ye were busy! At Castle Sinclair it was my duty to look after our clansmen and run the household."

"Well that is no' yer duty here."

"Well I am finding it verra difficult to figure out exactly what my duty is!"

"Yer duty is to be Lady of Clan MacKay."

"Which entails what? Embroidery and stitching tapestries! I am quite capable of doing more than simple woman's work, Ian."

"I am no' arguing that lass. I am just stating the fact that those things should no' be yer concern."

Keira was about to argue, but Ian quickly cut her off.

"But…I will look over yer list and see to what you believe needs to be done. But the next time ye wish to take matters into yer own hands, ask me first."

"I can agree to that as long as ye can agree to give me more responsibilities. I am no' use to doing nothing. I should help run the household."

"Nay lass. Yer place is at my side," he said, wrapping his arms around her and placing his lips on hers.

Keria slightly pulled back.

"Ye can no' cause my resolve to waiver by sweet kisses Ian!" she argued.

Ian's lips curled. Raising one brow he carried a smug look on his face. Before Keira could say another word, Ian pressed his lips hard against hers. His proud, cocky arrogance was not going to let her win this battle. She would let him win this fight and relish in his victory, but next time, she would not succumb so easily.

By the evening hours, Keira sought out Leland to see if her message from Laird Sutherland had arrived. She was grateful that it had arrived right on schedule. In the letter, Leland handed her, Isaac agreed to meet with her to discuss the terms of surrendering her lands since her letter to him did not include the details of the arrangement. Sutherland suggested they meet in the marketplace at Kildrummy; nearly a half days ride away the next afternoon. All she needed now was to convince Ian to allow her to go.

Chapter 26

Ian was quite displeased that his wife was so insistent on joining their journey to the market in Kildrummy, but he knew that she would not take no for an answer. Particularly, because she spent the better part of an hour arguing about it. She was insistent on inspecting the items they were to purchase for the castle, saying that Lady Farquharson had neglected her duties to make sure the household had been sufficiently stocked with supplies.

There was also the matter of acquiring a healer. Keira had the necessary skills, but she could not very well be in two places at once. Selfishly, he did not like the fact that had she taken on the role full time, it would have taken her away from him.

Since they arrived at Invercauld Castle, Keira kept herself busy with several mundane tasks that had been neglected, and Ian was adamant to find someone else to fill those roles, to free up her time.

He did, however, like the way she immediately took charge and fulfilled her role as Lady of the Clan. She certainly possessed the qualities to help lead his people and her actions were already winning the hearts of his clan.

Ian gave one of his guardsmen the list of items Keira had requested he buy. The list was long, but he was certain that they would find all of the items that they needed.

As soon as they passed the first stall, Keira's eyes lit up at the sight of all the marvelous items. Her innocent, childlike expression made him smile.

"Ian, if I were to bring my two *shadows* wit' me, would ye mind if I do a wee bit of sightseeing while we are here? I have never been to the market before and I still wish to get ye a wedding gift," Keira asked.

"Ye dinna need to get me anything, Keira. Ye are all that I need," he said as he took her hand in his and pulled her into his arms.

Keira leaned up on the tips of her toes and pressed her lips against his. She tried to pull away almost as soon as her lips touched his but Ian was one man who was not embarrassed by sweet kisses and showing his affection among crowds. He didn't care what others thought. If anyone deemed his actions inappropriate, to hell with them! He pressed his lips harder against hers and caressed her firmly in his arms deepening the kiss.

"Ian, people are staring at us," she whispered.

"Let them stare. Ye are my wife and I can kiss ye whenever I wish," he replied, brushing his hand along her cheek.

"If I promise to no' be long, will ye let me go?"

Ian smirked at her bright, eager expression. She was hard to resist. He knew allowing her to window-shop would please her, and with Seamus and William guarding her it eased his worry. He also hoped to steal a few minutes away to get something for her as well. The horse he had given her was not a proper wedding gift but a necessity, but there was one thing he did want to get her: a ring, a proper ring for a laird's wife. Ian had eyed a lovely ruby ring for sale at one of the market stalls they passed when they first arrived in the village but with Keira right by his side, he was unable to make an inquiry about it. Perhaps, this would give him the opportunity to do just that.

"Ye can go. But dinna wander off too far. We will meet back here within the hour."

"Thank ye," Keira said giving him a quick hug and dashing off in high spirits.

As Keira took off at a near sprint with Seamus and William trailing behind, Ian watched until they disappeared into the thick crowd before turning back to the jeweler's cart. As he reached the cart, he picked up the small ruby ring and inspected it.

"Ye have good taste, my Laird," the merchant complimented. "That there is a rare, special find. It was just imported this morning from the Orient. I get all of my best products from there and I can give it to ye at a good price."

Ian held the small ring between his large fingers. It had a gold band and a small ruby placed in the crown. He admired how it sparkled in the sun. Slipping it into the breast pocket of his vest, enthusiasm filled his heart for the moment when he would give it to her. Nothing pleased him more than to make her happy and see her smile.

"I'll take it."

~*~

As Keira, William and Seamus passed one of the taverns, two buxom women caught the men's attention. Keira pretended not to notice as she admired a market stall full of fine fabrics and linens. She had never seen so many wonderful things. The market had everything from chandlers selling expensive beeswax candles to mantua makers with the latest in ladies' fashion. With the coins Ian had given her, she purchased a few silk ribbons for her hair and a lovely dark green shawl.

Keira watched as her two escorts pathetically tried to fight off their two lady admirers, but she could tell that they were loving every minute of the attention and had it not been for their duty to watch over her they probably would have already been tossing up the maid's skirts.

"Ye know, there is no reason fer ye two to follow me so. Ye are more than welcome to enjoy a quick drink if ye like. By the looks of the women, it would be rude to no' offer them a drink," she teased.

"I see what ye are trying to do there lassie. Ye want us to get into trouble wit' our Laird. Ye are testing us!"

"Dinna be foolish, Seamus. I wish to purchases some of these fine dresses and will need to try them on to make sure they fit. I dinna think the Laird would be too pleased if ye accompany me in the changing room," she pointed out. "Now, go. I will be right here. And after ye have shared a drink wit' these fine ladies, ye can always return to my side."

The two men looked at each other and considered her suggestion. Keira crossed her fingers behind her, hoping they would accept her offer.

"Alright Mistress. But dinna ye go anywhere!" William ordered.

The two women practically pulled them inside the tavern leaving Keira alone and unguarded. If she were to meet Laird Sutherland, now would be the time.

Sneaking inside the tavern, she kept both Seamus and William in sight as she snuck toward the back of the room. Laird Sutherland was to meet her in the far back room where it would be quiet and private. The room was blocked off by a long red curtain that hung down to the floor, separating the dining area from the private room behind the bar. Keira moved the curtain to the side and stepped in.

The small space was empty other than a table and a few chairs. Just as Keira was about to sit down, she heard the sound of the curtain being brushed open but before she could turn around, she was forcefully grabbed from behind. Large, muscular arms held her waist while the other covered her mouth. To prevent her from screaming, her assailant stuffed a small damp rag inside her mouth and covered it with his hand.

Panic swept through her when she recognized the pungent odors of hemlock root and belladonna. As a healer, she knew almost instantly that the practice of combining the two herbs together created what physicians and monks called Dwale, a medicine referred to as the "deep sleep". It was a method used on patients to prepare them for surgery. By swallowing just a small portion, it would render the patient unconscious for several hours; too much could cause death.

Keira struggled violently against his hold but her body betrayed her, slowly giving in to the effects of the foul potion. Her limbs grew weak and heavy and she struggled to keep her eyes open. She became overwhelmed with fear as she became more helpless with every passing moment. She needed to fight. She needed to break free from this hold.

In the back of her mind her only thought was of Ian. He would come for me. He would save me. But as the minutes passed, there was no sign of him or his guards. He wasn't coming. He didn't even know she was here. How could he?

Keira's eyesight started to blur. Still, she fought with every last ounce of strength she had. She would not give up, not while she still had fight left in her and she would not falter, no matter how pointless it seemed. Unable to hold her own weight, her legs gave out and Keira was vaguely aware of collapsing in the arms of her assailant. Then, nothing.

~*~

"My Laird," Seamus called out as he ran towards Ian in a panic. "Has Lady Keira returned?"

Ian let out a sharp breath. Anger and fear coursed through his veins. His stomach twisted at the thought of Keira in trouble and if these two idiots were here and not guarding her as they had been ordered to do, he could only imagine what happened to her. Grabbing Seamus by the collar, Ian shook the man.

"What happened? She was no' supposed to leave yer side! God strike ye dead! If anything has happened to her, I swear it will be the two of ye who are to blame!"

"My Laird, she was out of our sight for a mere moment trying on dresses," William defended.

"And what were ye two doing? By the smell of whiskey on yer breath, I'd say it was far more than a moment wouldn't ye agree?"

Seamus and William both remained quiet but it was Leland who spoke up.

"I believe I may know who took her."

Ian shot a glance at his brother, confusion showing in the lines of his face. How could Leland know what had happened to her? He had been at Ian's side the whole time. If he did know something, why the hell was he just now speaking up?

"It is my belief that she was taken by the Sutherlands," Leland said.

Ian eyed him suspiciously.

"What makes ye believe such a thing? Did ye see them? Were they here?" Ian asked, fear gripping him, causing his muscles to stiffen as his heart began to race.

"Nay, I dinna see them. But I know that she arranged to meet with them," he confessed.

"Why would she go off and do something as foolish as that and why in bloody hell if ye knew about it did ye let her?" he snapped.

Ian's stomach twisted in knots. He felt as if he was caught in a bloody nightmare. He had to be, for his own wife and brother would never conspire against him. But in truth, they had. The fact that Keira had betrayed him ripped his heart in so many pieces that there would be nothing left of it. As his mind wrapped around the situation, his blood boiled. He would go save her, but did not know how he could ever forgive or trust her again.

Clenching his fists, he was ready to strike. Ian pointed to all three men. His eyes filled with rage and fear.

"Ian, listen," Leland began to say.

"Stay away from me. All of ye," Ian growled.

"Ian," Leland said but Ian stopped him before he could get in another word.

"I did no' say ye can speak! Betrayed, by my own brother. Ye are worse than them all. Ye are my brother no longer," Ian said with pain in his voice as he walked away from them.

"She did it fer ye, Brother!" Leland called out.

Ian stopped in his tracks, too hurt and angry to reply.

"If ye wish to denounce me as yer brother, then fine. But know this, ye are no' the only one who has sacrificed. Ye have lost Sarah and we lost our home, but Keira lost everything as well. Did ye take that into consideration? It was Keira who arranged to meet with Laird Sutherland. She was going to give up her title and deed to Sinclair Castle in exchange for our home. She was going to use her alliance wit' the Sutherlands and sacrifice everything she has left for *ye*! She dinna tell ye because she knew how ye would react. And I dinna tell ye because I believe in her."

Why would she do such a thing? Castle Sinclair meant as much to her as his home meant to him. Hearing that right now she could very well be in the hands of his enemy was maddening. He would do anything to protect her. She had been his light in the darkness and he would be damned if he did not get her back. With a stony expression, Ian turned to face his brother.

"I can no' lose her, Leland," he admitted.

Ian struggled to hold in his emotions, though his fear ran deep inside his core. He could not lose her. He needed her. He loved her. And he would fight with his dying breath to get her back.

"Then let us find the whoreson who took her."

Chapter 27

Keira woke with a start, as she was jostled upon a wooden floor. She could hear the hooves of the horses trotting along a rocky path and could feel the wheels of the cart she was held in hit the bumps in the road. It was dark. Nightfall had fallen, and the sky was lit by stars.

Her wrists burned; bound tightly together with rope and she could feel a nasty bump on the side of her head emanating pain. She felt as if she had woken from a long sleep. Her head felt groggy and her eyesight took a moment to focus in the dim light. Memories of what had happened in the market rushed to the forefront of her mind. Her body grew tense with fear.

Rolling over to her side, she looked up at the person atop the horse pulling the cart. But much to her dismay, his features were covered by a long dark cloak. With only the light of the moon, Keira knew that even if he had not been wearing the cloak, the darkness would still have masked his identity.

With each bump the cart hit, the pain in her head intensified. But the pain her body felt could not compare to the one in her heart. Her mind was drawn to Ian. She had been such a fool. How could she ever forgive herself? How could he? No matter what happened to her, she prayed that he would be safe. As she gazed up at the passing stars, she allowed her mind to drift. Her only comfort was that the same stars were also shining down on him.

They rode for what seemed several hours. Like soft whispers, voices grew closer in the distance. As they rode towards the commotion, Keira had little hope the men they were approaching would help her.

Her assailant led the cart to the middle of a campsite filled with men. Keira sat up and looked at the faces staring back at her. She recognized neither the men nor the plaid they wore.

Dressed in armor, they were prepared for battle. Keira took inventory of their weaponry. There were stack of quivers full with arrows, firearms with long barrels, and swords and shields stacked as high as their knees. There were at least forty warriors and they were well prepared to take on an entire regiment.

"Lady Sinclair, or should I call ye Lady MacKay?" a tall, black-haired man said as he walked up to the cart.

"Who are ye and why have ye taken me?"

"Allow me to introduce myself and my men. My name is Laird Thomas Chisholm, these are my men and ye were my intended bride until that bastard MacKay decided to steal ye fer himself."

"Laird Chisholm? But I saw ye in Inverness. Ye were tried and heading to the gallows."

"Aye, well, deception is only one of my many talents. The man ye thought was me was one of my many soldiers willing to die fer my cause. There are several men, if dressed up, that can be made to look like me. Apparently, I have been told I have a common face. But I can assure ye Lass, I am no' dead, nor common."

Not yet, she thought as she lowered her eyes to him.

"I am married to Laird Ian MacKay. He will come fer me. He will hunt ye down. And when he finds me, ye can be certain that he will no' spare yer life," she warned.

"It matters not. Ye are mine Keira. There's no point in fighting me and denying that fact. As for yer husband, I have little worry he will come. I should have killed him when I had the chance; an oversight on my part. He did, however, do me a great service. Now that all of Scotland thinks I'm dead I can continue my purpose."

"And what purpose is that?" she said with hatred seething from her lips.

"The same as yer father. Kill the king," he replied, his face devoid of emotion.

"Dinna ye dare talk about my father! He was a great mon!"

"Believe what ye will Keira. But yer father's soul is as black as mine. I know why yer husband and King James's men have been searching fer me. They wish to obtain this," he said as he pulled out a folded piece of paper from his pocket. "This letter is what James wants. This is what he has been searching fer; the detailed list of names of every Scot who signed their allegiance to the English Crown. This letter is worth more to him than his throne," Thomas revealed.

Slowly, he walked over to the fire pit and held the letter above the flames. The corner of the letter started to smoke as it caught fire. Keira watched as flames sparked and the paper crumbled into ash.

"As for yer father, I made a promise to him before he was taken. That I would protect his daughter, even if I had to protect her from herself. I stand by my end of the bargain."

"And what did my father get from ye? To die without honor at the end of the noose? Ye will ne'er get away wit' this!"

Chisholm laughed wickedly as if he suffered from hysteria. The cold look in his eyes did not once waver at her threat. The rider dismounted and came to stand at the man's side. As he lowered his cloak, Keira gasped in disbelief. His familiar eyes regarded her but remained unmoved by her reaction. She felt faint. Her throat tightened as she struggled to breathe and her heart pounded faster in her chest.

Swallowing hard, she whispered in a strained voice, "*Father?*"

Keira's knees gave way, and she collapsed to the ground.

~*~

Ian, Rylan and Leland, followed by a dozen of their warriors, set out northward following the tracks the cart had left behind. After struggling with a forgetful barmaid for almost an hour to get a proper description of the man who took Keira, the maid led them out back where Ian found a set of prints left in the mud by a horse-drawn carriage.

For hours they rode down a well-beaten path losing hope that they were on the right track. But Ian would not give up. He would search every home in the Highlands if he had to.

Driven by anger and fear, flashbacks of his village burned in Ian's mind. The smell of burning wood and hay from the cottages and cries of the villagers as they mourned their loss still haunted him. When he returned from battle, never could he have imagined the carnage he saw in the village. As he rode into the settlement, he raced towards his home. There, he found his dear young wife Sarah lying on the bloody ground.

He recalled dropping to her side and cradling her in his arms as he wept. Leaving her unprotected in the village was a foolish mistake. She should have stayed with his family in the castle but she fought hard with Ian to stay close to her family. Believing his clan would be safe, he foolishly gave in to her request.

If Laird Sutherland took Keira away as he had taken Sarah, there would be no place safe for him. Ian would hunt him down until his dying day.

There was a dark side to Ian, a beast within, that when provoked and angered no man could rein him in and stop him.

Ian had to bury his emotions deep inside his core. If he allowed his fear and anger to control him, he would lose not only his focus but all sense of himself. He would go mad with revenge. A man driven by anger was like a loose cannon. And if he wanted to save Keira, he could not continue being hell-bent on vengeance. He had to think like a warrior and not a love-sick fool.

"Ian," Leland called out. "We must stop. We cannae see their trail in the darkness. We will pick up again in the morning."

Curse the sun!

"Set up camp and put men on guard. I will take first watch," Ian commanded.

"Ye should rest," Leland suggested. "Ye will be no' good to her if ye are weak and tired. I will send men ahead to continue the search."

"I will join them," Rylan offered.

Ian stared in awe at the way his brother took command. Leland, a lad less than two years younger than he, had always been a free spirit and considered too reckless for Ian's high standards of discipline and duty. Ian had no idea how, but he knew his sudden change in disposition was because of Keira. It was more than just Leland's sense of honor to protect his Laird's wife, but that he actually cared for her. Keira had managed to charm many of his clansmen and every single one of them would risk their lives to protect her. Never had Ian felt so proud of his clansmen until this very moment.

Ian went to lay near the fire. Rolling on his back, he looked to the stars and sent up a silent prayer for her safe return.

"I'm coming fer ye lass. Ye just have to hold on a wee bit longer," he whispered.

~*~

Keira awoke to the sound of men's chatter from outside the tent. It was pitch black outside and the only light she had was from the fire burning brightly outside her shelter. Scurrying to her feet, it took a moment before it dawned on her that she was no longer bound. Rubbing her wrists where the skin tore from the tight restraint, she wondered why they released her. Were they foolish enough to believe she would not run?

At the sight of her father and Laird Chisholm, both alive and well, she felt that either she was dead or was having delusions. The last she had seen her father he was shackled, chained, and being escorted to the gallows. How did he escape? It didn't make sense. Nothing made any sense in this extravagant spectacle her father was involved in. She couldn't help but feel heartbroken as she was made out to be the fool.

For several minutes she watched and waited as shadows moved along the tent wall. When the noise of shuffling feet silenced, Keira slipped out of the tent but was greeted instantly by Laird Chisholm who stood guarding her exit.

"Ye are awake," he said.

"Where is my father? I wish to speak to him."

"In a moment. It is my desire to speak to ye first."

"I have no desire to hear anything ye have to say!"

"Even if it has to do wit' yer husband?"

His question caught her off guard. What did he know of her husband? She turned to look at him waiting for him to continue this ridiculous game he was playing.

"I am a powerful mon Keira. And I am a mon who gets what he wants. If ye submit to me, I will see to it that Varrich Castle is restored to Clan MacKay and that they will no' have trouble wit' Laird Sutherland. That is what ye wanted after all, was it not?"

"How do ye know that?"

"Truth be told, that one of my men intercepted yer message to Laird Sutherland. He never received yer missive, my Lady, but received mine instead."

"Ye bastard! What did ye do?"

"As we speak, yer husband is heading into a trap. That is, unless ye agree to submit to me."

"And if I did?"

"Then I would keep my word and call off the attack. And yer husband shall live, I would imagine."

Keira thought hard on the proposition he offered. Returning Ian to his rightful place was everything she wanted. He would finally be able to go home. But giving herself to Thomas Chisholm was not what she was willing to bargain for.

"I can be a compassionate mon, Keira."

Keira saw little choice in the matter. If she had to give herself to Laird Chisholm to keep Ian safe, she would, and she'd not regret that decision.

"May I have yer word," she asked, remaining steadfast in her decision.

"On my honor of my clan and of Scotland. Ye have my word."

"Then I agree to yer terms."

Laird Chisholm walked towards her so that he stood nearly a breath away. Keira clenched her fists against her sides and turned away from his foul stench.

"I want ye to prove yer alliance to me," he said stroking the side of her face. "Kiss me. Kiss me as ye kiss yer husband."

Tears burned Keira's eyes. She tried to look away, but Thomas turned her head forcing her to face him.

"Do it," he ordered, his voice deep and commanding.

This man brought fear unlike any man she had ever met and there was no stopping him. Keira let out a breath and hesitantly leaned towards him. She couldn't get herself to do it. All she could think of was Ian.

Before she could refuse, Thomas pressed his lips against her. Sweeping his tongue across her lips, he forced her mouth open, and slipping his tongue inside. Keira tried to resist, but Thomas kept his hold firm.

His kiss did not taste as sweet as Ian's nor was it gentle. Cupping her breast, he squeezed and fondled it

Heart of the Highlands: The Beast

with his hand. Chisholm's men watched with sinister eyes and wicked smiles as he groped her body freely.

"Do no' resist me! Ye will only make it worse fer yerself. If ye do what I say, I will no' hurt ye."

Keira choked on her tears. "I would rather rot than have yer hands touch me again!" she replied.

Chisholm smirked and pushed her backwards into the arms of one of his guards.

"Put her in the tent. I will deal wit' her later," he instructed.

The guard nodded and followed his order. Placing his large hand on her thin waist, the guard picked her up and carried her off inside the large canopy tent. Once inside, he tossed her on the pallet, leaving her alone. Curling herself into a ball, she wept.

Ian. His name resonated in her mind. She prayed for his safety and hoped he would find her before it was too late.

~*~

Thomas stepped inside the marquee where his highest guards were stationed. The round pavilion had high walls and space to accommodate fifty of his soldiers. Leaning back on his chair, he listened as they discussed their advance toward Linlithgow, where James had returned. He watched as Magnus Sinclair instructed his men the best route to travel through the lowlands. Thomas could see the worry in his eyes as the man held back his frustration and worry over his daughter. Though he was an ally, Magnus was no more to Thomas than a puppet. And once his services were no longer needed, Thomas would rid himself of both Magnus and his daughter.

His plan was working magnificently as all of his plans usually did. Second son to Laird Farrell Chisholm, Thomas was used to having to fight for what he wanted. Second in line, he was a shadow; often ignored by his father and his eldest brother Creighton, who reaped the benefits of Lairdship of their clan.

With an abundance of time on his hands, Thomas grew up studying politics, theology and law. In his younger years he thought to pursue a military position against their English enemies, but after the fall of his father's regime, their clan suffered several casualties; left with nothing but a damaged castle and a broken spirit. Until he happened to run across another man bent on revenge against James, Archibald Douglas; the king's step-father. James banished him from Scotland and the man was just as eager for vengeance as Thomas was.

With no great position, there was little Thomas could do, which led him to killing his own brother and securing his place as Laird. After that, the pieces fell into place. Thomas was stronger than his brother and much more intelligent. He managed to unite his clan with several others. With Thomas and Archibald Douglas feeding each other information, both of their power and influence grew stronger.

With Thomas's alliance with Douglas, he was promised titles and land in England as well as a proper position within the king's army, which would grant him nobility. The reward could not be sweeter if the King of England himself wrapped it up in a bright red bow.

James was young, inexperienced and easily influenced by his councilmen. He was not fit to be king.

Chapter 28

"Ian!" Leland hollered. "The men have returned."

Ian pushed himself off the ground and stood up. He could see the men Leland had sent to scout riding toward them.

"My Laird, we spotted Sutherlands no' too far from here. But we did no' see any sign of Lady MacKay," Rylan informed him.

"How many?" Ian asked.

"At least twenty men."

Leland turned to Ian and asked, "What are ye thinking?"

Ian looked out over the horizon and pondered his next move. Like any game of war, Ian knew that he must first plan out his strategy in order to find Keira; much like in a game of chess. Most warriors well-trained in battle moved their men into position and then struck. But if the warrior expected to win, he must predict his opponent's movements first. Any man can run out onto the battlefield waving his sword around, hoping to hit its target, but a smart man waited to make each strike count.

Ian waged that if Laird Sutherland took Keira, he would not want her in harm's way. He would want to keep her safe and away from his battalion. She would do him no good if she were dead. Therefore, chasing after his men would only put a greater distance between him and Keira and very well could result in unnecessary loss of life. If his men were directly north and the sea was directly to the east of their position his only option was to head west.

"We head west!"

"But what of the Sutherlands?" Rylan asked. "Ye surely dinna intend to just leave them?"

"Lady Keira is my only concern. Perhaps we should leave a few men behind. If they believe we were too busy fighting off their men, we can surprise them when they least expect it."

"I will stay wit' a few of the men. We are no' too far from Fraser land. We will find refuge there," Rylan suggested.

"Take care, my friend. God speed," Ian said holding his arm out to Rylan.

Rylan took his hand in his.

"I will. Dinna worry about the Sutherlands. I will have them chasing their own tails by nightfall. It is my plan to head south in the morning. I will send word once I petition the Duke of Annandale for my pardon. Once it is granted, I will be a free mon and will be able to return home once again in the Highlands."

Rylan and four others mounted their horses and headed north. As for Ian, Leland and the remaining warriors, they headed into the westward winds.

After nearly an hour of riding, Ian spotted the same wheel tracks they had seen and followed yesterday. His hope was renewed the moment he saw them. The tracks were still fresh and he knew that it would be only a matter of time before he came upon their camp. The more westward they traveled the thick density of trees faded to patches of woodland, dwarf shrubs and open pastures.

Crossing the expanse of the terrain they entered the foothills of the stony mountains of Beinn Dearg. With its summit a steep incline and reaching more than three thousand feet in the air, no horse or cart could travel up the mountain side. Its only safe passage was by passing through the glen between the valleys of mountains.

As they continue upward, the air thinned, causing the men to breathe heavily. Strong winds blew fiercely as if a storm was approaching from the north.

Leading his men into unprotected, open terrain never sat well with Ian, but Keira's safety weighed heavy on his mind. The longer she sat in the hands of his enemy, the more danger she was in, leaving Ian no choice but to continue onwards.

~*~

Night turned into day slower than usual. Perhaps it was because sleep eluded her or perhaps it was because time itself had unnaturally slowed. Keira laid on the pallet, her eyes dry from crying. Staring into nothingness she waited for an audience with her father.

His disloyal deceit burrowed a hole so deep in her soul that she felt he might as well stab her in the heart with his own dagger. At least then she would have the dignity to look into his eyes before he betrayed her instead of him cowering behind the façade he created.

It had been nearly two days and there was no sign of Ian. Her faith weakened with each passing moment, her hope in shreds. She had no idea why she held onto hope at all. Thomas assured her that Ian would be facing the Sutherlands in a surprise attack which he'd orchestrated himself, and she had no doubt he meant every word that he said. She knew Laird Chisholm to be an influential man. How else would he have been able to convince so many Scots to go against their king?

These were dark days for Scotland. If Thomas succeeded in his plan, the English Throne would take precedence over Scotland. But if that happened, what would remain of the Scots loyal to James? No doubt Henry, the English King would weed them out like rats and Scotland would forever lose the independence that it has struggled to retain for hundreds of years. What would their forefathers think? So many great men had died for Scotland's freedom and now Scotland was at the hand of one man's mercy.

Thomas's malevolence was sickening. She did not understand his motives or what he would gain by handing Scotland over to the English crown. His treachery must be worth its weight in gold, but Keira would not be surprised if the English failed to follow through with their promise.

King Henry would, however, have the support he needed to advance his war against the France. Perhaps that is what all of this was about. It was common knowledge that England and France were at war against one another.

Keira scolded herself for not paying better attention to the world of politics. Had she known at least a little more, she would have been better equipped before becoming a pawn in this game.

The flap to Keira's tent opened and her father stepped inside. Keira took notice of the guard standing post outside her tent. Did Chisholm not trust him either?

Keira looked at her father as his expression remained unchanged. She hoped he felt shame and humiliation for disgracing his family. She hoped he felt riddled with guilt and that it clawed at him from the inside.

Before he even stepped inside the tent, Keira had already decided she would accept no apologies or excuses from the man. There was nothing he could say that would make her change how she felt. To her, he was already dead, and she had already said her goodbye. This man who stood before her was just a mere shell of what was once her father.

"I have nothing left to say to ye," she said, looking at him in disgust. "The only question I have is did my mother know?"

Keira's father held his head high, which angered her more. She had hoped he would fall to his knees and beg her forgiveness, but instead he stood tall and steadfast.

"Nay, and neither did yer sisters," he responded. "I did what I had to, in order to protect my family," he said, with no feeling in his voice.

"Nay Father, ye did what ye had to, only to protect yerself. Ye thought naught of yer family or yer clan. Mother would be disgraced by what ye have done," she replied, her words piercing like swords.

Keira's father stepped forward and slapped her across the face. She fell back a step by the force of his hand. Her eyes welled with tears as her cheek stung from his open-handed blow.

"I will no' have ye speak to me that way," he said in a deep, angry tone. "Ye are still my daughter."

Keira clenched her teeth, desperate to lash out at the man, but for the first time in her life she feared him. In a life-changing moment, he stripped her of her words. Her father had been a hard man but never once did he strike her or her sisters. She grew up admiring him as any child would adore their father, but this man was no longer her father. He was a monster!

"Ye will do what Laird Chisholm tells ye to and that is final," he barked his order, his eyes as cold as ice.

"Laird Sinclair," the guard said, poking his head inside the tent. "We have company. Riders have been seen along the ridge heading this way."

Magnus gave a sharp nod and glanced back at Keira, his look of warning that she yield to his words causing her to hate him even more. He coldly turned from her and exited the tent.

Keira's heart leapt at the knowledge of riders approaching. She wanted nothing more than for it to be Ian. She didn't know whether to leap for joy or keep herself grounded to save herself from disappointment. Folding her hands and bringing them to her chest, she prayed, pleaded and begged for it to be him.

Nothing would please her more than being back in her husband's warm and safe embrace. She swore that she would never leave his side again.

~*~

As Magnus stepped out of the tent, Thomas charged toward him, blade drawn, heated with fury like a raging bull.

"Ye bloody eejit! Ye led them right to us!" Thomas yelled, his voice resonating around them.

"I did no such thing!" Magnus loudly defended.

"How else would they have found us? This hideout is far from the road and from peering eyes! Ye were careless!"

"I did exactly as ye instructed. They were supposed to head north and be greeted by the Sutherlands. Perhaps it was Sutherland who can no' be trusted! Ye even said it yerself that Sutherland is a lying, cheating bastard! Do ye remember what I told ye at Inverness? I ne'er trusted the Sutherlands!"

Thomas eyed Magnus suspiciously. Perhaps, it was Thomas who could not be trusted. When Thomas first approached him about the alliance, Magnus was hesitant to agree, but who could blame a man who was not of a sound mind? He had given up on caring about the world after the death of his wife and his mourning led to the breakdown of his own clan.

Thomas offered salvation. The world was ever-changing and Magnus was eager to change with it. Thomas promised him many things, including the protection of his daughters and an estate in England where he could peacefully live out his days away from the politics and pressures from the church.

After five long years, it took him until just now to realize that he was not fit to be Laird of his clan. He couldn't even take care of himself, let alone take care of his clan. He looked at Chisholm as a mentor who would lead Clan Sinclair into victory. But he was wrong. He should not have let Chisholm help him escape the clutches of the King's guardsmen at Inverness. He should have died that day on the gallows instead of allowing this farce to continue on.

Magnus stood proud in front of the Sherriff of Ross-Shire as he admitted his crimes. He knew his crimes would one day have to be answered; but he deeply regretted getting his daughter Keira involved. She was never supposed to be involved. It was the only reason he agreed to the marriage with Thomas Chisholm. He was meant to keep her safe.

Magnus looked over his shoulder to steal a glance at his young beautiful daughter. The moment he saw her red eyes he felt pain-stricken. God, she looked like her mother. Magnus clutched his fists at his side. Full of shame and remorse, he would never forgive himself. No child should have to watch their father shamefully hanged by the noose. The image he imaged would haunt her forever, no matter how mad she was at him.

Until the king's guards stepped in, he accepted his fate at the end of the noose. If he was going to die, he would maintain his honor and integrity until his very last breath. But as the guards approached, one man stood out from the crowd, Laird Thomas Chisholm; disguised as one of the King's guards. No one recognized him, other than Magnus.

He stood with a crooked smile staring at Magnus. Silently, he nodded and Magnus knew that his saving grace had arrived and death would not greet him this day.

Thomas and another guard grabbed onto Magnus's arms and led him out the back door of the courtroom, but instead of heading towards the gallows, they turned down a dark corridor that led down to a small open shaft outside of the castle.

Magnus peered down the open hole and glanced at the murky waters of the moat that circled the castle.

"Jump," he heard one of the men behind him whisper.

Magnus did as he was instructed and leaped into the waters below. With the impact of his weight and size the water made a loud splash but was muffled beneath the loud chants of onlookers near the gallows. The other two men jumped in the water behind them and the three men swam down the small channel until they were a safe enough distance away out of view from the castle guards who stood post atop the castle walls.

"Trust is becoming something of a rarity these days, would ye no agree?" Thomas asked. "I have put trust in many men and do ye know what I have learned?"

"What is that?" Magnus impatiently asked.

Thomas stepped closer. Letting out a breath, he stood quietly and stared at the ground.

"That if ye want something done," he said as he took his dagger and forcefully thrust it deep in Magnus's side. "Ye have to do it yerself."

Thomas's twisting the knife back out hurt worse than the initial impact. Magnus's hand flew to Thomas's shoulder as he felt faint from the pain and loss of blood as it pooled down his leg. Digging his fingers hard into Thomas's shoulder, he let out a breath and violently tumbled to the ground. With his eyes barely open, he watched as Thomas stepped back and wiped off his blade with his sleeve.

Thomas looked at him with no emotion. Wiping his brow, he bent down and gently placed his hand on Magnus's back. Magnus grunted at the contact though his body was too weak to move. He was dying.

"Tis a shame my old friend that things had to turn out the way they had. But the truth is, ye needed me more than I needed ye," Thomas whispered.

They were the last words Magnus Sinclair would ever hear.

Chapter 29

Standing atop the cliff, Ian looked down the long expanse of the ravine below. It took him nearly an hour to climb the steep face to the summit but he knew it would allow him to see the landscape below for miles. The moment he saw the smoke rise from the trees, he knew for certain that was where they held his bride.

Had Ian not journeyed up the mountain, he might have missed it as their camp was nestled between hills in a deep valley with no visibility beyond the mountain that encircled it. His enemies likely never thought he would make such a climb, for it was no easy feat, but Ian was full of madness today. And he would go to any length to find Keira, his heart ached for her.

The grade of the vertical summit was nearly straight up. Without rope or a harness, fueled by adrenaline, he made the journey alone. Once he reached the top and could survey the land, he would make his way back down and return to where his men waited below.

The location of the smoke was not going to be easy to get to on horseback, but it wasn't impossible either. Ian had ridden his horse in worse conditions. He didn't name her Storm Fighter for nothing. She was a tough and spirited horse who had earned her name.

Making his way back down the incline he rejoined his men.

"What did ye see?" Leland asked.

"I saw the camp where they are holding her, but it is no' easy to get to. Tis on the other side of the mountain nestled deep in the ravine. We will have to follow the river to get there," Ian advised.

With his men loyal by his side, Ian rode ahead following the shallow, meandering river that weaved around the hilly terrain. The smell of burning wood grew stronger. They were close.

Ian drew his claymore strapped to his back as he approached the trees. As they climbed the hill they were met by nearly a dozen warriors standing on the top of the incline, each one armed with a loaded rifle in his hand.

Ian's heart pounded thunderously. The last time he saw weapons like those was during a brief journey to France. He had seen firsthand their capability and deadly potential. They were not a Scotsmen's choice of weaponry as Highlanders lived by their sword, but the firearm, known as an arquebus, had the ability to shoot at great distances, and gave the bearer the advantage. And now, Ian stood staring at a dozen barrels pointing directly at him. Twelve to one odds were not in his favor.

Ian kept his eye trained on the twelve warriors that were about to engage. Though they had the upper hand, he could sense the fear in their eyes as Ian's men approached. He could see their hands tremble as their fingers hovered over their triggers. These men did not show signs of being seasoned warriors and clearly were even afraid of their own weapons. An advantage Ian would be happy to exploit. They were, however, Scotsmen, so he knew they would be relentless.

So focused on their weapons was he, Ian never noticed the red and green color of their kilts until now. *Red and Green.* Ian repeated the colors in his head. Why had he not realized that until now? These were not the blue and green colors of Sutherland men. They were Chisholms! Scanning the area and the men who would soon meet their deaths, he spotted Thomas Chisholm at the far end of the encampment. Rage burned in his blood like boiling water. He knew the man who claimed to be Chisholm at trial was a fake. He knew catching him would never have been that easy. Chisholm had successfully planned his own death, but it was all for naught, Ian thought, as he imagined he would enjoy taking the man's life.

Gripping the hilt of his sword, Ian charged forward as ear-piercing shots fired around him. He felt the wind on his face as he drove his horse forward breaking their line, causing the men to scatter. As they reloaded their weapons, the momentary relief gave Ian the opportunity needed to strike.

Raising his sword high, he turned his horse around for his second wave of attack. His men fought aside him, knocking several of their enemies to the ground. Ian could hear the swooshing of his blade slice through the air as he impaled his sword deep in one of the men.

As metal clashed and the wind howled, a feminine voice penetrated above the noise.

"Ian!"

Ian spun the horse around, his eyes searching frantically until they locked onto Keira standing on the far end of the encampment. One guard held her back from running toward him. Ian was about to charge when a close range, low sounding boom from an arquebus abruptly immobilized him. He did not feel the pain at first as it came in waves and grew intense with each beat of his pulse. Ian's sword clattered to the ground as he wrapped his arm over his stomach and pressed his hand firmly against his side. He was bleeding freely though he was unable to detect how deep the bullet had gone. His eyes stayed fixed to Keira's as he fell from the horse. For a moment, time stood still.

~*~

At the sound of thunder unlike anything she had ever heard, Keira bolted from the tent but was quickly stopped but a guard standing watch near the canopy. From across the field she could see Ian and his men charging toward the armed guards, their swords raised in the air.

After another ear-piercing blast, Keira's breath caught in her throat when she saw Ian fall from his horse after being shot by one of the assailants. The blast from the rifle was deafening as if a lightning bolt had struck the ground around her. The noise startled her as bright light accompanied the sound. Her chest squeezed tight as if she had suffered the blow herself.

Her mind and pulse raced faster than horses. She could see the blood spewing out from his side. The lead needed to be removed, and he needed to be bandaged; and quick. If he lost too much blood, she worried he would blackout and never wake.

Struggling to break free from the guard who held her arm, she watched as Ian's men circled around him, fighting off Chisholm's guards. They were holding the line of warriors back but she did not believe Ian was going to be able to last much longer.

Keira looked up at the tall giant holding her captive and was reminded of Brodie and the story of David and Goliath.

The bigger they are the harder they fall, she said to herself.

Keira angled herself to face him. Lifting her leg back, bending at the knee, she kicked him as hard as she could on his shin. The man yelped in pain, releasing his hold on Keira's arm and dropped his hands to his shin.

"Ye bitch!" he shrieked, after letting out a mass of curses.

Scooping the air with his hands, he tried to grab her but was unsuccessful as Keira ducked. Momentarily, she glanced back at Ian. It was her intention to run toward him but to do so would be absurd. Men circled around him like a ring of fire. She would never make it.

Time seemed to slow as if the last grain of sand had gently fallen from the top half of an hour glass. The thunderous clamor of battle seized, and the only sound she heard was the sound of her own hard breaths.

Keira had to think fast. She had to have faith in Ian's men that they would save him. She had to have faith in Ian. He would not allow death to take him so effortlessly. In all things, she knew that God had a plan for her and she refused to believe that that plan did not include Ian. She could not picture a world with him no longer in it. Simply put, she was meant to be with him.

Keira looked away from the fight out toward the trees. To run would not be cowardly but staying would only put her in unnecessary risk. She had no weapons to fend off an attack, nor did she have the strength to run into battle. The only way to save Ian was to save herself. Once Ian's men managed to fight off the warriors, she trusted they would help him; keeping him safe from further harm.

She began to run toward the trees, her long muscled legs pumping fast in an effort to flee her assailant. He was gaining on her but she was smaller and more agile, dodging the trees and shrubs, weaving in and out like a wee banshee. She had no idea the direction she ran. All she knew was she was heading in the opposite direction of Chisholm's men. Tripping and stumbling over exposed tree roots and forest debris, fear boosted her adrenaline.

Keira came to a wall of rock at the base of the mountain. Looking up, she felt like an ant beneath a tree.

Offering up a prayer, she accepted the challenge and started to climb. Using the cracks in the wall and bits of rock that unnaturally stuck out, she scaled the mountainside. As she was nearly twenty feet from the ground, her assailant started to climb, but his weight and large feet prevented him from getting good footing, and he slipped back down to the ground.

Keira continued her ascent until she reached a flat outcropping of rock. Looking down, she was relieved to see that the Chisholm guard had given up, as he was nowhere in sight. She rested for a few moments until she continued her way up the tall incline. She estimated that it would take at least a quarter past an hour until she reached the top.

The wind blew strong at this height, which worked against her. It was a good thing she did not have a fear of heights for if she had; she would have never attempted this grueling climb.

Once she reached the top of the hill, Keira was able to see the entire expanse of the landscape from the cliff. She would find refuge here and wait until she saw Ian and his men.

~*~

The pain radiating in his side burned like the fires of Hades. With his men shielding him, Ian carefully ripped off his shirt and tied it tightly around his waist. It would stop the bleeding but do little for the pain.

Relief rained down on him when he saw Keira run off into the woods. She was away from the fight but still in danger with one of the guards chasing her.

Seeing his sword lying on the ground only a few feet away, Ian leaned toward it and picked it up with his left hand. The sword felt heavier in his non-dominant hand as he gripped the handle but not so that it would render him useless. Pushing himself to a standing position, he rejoined the fight.

Men scattered, swords clashed and his men fought victoriously. It would be a story told for generations. As his men slayed many of the Chisholm warriors, others fled in fear.

Thomas, however, stood his ground; refusing to withdraw. Ian walked toward him, sword in hand. He wanted that man's head on a stake; James wanted him alive. At least long enough to kill the man himself.

Charging toward Ian, Thomas swung his sword in the air. He fought with rage but not with his head. He swung wildly, missing his mark. Ian's sword met his, the clang of metal colliding, the force of the collision vibrating down his arm. Thomas circled Ian, swinging his fist and making contact to Ian's wound, causing Ian to stagger in pain, dropping his sword.

God damn bloody hell!

Thomas held an appalling, sinister look then tossed his sword to the ground as well. Raising his fists, he waited for Ian to make the next move. There was nothing rawer, more elemental than fighting in hand to hand combat. To kill a man with only their bare hands offered a certain kind of dignity and power no sword could ever provide. It was savage but exactly how a true warrior would want it. It was a more honorable way to die. But death would not come for Ian this day.

Ian tackled the man to the ground. Fists swung, blood spilled, and moans and grunts echoed around them. Like two wild dogs, they fought to the death. He felt yet another blow from Chisholm and barely held on to consciousness as his vision blurred, but thoughts of Keira renewed his strength. He drew back his arm and with all the energy that he could muster he swung a mighty blow to the bastard's head. Feeling Chisholm's body go limp beneath him, he knew victory was his, at last.

Covered with blood, grime and sweat, Ian collapsed to the ground, next to the corpse of Thomas Chisholm. His hands were bloody and swollen, his ribs and side ached like the devil, and a swollen right eye nearly blinded him. He heard shouts and noises as they came near, but could not make out the words. The world above him spun as darkness pulled him under. He fell into a peaceful sleep as he dreamt of bathing in a vat of whiskey. He must be dead and *this* must be heaven!

~*~

Keira's heart sank deep in her chest when she spotted Leland and the others ride toward her. She searched their faces but there was no sign of Ian. Their mournful expressions stole her breath. Keira's head lowered as she focused on her breathing, feeling faint. Her knees trembled violently. Her husband was dead.

Leland rode to her side, Ian's body draped over the back of the horse behind him. She ran to him and placed her hand gently on his cheek. It was still warm under her touch.

"Is he…"

"Nay! No' yet but he sleeps harder than a rock," Leland assured her.

"I was afraid of that. I must tend to his wounds."

"It'll have to wait, my Lady. Chisholm's men are still verra near. We are no' prepared fer another attack."

Keira assessed Ian as best as she could. His skin had paled.

"He cannae wait, Leland," she whispered. "I need enough time to stop the bleeding."

Leland let out an annoyed sigh.

"Alright, do what ye must but be quick about it."

Leland and two of the guards helped lay Ian down on the ground. The shirt he had tied to his waist was soaked in blood. Carefully, she removed it, exposing the open wound. Thank God, the projectile had gone clear through. She wouldn't have to dig in his side to get it out. Fever and bleeding were the only risks, and they were grave.

"Does anyone have a flask of water? I must clean it first before I attempt to close it."

One of the guards rushed to her side and handed her his open flask. She poured the contents on the wound. Using the torn, bloody shirt as a bandage, she instructed on of the men to start a small fire.

"Lass, we dinna have time fer this," Leland warned.

"I must seal the wound. Once the fire is lit, take yer dagger and hold it over the flames. Make sure it is good and hot. Be quick about it unless ye want Ian to bleed to death or die from fever after all this," she instructed.

Leland did as she asked and held the blade in the flames. Several moments later, Leland returned to her side and handed her the knife. Keira exposed the wound once more and pressed the hot metal against this wound. The smell of burning flesh enveloped her as his skin sizzled.

"I think I'm going to be sick," Leland said, walking away quickly with his hand covering his mouth.

Keira waited a few moments longer until she peeled the blade from his skin. It would leave a horrific scar but at least if her were to die it would not be because he bled to death.

Running her hands down his chest, his arms and his legs, she searched for additional wounds. She noted less serious wounds such as three cracked ribs, two broken fingers and a possible sprain to his ankle. But those things would have to wait till later. Once they found shelter and she had the proper supplies, she would reset his fingers and wrap his chest so the ribs would heal. It would be a long recovery but once she fixed him, the rest was up to God.

As she continued to minister his wounds, her mind went to her father. Ian wasn't the only man she worried about. Even though she was madder than a crazed rabbit, Magnus Sinclair was still her father. He'd managed to escape one death, but she feared he had not been given the luck of the saints to escape another.

Softly she asked, "Leland, did my father survive?"

She was unsure whether she wanted to know the answer but thinking of her father left for dead disturbed her thoughts.

"Nay, lass. We found his body after the fight. But 'twas none of my men. He was already dead before we ever got there," Leland replied.

Keira nodded her head. She figured that had he not died in the fight, he would have simply ran off, but after her brief time with Laird Chisholm she knew that neither she nor her father would be allowed to live. Sending up a silent prayer to the heavens, she asked God to forgive his sins and pray that he would now rest in peace in the company of her mother.

Leland led them to a nearby abbey that offered them shelter. With the help of the monks, Keira bandaged Ian's wounds and left him alone to rest. Each day Keira paced anxiously across the floor at the foot of Ian's bed waiting for him to wake. It had been nearly three days and he had still not wakened.

"Ye be worrying yerself sick, lass," Leland said. "Ye should get some rest. I can fetch ye if he wakes."

"I can no' sleep, Leland. I know his body needs the rest to heal, but if he doesn't wake soon, I'm afraid he will starve to death."

Leland lowered his head. He too worried greatly over his brother though he tried to keep optimistic. Ian was a hard man and a fighter; he was not one to easily give up.

"I promise I will rest soon. I just wish to stay a bit longer," she said as she went to sit near Ian's bedside.

"Alright, lass. Come find me if ye need anything. I will be down in the kitchens. I will come to check on ye and Ian later."

"Thank ye Leland. Ye are a good brother," she said thinking of her own siblings. "Leland, if Ian does no' wake, I wish fer ye to take me home to Castle Sinclair."

"Ye cannae be talking like that. He will wake!"

"I know, but if he doesn't. I need to be home wit' my sisters. They are all alone and they dinna know what has happened. Promise me, please!" she said somberly.

Leland regarded her with sad eyes.

"Lass, dinna worry about yer sisters. If it makes ye feel better, I will go myself and bring them back wit' me to Invercauld," Leland offered.

"Ye would do that?"

"Of course, ye are my brother's wife, and I dinna like just sitting here waiting to find out whether or no' Ian is going to get better. I could use the distraction. Besides, how much trouble could four young lassies be?"

Keira stood from her chair and wrapped her arms around Leland.

"Thank ye Leland! Ye dinna know how much that means to me!"

"Tis no problem, my lady."

Leland offered her a slight smile and left the room. With the comfort knowing her sisters will be safe in Leland's capable hands, she felt some relief. Keira leaned over to grab a wet rag from the basin. Wringing it out, she blotted it along Ian's forehead, grateful he had not succumbed to fever. Setting the rag under his chin, she grabbed a small cup of broth and held Ian's head as she forced the liquid down his throat.

"Ian, ye must wake up. Ye must eat," she said in desperation.

She felt drained of energy, and emotionally exhausted as she had not slept in almost three days. Dark smudges had begun to appear under her eyes, her skin was pale, and her cheeks were sunken. But she refused to leave Ian's side. Every few hours, she would redress his bandages, wipe the sweat off his brow and try to get him to drink some broth. His wounds, remarkably, were healing much better than she had initially anticipated. Now all she needed was for him to wake.

Keira placed her hand on top of Ian's.

"It was my fault that ye got hurt. I should have told ye what I had planned. I should have trusted ye. Ye have lost so many things in life that I just wanted to see at least one of those things returned to ye. I am sorry I failed ye. Please wake up, Ian. I am no' ready to say goodbye," she said softly, hoping he would hear her words and wake.

Kissing him on his forehead, she rested her head on his shoulder and placed her hand on his chest. Closing her eyes, she listened to the strong beat of his heart.

"I love ye, Ian MacKay," she said as she ran her fingers up and down his chest.

"I love ye too," Ian responded with a dry, scratchy voice.

"Yer awake!"

Tears filled Keira's eyes as she flung her arms around him.

"Easy, lass!" Ian said, calmly.

"I thought I was losin' ye. Oh Ian, I am so sorry fer what I did. Will ye ever forgive me?" she asked as tears fell from her eyes.

"I am no' mad at ye lass. It took me some time but I understand why ye did it, but it was no' necessary."

"But what of yer home? How will ye get it back?"

"Ye are more important to me than a castle, Keira. I dinna ever want to lose ye again. Ye are my wife and I love ye. Ye are the reason fer every beat of my heart, every breath I take, every smile. I promised ye from the beginning that I would do right by ye. To love and cherish ye fer all my days. My word is my vow and someday we will return home, I promise ye that."

Keira held her husband tightly in her arms knowing that whatever challenges they faced, they would face them together.

Heart of the Highlands: The Beast

Other books by the Author

Protectors of the Crown Series

Heart of the Highlands: The Beast (2015)
Heart of the Highlands: The Wolf (2015)
Heart of the Highlands: The Dragon (2016)
Heart of the Highlands: The Lion (2016)
Heart of the Highlands: The Stag (2016)

The MacKinnon Clan Series

The Honor of a Highlander (2013)
Escape to the Highlands (2014)
Highland Daydreams (2014)

Stand Alones

Legend of the Fae (2015)
Stones and Stars: A Highland Holiday novella (2015)

Heart of the Highlands: The Beast

About the Author

April lives in central Minnesota with her husband and son. She developed her passion of historical romances through her love of history and genealogy. Over the last several years she has compiled her family tree finding over 350 bloodline grandparents dating back to the 900's from England and France.

When not working or writing, she enjoys spending time with her family, reading and being outdoors.

Check out the author's website, Twitter and Facebook page for updates on upcoming books, cover reveals and giveaways.

www.facebook.com/author.april.holthaus
https://twitter.com/AprilHolthaus
http://myromanticenchantments.blogspot.com/

Made in the USA
Charleston, SC
31 July 2015